"How did you get in here?" Olivia asked.

She'd been soaking in a tub of warm water. And, as she'd relaxed, her thoughts had settled on one Campbell Raines—all six-plus, muscular feet of him.

But now he stood in the middle of the room, and she stared at him in confusion.

"You invited me in, remember?"

"I did?"

"Yes, Olivia. You wanted me here, where I could touch you."

"Bite me?"

"Only if you want me to."

Did she want that? No, of course not. But something else? She walked closer and looked up at his handsome face. Yes, she definitely wanted something else. "Kiss me."

Books by Trish Milburn

Harlequin Nocturne

Out of the Night #170

Harlequin American Romance

A Firefighter In The Family #1228
Her Very Own Family #1260
The Family Man #1300
Elly: Cowgirl Bride #1326
*The Cowboy's Secret Son #1386
*Cowboy To The Rescue #1396
*The Cowboy Sheriff #1403
**Her Perfect Cowboy #1450
**Having The Cowboy's Baby #1468

*The Teagues of Texas
**Blue Falls, Texas

TRISH MILBURN

writes paranormal romance for the Harlequin Nocturne line and contemporary romance for the Harlequin American Romance line. She's a two-time Golden Heart award winner, a fan of walks in the woods and road trips and is a big geek girl, including being a dedicated Whovian and Browncoat. And one of these days, she's going to cosplay Selene from Underworld at Dragon*Con.

OUT OF
THE NIGHT

—

TRISH MILBURN

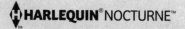

Recycling programs
for this product may
not exist in your area.

ISBN-13: 978-0-373-88580-0

OUT OF THE NIGHT

Copyright © 2013 by Trish Milburn

Printed in U.S.A.

HARLEQUIN®
www.Harlequin.com

Dear Reader,

I am beyond thrilled that my first Harlequin Nocturne, *Out of the Night,* is available this month. It introduces V Force, an elite group of cops who just happen to be vampires. Leading the New York City arm of V Force is Campbell Raines. His one reason for existing is to keep law and order—until he meets Olivia DaCosta and begins to yearn for more. But can a human ever love a vampire?

I might be a gal who spooks easily in the real world, but I have a definite love for things that go bump in the fictional night. Considering my love for the *Underworld* movies, *The Vampire Diaries* and *Supernatural* TV shows, Gary Oldman's turn as Dracula in *Bram Stoker's Dracula,* and several vampire-centric book series, it was only a matter of time before I put my own spin on a vampire world. I hope you enjoy the world of V Force.

Trish Milburn

To Tanya Michaels, my fellow geek girl and conference roomie extraordinaire. I love that you don't think it's weird to dress up like a favorite character and stand in a Dragon*Con line for two hours to see a panel of actors from *The Vampire Diaries, Battlestar Galactica* or *Firefly* because you're right there next to me. Here's to many more conferences with you and Bob the fan.

Chapter 1

Olivia DaCosta banged on yet another door as the shadows lengthened ominously over Lower Manhattan. Her knuckles throbbed and were already bruising from countless other such attempts to get a response. Each time her pleas for entry went unanswered, she grew more desperate and her pulse ratcheted up another notch, just the response she didn't need.

Despite the soreness in her hand, she banged again, louder this time. "Come on, come on!" She prayed someone would be brave enough to open this door and let her in before the last faint light of day disappeared. Already the shadows seemed to move and reek with dread. If she didn't find shelter before they totally consumed the final hints of daylight, she'd be dead before the night was through.

Movement beyond the curtain caught her attention and she hammered on the door with even more force, sending sharp pains up through her hand into her lower arm. "Please, let me in!" she called out, wondering if she could claw her way through the door. But when the banging and pleas didn't bring anyone to the door, she had no choice but to choke down a sob and move on.

She checked her cell phone yet again, hoping for a miraculous resurrection. But the battery was still dead. If she made it through the night, she would never forget to charge her phone battery again.

She walked at the edge of the sidewalk closest to the street, as far as she could get from steps that led downward into the lower levels of the dwellings. The shadows gathered in those stairwells made her heart beat too fast, turning her into a shining beacon for the city's vampires.

God, every time she even thought about them, part of her still couldn't believe they were real, that they had roamed the earth for centuries. She wanted to reject the very idea of them as something horrible created by her brain. Not so many years ago, they had been the stuff of fiction. At least all sane people had believed so. Now their emergence in the wake of the massive die-off caused by the Bokor virus made going out for a night on the town, taking a romantic moonlit walk and even stargazing things of the past for humans. Those once-enjoyable activities were as much a part of humanity's collective history as the Roman Empire or the belief that the world was flat.

As soon as the sun hit the horizon, everyone without a death wish retreated indoors and didn't step foot outside for any reason. If someone had a heart attack or any medical emergency in the middle of the night, they faced an impossible choice—risk a mad dash to the hospital or hope they'd last until daylight. Either came with the very real possibility of death. But there were no ambulances running between sundown and sunrise. What was left of humanity couldn't risk losing its remaining health-care professionals with suicide runs.

Olivia tried not to dwell on the realities of the cruel new world. Nothing mattered beyond finding shelter right now. She passed the next doorway because it was padlocked from the outside with a rusty lock and chain. She fought panic and dwindling hope as she tried to rouse someone at the next three residences. When she noticed a thin line of blood on her middle knuckle, she picked up her pace even more. The only thing worse than being caught out after dark was adding fresh blood to the mix. Forget about being dead before morning. She'd be lucky to last five minutes.

She couldn't believe she was in her current situation. What was the old saying? No good deed went unpunished?

Normally, her runs to the city's parks, where the homeless and poor spent their days, were over and she was safely back in her own home well before sunset. But today, when she'd returned to the parking area where she'd left her car near Battery Park, it was gone. Where once the realization of a stolen car might have brought about anger and frustration, now it was cause for pure and utter terror. When a call to her best friend, Mindy, went unanswered and her phone then chose that moment to die, Olivia had started running and trying to find a building where she could spend the night.

If only she'd noticed her car had been stolen before the last city bus of the day had made its stop at Battery Park, picking up the homeless to transport them to whatever shelters had space. A night on the floor of a shelter would have at least guaranteed she'd live to see tomorrow.

Considering how many people had died during the virus outbreak, it was a sin there were even homeless people anymore. Even with the increasing immigration from other hard-hit parts of the world, there were more than enough apartments and even empty office space to hold the homeless now, not to mention the hotel rooms. But despite everything that had passed during the past two years, greed still reigned supreme in the hearts of many. They banked on fear of the night ensuring their survival in this dark descendant of what New York had been such a short time ago.

And with society on the edge of disorder, with thugs and gangs posing almost as much danger as the vampires, there was plenty of fear to go around.

Movement out of the corner of her eye caused her to gasp as she jogged down yet another stoop. But it was only a gray-and-black tabby cat. He stopped and stared at her for a moment before continuing on his way. Unlike her and the rest of the human population, he had no more worries than he'd had before the pandemic. Unless he'd lost his owners and thus his fancy cat food, and really that was nothing in the greater scheme of things. At least the disease hadn't jumped species, and vampires couldn't feed from any living creatures other than humans.

Lucky us.

It was full-on twilight now. Not even the highest floors of the surrounding buildings or the distant skyscrapers were bathed in sunlight. Olivia imagined an increased ticking in her head, counting down the minutes she had to live. A part of her whispered to just accept her fate, to take a seat on someone's cold concrete steps and wait for the inevitable. Why spend the last moments of her life engaged in fruitless, panicked flight?

But that wasn't who she was. She'd survived the world's worst pandemic when so many hadn't. She owed it to whomever or whatever had saved her from that awful death, owed it to herself and the people she helped each day, to survive yet again. Owed it to Jeremy and all the good the world lost when he'd succumbed to the unstoppable disease.

So she kept moving, kept knocking on doors, would have considered breaking out a window and forcing her way inside if all the windows weren't barred. She doubted any inhabited lower-floor residence in Manhattan was without those bars. The irony was that they weren't there to protect the residents from vampires, since vampires couldn't enter any human-owned building without being invited. No, the bars were there to prevent people like her—those seeking sanctuary—or the city's criminal element from committing home invasions. Sadly, when the world came down to pure survival, the veneer of civility and kindness too easily slipped away. Many had died at the hands of the frantic and the criminal.

A gust of wind from between two buildings slapped against her. She pulled her jacket closer around her body and continued scanning the buildings she passed, looking for what she wouldn't find—a way inside, a portal to safety for another night.

One more day of living and breathing.

The moment the deadly sun slipped to bed below the horizon, Campbell Raines signaled for his V Force team to load up. Time to go to work patrolling the dark streets of New York to make sure the vamp population was behaving itself.

Colin O'Shea slid into the driver's seat of the black armored vehicle, much as he'd done in fire engines prior to his turning. Travis Wright took shotgun as he always did, a victim of motion sickness if he rode in the back despite being immortal. Campbell climbed into the back with Sophia Tanis, Kaja Belyakova, Len McBride and Billy McGoin.

"Where to?" Colin asked as he put the truck in gear.

"Head down to the Financial District. We got a tip that the black market has gotten more active in that area," Campbell said.

"Imagine that, bloodsuckers on Wall Street," Len said as he adjusted the sharp stakes and blessed handcuffs at his waist.

Travis, a former stockbroker, flipped him the bird from the front, drawing a deep laugh from Len.

Colin left their underground garage near Central Park and headed toward their first destination of the evening. No matter how long he'd been a member of the undead, Campbell still chafed at being able to move about freely only at night. Although the idea of going up in a sizzling ball of flame didn't hold a whole lot of appeal either.

As they moved down Broadway, Campbell eyed the vamps lined up outside the Times Square blood bank, one of several scattered throughout the city. It was here that humans gave blood during the day to feed the hungry vampires at night. It gave them a false sense that they were making the night marginally safer for humanity, though most of them weren't stupid enough to test it. But no matter how much they gave from their veins, the night was lost to them. He doubted they'd ever be able to reclaim it, even after generations of births helped to repopulate the planet. For now, too few humans meant too many hungry vampires.

That was the real reason the blood banks had been established—to curtail panic in the vampire community and protect the remaining food supply.

He swallowed against his own mounting thirst. He'd gone to the blood bank the night before, but as usual the AB-negative was in short supply. He'd given his allowance to a young vampire who'd been already cramping over from thirst. She'd broken his heart when he'd seen her, not more than fifteen at her turning. Her human life had been taken before it had even really started.

As their truck rolled by the blood bank, Campbell didn't see or sense anything wrong, but he did catch the eye of a tall beefy vampire who didn't disguise his hatred of the V Force. No doubt this guy had been a thug in life and had brought his lawbreaking ways and contempt of law enforcement into life after death.

"We have a fan," Colin said, picking up on the guy's

pissed-off vibe. "I'm guessing he's not looking forward to the bagged stuff."

That was nothing new. Even Souled vampires such as his team had to admit fresh blood tasted better. They just weren't willing to risk tapping into a pumping vein to get it. In addition to the practice now being illegal, they ran the risk of being overtaken by bloodlust and killing someone. And they knew better than anyone what happened to vampires who killed humans. V Force took them out. As odd as it seemed, even immortals could die.

He made a mental note to stop by the bank himself later to see if they'd restocked the AB-negative supply. It'd been seven days since he'd fed, and that was the max before a vampire tipped over into the danger zone. Just another of the odd quirks of his species. He shook his head slightly. Even after all the time that had passed since his turning, it was still surreal to think that he'd actually changed species that night. It was like a bad late-night horror movie.

He pushed that thought away and stared out the tinted window. If he didn't feed tonight, he was going to have to take himself off the work rotation until he could replenish himself. Already he could feel the edginess clawing at him, whispering to him to jump from the vehicle and drain the first human who met his body's needs. That whisper was going to increase in volume throughout the night until it was screaming at the ravenous animal he'd become.

Campbell hated the double-edged curse of having the rarest blood type before he'd been turned. Since vamps could only feed on humans who had the same blood type the vampire had before being turned, he had fewer sources of sustenance. Campbell and all the other AB-negative vampires were less likely to walk into a blood bank and find an adequate supply of blood, especially after the Bokor die-off culled the human herd. The irony? When he did feed, he experienced a huge rush and came out the other side with greater strength than other vampires.

He noticed Kaja staring out the window with an odd look on her face, almost like longing. That was strange for Kaja, who more than any of them liked being a vampire because it meant she'd never get old or lose her beauty. Well, she didn't particularly like drinking blood, but she took the bad with the good. He should probably ask her what was bothering her, make sure it wouldn't impair her ability to do her job, but asking a woman a question like that was a potential minefield. He ended up not having to since she noticed him staring.

"You ever go see a show before you were turned?" she asked.

He looked out the window at the darkened marquees and shrugged. "A couple of times, on dates. Wasn't really my thing. I much preferred a good Yankees game."

"At least you can still see that."

"On TV isn't the same as sitting in the stands drinking beer and eating a giant hot dog."

"Ugh."

He laughed at the look of disgust on her flawless face. He very much doubted Kaja Belyakova had ever deigned to eat a hot dog.

"What's wrong, princess?" Colin asked from the driver's seat. "Hot dog not on the model diet?"

"Shouldn't have been on anyone's diet. Gross." She shuddered with her normal amount of drama, eliciting laughs from most of the team and an eye roll from Len McBride. He was a former ironworker, and his life experience had been about as far from Kaja's parade of fashion shoots as a person's could get.

"You ever been to the Damask?" Sophia asked Kaja, referring to the former Broadway theater vamps had appropriated for their own, the only one to still stage productions at night.

"Once. The acting was terrible, so I never went back. You'd think vampires could put together a decent drama."

Things outside the truck remained pretty quiet until they passed into Tribeca. Almost as one, they all sensed it. Fear. The air was ripe with pulse-pounding, raw human fear.

Olivia knew she was in trouble the moment she looked over her shoulder and saw the pale blue eyes in the dark. Her heart rate picked up even more as she launched herself onto another stoop and banged on a final door in a last-ditch effort to save her life. She knocked with one hand while slipping a knife out of her pocket with the other.

Please don't let anyone look out and see those vampire eyes. If they did, she had no hope.

"Help me!" She pulled back her fist to bang again, but cold hands latched on to her wrist and pulled her off the steps as if she weighed no more than a string of spaghetti.

"Careful," one of the vampires hissed. "We need her alive if we hope to get paid."

Olivia slashed at the vampire holding her, but he was too fast and her knife went flying across the street.

A blinding panic exploded inside Olivia and she struggled in vain to free herself, even knowing her mere human strength was no match for one vampire, let alone two. These vamps weren't going to feed, didn't need her type of blood, but she was smart enough to know she was a valuable commodity on the vampire black market. With the cut on her finger, they could smell her blood and thus tell her blood type. She didn't understand how it worked, but it must be like a human being able to tell the difference between the scent of grilling meat and fresh cookies. Even if she didn't have exposed blood, it wouldn't be difficult for a vampire to determine what type of blood she had. All they would have to do is break into a blood bank and access the records then target their victims.

She'd heard the stories about the vampires' black market. Part of her had wondered if they were true or simply a product of fearful minds. As she stared the possibility of becoming a blood slave in the face, she no longer doubted.

She'd rather be bled dry and left in the street than endure what they no doubt had planned for her. At least then it'd be over in a matter of moments. Her agony wouldn't be stretched out possibly for the rest of her natural life.

She kicked and wriggled, scratched and screamed against the viselike grips of her two abductors. She had to get away somehow, and she racked her brain for some miracle of a solution.

"I'll donate more blood. Just please let me go."

One of the vamps laughed at her, and she had the impression that his breath would be hot and foul if he were still alive.

"Why would we do that when you're our ticket to a life of leisure?"

She bucked like a wild horse determined to be free. Though it likely made no difference, she clawed at the vampires' cold skin and did her best to kick them. She would fight until her last breath. If she died tonight, she wasn't going quietly or easily.

"Let me go!" she screamed, then spit at the taller of the two vamps. She eyed his mouth and imagined head-butting him so hard his fangs would fall out.

One of the vamps clamped down harder on her arm, causing her to scream. She'd swear her bone was on the verge of breaking.

"Stop making so much damn noise," he said.

That was when she noticed dark shapes coming out of the alleyways, more vampires who'd scented her and planned to take her off her abductors' hands for their own profit—or their dinner. God, she was going to be the prize in a vampire fight.

Despite the white-hot pain in her arm, she struggled even

more, desperate to get loose, to run as fast as her feet would carry her while these vamps fought over her. She jerked her body, writhed like a snake, made every movement she thought might make even the slightest difference in the state of her capture. Panic welled in her so much that she feared her heart would simply burst with it.

"See what you've done," the bigger of her two captors said with disgust.

He tossed her aside so quickly that she didn't have time to process that she was free before her back slammed into something hard and unyielding. She cried out as she realized she'd hit a fire hydrant. She tried to draw in a breath, but the pain caused her to stop and her eyesight threatened to abandon her. Pain radiated out from the spot on her back where she'd hit. Her vision blurred so much that she had to close her eyes to keep from vomiting. If she'd broken any bones, that would lessen the minuscule likelihood that she could slip away while the vampires fought among themselves.

She swallowed and tasted the salty, coppery taste of blood. She must have bitten her lip or the inside of her mouth in the struggle. Her stomach revolted at the idea of swallowing blood. The very idea of being turned frightened her a million times more than being killed. Being like these beasts, feeding on the lives of humans, was a horror beyond comprehension.

She did her best to take slow, deep breaths and blinked to clear her vision. Neither tactic was working very well, and she couldn't get her body to obey her mind's command to get up and move.

The sound of brakes, slamming doors and boots on pavement broke into the melee of curses and rock-hard fists doing battle. Her brain must have been rattled loose, because she'd swear black-clad soldiers had jumped into the fray.

She watched as they broke apart the warring parties as if they were separating snapping dogs, only to be jumped by even more. Grunts and the thuds of fists hitting flesh rose up out of the melee. The vamps reminded her of an anthill with an endless line of ants filing out of the darkness. Or maybe she was seeing double or triple.

A tall blond guy wrenched the hands of a smaller vamp behind his back and slapped handcuffs on him. She squinted, wondering if she was really seeing what she thought she was. How could handcuffs possibly hold a vampire?

Why was she sitting here asking herself questions when now might be her only chance to get away and find safety? It'd take a miracle, but she had to try. She winced as she finally dragged herself to her feet and attempted to run, only to realize her ankle had gotten badly twisted sometime during her struggle. Still, she moved as fast as she could, biting her lip against the pain so hard she drew more blood. Even if her foot came off, she was going to keep running.

"Campbell, no!"

Olivia heard the woman's voice on the cold wind a moment before another iron grip latched on to her arm. The vamp spun her toward him.

She thought she'd known fear before. But that was before she'd stared into the red eyes of a vampire in the unrelenting grip of bloodlust.

Chapter 2

Campbell shook with the effort not to bite the woman in his grasp, to not totally give in to the vampire. To the outside world, he would appear to be nothing but a vampire, but he stubbornly held on to the scrap of humanity he still possessed. Though it was never harder than at moments like this, when the animal inside him roared with need and threatened to wipe out the man he'd been once and for all.

He pressed his teeth together, his fangs digging into his lip, as he tried to focus on the sound of his team's voices, on the expression of abject terror on the woman's face. He could tell she knew in the deepest part of her instinct that she was about to die. He was her worst nightmare, the worst nightmare of all of humanity.

Saliva pooled in his mouth. He could already taste her, imagine the sweet, warm richness of her blood as it coursed over his tongue, filling him with the closest thing to life he'd ever have again. He leaned toward the racing pulse in her neck, losing the battle with himself.

Len and Colin yanked him backward with all their strength, and Billy snapped a pair of blessed cuffs on his wrists behind his back. He growled and jerked against them as his fangs retracted, anger hammering inside him that he'd been denied the thing he desired most. His eyes met those of the woman whose body held what he needed. The thought that he'd never seen eyes that wide managed to push its way through all the ones based on pure instinct that said simply, "Take. Feed."

If he'd been alone, she'd be dead. And he'd be no better than the Soulless vampires who never gave the miracle of life a second thought.

"Damn, Camp," Colin said next to him. "Why the hell didn't you tell us you were so far gone?"

He said nothing. Too much of the animal still had possession of him. He wasn't sure he could form human words if he tried. Instead he concentrated on taking slow, unnecessary breaths.

Gradually his bloodlust dimmed. The red tint to everything didn't disappear, but it lessened enough for him to feel marginally sane. He became more aware of the stares of his team and the harsh reality that he'd failed them by going out when he was too close to the edge. If he'd killed the woman, they would have had no choice but to eliminate him, friend or not. And the way things were going lately, V Force couldn't afford to lose anyone. They needed boots on the ground to combat the rising tide of vampire crime, to keep humans safe from the blood slavers—for everyone's sake. Each person lost to a slaver was one less who could donate to the blood banks. One less person available to help rebuild the human population, to live a life now denied to vampires like Campbell.

Sophia stooped next to where the woman had fallen onto the sidewalk when he'd been jerked away from her. "Are you okay?"

Though it didn't seem possible, the woman's eyes grew

even wider. She tried to scoot backward, as if she could ever move fast enough to get away from even the weakest vampire. Even so, he saw her scan her surroundings for a weapon. She might be human, but she was a fighter. But she must be injured, because she winced and drew in a sharp breath. The animal in him stirred again, instinct pushing him to dive on the injured prey.

He forced himself to refocus his gaze on Sophia. The young African-American woman, the team member with the softest heart, held up her hands, palms out. "You're okay. None of the rest of us has your blood type. And Campbell is under control."

If he weren't aware of every heartbeat in the woman's chest, he wasn't sure he'd be able to tell she was breathing. It was as if she'd forgotten how, as if she'd been frozen by a fear so intense that even her body's fight-or-flight response had ceased to function. He strained against the cuffs, and his fangs ached with the need to descend.

"I need to feed," Campbell said past his gritted teeth, his voice gravelly and deeper than normal.

Kaja sauntered into his line of sight. "Well, you're not feeding from her."

"Blood bank. Now."

Sophia eased toward the woman, talking to her in soothing tones that grated on Campbell's nerves. "Shh, it's okay. I swear no one here will hurt you. We just want to get you to safety."

The woman made a final attempt to scramble away, grabbing a discarded beer bottle to defend herself, and Sophia let her. She made no sudden moves. She'd probably been a damn fine nurse before she'd lost that life forever, the queen of bedside manner.

A little cry escaped the woman again, as if she'd hurt whatever injury she'd sustained. Sophia smiled at her, and with her fangs hidden she looked just like any other normal human woman.

Sophia stood, lifting the woman to her feet with next to no effort. "We need to get this one home before any more of the less-than-desirables crawl out of the muck."

Campbell's body vibrated with need, as if a raging fire were about to consume him, as if giant metal claws were raking at him from the inside out. "Blood blank. Now!" he repeated, with more force this time. He had no idea what he sounded like to the woman or the rest of the team, but inside his head his voice sounded like a lion's roar.

"Okay, Thirsty McThirsty," Colin said. "Don't get your knickers in a bunch."

Team 2 of V Force pulled up to transport the arrested vamps to Detention, leaving Campbell's team free to take the human woman home and him to the blood bank.

Despite the hated instinct within him, Campbell didn't fight as the guys dragged him back to the truck, tossed him inside and used his cuffs to lock him to one of the thick metal rings on the wall. He concentrated on slowing his breathing. Vampires didn't have to breathe anymore, but old habits died hard.

He might not have struggled, but the human woman remembered she should as Sophia and Kaja pushed her inside the truck. The woman brandished the bottle as if it would do her any good, even after the back door latched and any tiny hope for escape was extinguished.

"Please, let me go." The panic in her voice only served to toss more fuel on the fire within him, making him want to take her vein even more, to drink from her until there was nothing left and she was no more than an empty shell.

And the sane part of him loathed himself for that thought and for how he strained against the cuffs.

"We can't do that," Sophia said. "It's more dangerous out there than in here, trust me."

Campbell almost laughed. How in the world did Sophia expect a human to trust a vampire when vampires looked at humans and saw lunch? When all vampires were little more than single-minded beasts when they weren't well fed?

He saw the woman's lean muscles bunch as if she was going to bolt for the door. He growled and stared hard at her, then roared a single command. "Stop!"

She froze, an animal caught in the crosshairs of her most feared predator, her eyes so wide that he could see white all the way around her irises. With his vision still tinged with red, he couldn't tell what color they were. He forced himself to take a long, deep breath before he spoke again, reminding himself that he was more than an animal bent on slaking his thirst with no regard for the cost.

"The sooner I can feed, the sooner you get to go home." He was never, ever going to let himself get this hungry again.

Though he told himself to stop looking at her, to stop staring at his biggest temptation, he couldn't. And it wasn't just because of the bloodlust scorching his entire body. Enough of the man who lived side by side with the vampire was present to suddenly realize she was beautiful as only a living, breathing woman with color in her cheeks could be. He wondered how much more beautiful she might be if she weren't scared to within an inch of her life.

Scared of him.

Sophia tried to soothe the woman by patting her lower arm, but she flinched and scooted as far away on the bench seat as she possibly could. He wouldn't put it past her to start clawing at the thick metal of the back door in an attempt to get away. If the tables were turned, he'd do the same thing.

But they weren't. No matter how much he might want it to be otherwise, there was no going back. Like every other vampire roaming the world, he had exactly two choices—remain a vampire for eternity and deal with all that entailed or end his existence forever. Most days he lived with what he was without much second thought because he told himself he was still doing good in the world, protecting the members of the species he'd once called his own.

And then there were the other days, the ones when he wanted to take out as many vampires as he could before ending himself once and for all.

With more effort than he would've liked to admit, he ripped his gaze from hers and forced himself to stare at the floor between his feet. He stared so hard that he wouldn't have been the least bit surprised if the metal had started to melt, allowing him to see the surface of the street below.

A street he'd once patrolled as part of the NYPD back when he was human. Before the Bokor virus began its rapid spread in Haiti. Back when a beautiful woman would have generated a much different reaction from him.

Olivia didn't dare breathe as the vampire driver raced through the dark streets of New York. She didn't want to do anything to draw any more attention to herself. Instead she tried to focus on the sliver of the outside world she could see through the windshield. Buildings slid by in an inky blur.

Not so many years ago, covering this much ground so quickly wouldn't have been possible. Back then, honking cabs, people on bicycles and countless pedestrians would have filled the night with activity. Amazing what a 75 percent decrease in the population and deadly predators roaming the streets could do for gridlock.

When nausea threatened, she ripped her gaze from the window. It landed on the big vampire who'd attacked her. Thank God he'd stopped looking at her as if she were a fat juicy steak. Now he kept his head down, seeming to stare a hole in the floor of the armored truck. Even confined, he radiated power. He frightened every inch of her, but there was a scary magnetism about him, too. The kind that made you do crazy things against your better judgment. As she stared at his big hard body, she got the oddest feeling he was feeling guilty. Something about the way his shoulders hung off his large frame.

But that was crazy, wasn't it? Could vampires even feel human emotions such as guilt? She considered how the female had approached her carefully and with empathy in her expression. Olivia dared to close her eyes. The more she thought, the more confused she grew.

"Why were you out on the street?"

Olivia jerked at the question and redirected her attention to the petite dark-skinned woman who sat across from her, the one who'd approached her before. Despite those spooky pale blue eyes, she looked…kind. She'd done nothing so far to indicate she planned to cause Olivia any harm, had sworn the exact opposite. Olivia found herself wondering about the woman she'd been before she'd been turned. Was she a recent turn or had she been walking the earth for hundreds of years? You could never tell a vampire's age by looking at them. Strange as it might seem, that was one of the creepiest things about vampires, the end of aging. It seemed even more unnatural than the thirst for blood.

Whether it was nerves, insanity, a need to fill the tense quiet or even an insane sense that this vampire wasn't so bad, Olivia found herself answering the other woman's question. "I… Someone stole my car, and I couldn't find shelter."

"What kind?" The question came from the dark-haired guy who rode in the front passenger seat. He caught her gaze in the rearview mirror. "Your car, what kind is it?"

Olivia felt as if she'd fallen into a darker and creepier version of Oz. "A silver Versa."

"Get me the VIN and we'll look for it."

Olivia simply stared at the back of the guy's head, wondering if maybe she was having the world's weirdest nightmare. Why would a vampire care anything about her missing car?

"Travis is good at finding stolen stuff," said the vampire sitting next to the woman who'd been talking to her. He looked maybe twenty with blond hair down to his chin. Before the world went to hell, she could imagine seeing him performing tricks at a skate park. Now he was an animal just like the rest of them, no matter how harmless he looked.

"I think I have it at home," she finally managed to say in answer to the other vamp's request.

The driver, a tall guy with curly dark blond hair, pulled over onto the side of the street. He glanced back at the five vampires in the back with her. "I don't want to go any closer," he said, then nodded toward Olivia. "Not with living, breathing AB-neg in the truck."

The big blue-collar-looking guy in the back who hadn't spoken yet nodded. He and the tall, stunning brunette unlocked the hungry vampire. Olivia shrank against the wall, wishing she could fade into it, as they guided him out. He met her eyes, and for a moment the fact that he was a vampire faded and she saw the man he'd been before. A gorgeous man with dark hair and a toned, sculpted body who made something stir in her that had been dormant so long she'd assumed it was dead. Her reaction frightened and fascinated her at the same time.

He glanced over his shoulder. "Take her home."

The authority in his voice brooked no argument and left no doubt who was in charge of this odd band of vampires. Nothing about tonight made sense, but she was still alive and for that she was immeasurably thankful. Even if it made no sense that she had vampires to thank for that fact.

Her attacker's eyes met hers again, stared so deeply she had to force herself not to squirm. "I'm sorry," he said.

She couldn't have been more surprised if he'd admitted to being Dracula.

By the time Kaja and Len dragged Campbell into the blood bank, his veins felt like a lit fuse. When some of the curses from the vampires waiting their turn to feed made it past the haze covering his brain, he turned his head toward them and growled. If he hadn't been cuffed, he would have bared his fangs, perhaps ripped out a few throats.

Len jerked him toward the door to the back and Kaja pushed him from behind. Once they got him inside the feeding room, they shoved him down in a chair and held him there. He shot every vile word he knew at them.

Kaja slapped him on the back of his head. "Behave yourself, potty mouth. You're the one who allowed yourself to get in this state."

He bit down on another curse because despite how far gone he was he realized she was right. He was so dangerous at the moment, in fact, that it wasn't one of the nurses who came in but Ethan Ferris.

"Hey, Doc," Len said. "We've got a hungry moron for you."

"So I see. And I'm not a doctor." He'd said the same thing to the various members of V Force's Team 1 a thousand times if he'd said it once, but for some reason Len and Colin refused to call Ethan anything else. Though he had been on the verge of getting his medical degree when he'd been turned.

Ethan went to a refrigerator in the corner and pulled out three bags of blood. "We're running low on AB-neg, but I think we have enough to give you a full feeding."

The moment Kaja uncuffed him, Campbell grabbed the first two bags and downed them in a handful of gulps. The red clouding his vision began to lessen.

The radios hanging from Len's and Kaja's belts crackled to life.

"Guys, we just got a call about the movement of a blood slave," Colin said.

Campbell started to stand, but Ethan pushed him back down. "Oh, no, you don't. You still need more before I'm letting you out of here."

Campbell met Len's gaze. "Go, both of you. I'll catch up."

They didn't look convinced that was a good idea.

"That's an order."

Ethan motioned that it was okay, so Len and Kaja hurried out the door.

"Don't let the bastards get away!" Campbell yelled after them.

It was all he could do to sit still long enough to feed. Ethan, being a smart man, didn't comment on his agitation or the fact that he'd made a colossal mistake in letting himself get so hungry.

When he finally sated his craving, draining a good half of the blood bank's AB-negative supply, Campbell stood and pitched the last empty blood bag in the trash. He shook the kinks out of his arms and rotated his wrists where the cuffs had dug into his skin as he'd pulled against them. Renewed power surged through him, and new urges took over—to fight and have sex, but not with the same person.

A picture of the woman he'd nearly killed popped into his head, quickly followed by an image of pushing her against a wall and having hot, sweaty sex with her. He'd always had a healthy sex drive, but when he'd been turned, it had ratcheted up a few hundred notches. Seemed that was part of the vampire prize pack.

So the last thing he needed to do was be anywhere near a human woman, one he could break in half with two fingers.

Humans were too fragile. He'd seen that firsthand, beginning on the night he was turned.

With a curse, he stalked toward the door.

"You okay?" Ethan asked.

"Peachy."

Ethan gave him a disbelieving look.

"Nothing some ass-kicking won't cure."

That and shoving those long-ago memories of Bridget Jameson back down to the dark depths of his brain where they belonged.

Chapter 3

Olivia held on to one of the metal rings on the truck's wall as Colin, the vampires' driver, careened around a corner.

"Sorry, looks as if it'll be a little longer than we anticipated before we can take you home," the female vampire said.

She'd heard the others call the vampire woman Sophia. The other female was Kaja, and she looked familiar for some reason.

"Just let me out anywhere," Olivia said, about at the end of what her nerves could take.

Kaja stared at her. "Are you stupid?"

"Kaja!" Sophia gave her a scolding stare.

"Well, she can't be that bright if we save her from the streets crawling with vampires and she wants to go right back to that."

"You're vampires," Olivia said, wondering if maybe she was indeed stupid the moment after the words left her mouth.

"Yes, but we're not hauling you off to a blood den, which

is what there'd be a fifty-fifty chance of happening to you if we tossed you out."

Olivia's skin crawled with that image, or the other option of simply being drained and her body being tossed aside like useless garbage. God, she'd been dumped into a devil-you-know situation, one in which it felt as if the night would never end.

"Don't worry," Sophia said. "We'll take you home, just as soon as we take care of this call. We have to move fast when we hear about a blood den or the trail goes cold."

"Then they're real?"

"Very."

Olivia went silent as Colin sped through Midtown so fast that the buildings looked like no more than blurs through the windshield. By the time he stopped, she had no idea where they were. Colin looked back and met Olivia's eyes.

"Stay here, out of sight. I don't like leaving you here, but we don't have any choice. We don't know what we're facing inside, so we need to go in full strength."

The vampires filed out of the truck, Sophia going last. "Please, don't try to run."

Olivia didn't say anything, not even when the door shut behind Sophia and she heard the locks engage. Alone, she became acutely aware of the rapid thudding of her pulse. Could the vampires outside hear it? Would they be able to get inside? Her hand tightened on the beer bottle in her sweaty hand. It was a useless excuse for a weapon, but she still couldn't let go of it.

The minutes stretched along with her nerves. Her ears strained to hear some indication of what was going on outside. Were the vampires who'd brought her here even out there? Had they gone inside one of the surrounding buildings?

Something heavy landed on the roof of the truck, causing her to scream before she thought that wasn't the smartest move. She raised the bottle and stared at the back door, ready to fight. She jerked her attention to the front when the sound of tearing metal sent her heart into overdrive again.

From where she sat she watched, horrified, as the locked driver's-side door peeled away and was slung to the street by a powerful arm. In the next moment, an incredibly pale young woman was flung into the back with her, landing at Olivia's feet. Olivia started to lean forward to help her but froze when she saw the vampire staring at her. He was huge, and his fangs made her think of a saber-toothed tiger. And they were bloody.

"Bonus," he said as he slipped into the driver's seat, stripped the steering column and started the truck in what seemed like one fluid motion.

Before she could grab the injured woman and make a run for it, he shoved the truck into gear and took off. Every time she thought this night couldn't get worse, it did. She was still frightened of the other vampires, but her survival instinct told her that this one was way worse, that if she let him flee with her and the other woman, they were doomed.

She'd had enough! Careful not to fall in the moving vehicle, she stood and stepped over the woman, who was weakly trying to pull herself to a sitting position. Before Olivia lost her nerve, she slammed the beer bottle against the side of his head.

It didn't faze him. He simply glanced at her with an angry look on his face then shoved her back so hard that she bounced off the wall of the truck and crumpled to the floor beside the other woman. Pain like she'd never experienced before consumed her, and she couldn't breathe. She collapsed to her side and stared at the other woman, who was so incredibly pale and whose neck bore obvious puncture wounds.

Dear God, she was going to end up the same way.

She blinked hard against the black spots invading her vision. For the second time that day, she faced the very real possibility of her death.

Campbell reached the blood den just as Colin and Len raced out of the building onto the sidewalk. Colin cursed a mighty blue streak.

"What?" Campbell asked.

"This big bastard took the truck after he made me feel like a stupid rag doll," Colin said. "We got the rest of them, but he jumped out the flipping window."

Campbell's anger roared to life. They didn't need a V Force vehicle in the hands of a criminal. He glanced at something in the middle of the street, the door to their truck.

Len and Colin saw it, too. "What the hell?" Len asked.

"I'm telling you, this guy is strong, as if he's juiced up on 'roids or something," Colin said as he kicked the mangled door.

The sounds of squealing tires and horn blasts in the distance gave Campbell a good idea where the truck was. He glanced over as Kaja, Sophia and Billy came out of the building with the vampires in custody as well as the former blood slaves. The humans all needed medical attention. "Get Team 2 over here to help with this mess. I'm going for the truck."

"This guy's powerful, Camp, like nothing I've ever seen," Colin said.

"So am I." With a fresh supply of blood amping him up, he was ready to do some damage. And with AB-negative vamps being stronger than other vampires after they fed, he was their best bet for retrieving the truck.

Colin grabbed his arm as Campbell turned to leave. "The girl's still in the truck, along with one of the captives."

"Bloody hell." Powerful bruiser or not, this guy was going to pay.

Campbell took off at a dead run, pausing occasionally to listen for sounds to lead him in the right direction. As he rounded a corner, he caught the ripe smell of human fear. He recognized it as the woman from earlier and followed her scent.

By the time he caught up to the truck, it was heading toward Brooklyn. With an extra burst of speed, he leaped onto the back bumper and grabbed one of the handholds next to the door. Just as his hand wrapped around the grip, the driver swerved wide, causing Campbell's boots to slip off the bumper. He swung to the side but managed to hang on. As the driver steered sharply in the other direction, eliciting a chorus of car horns from other drivers, Campbell used the momentum to swing himself onto the roof of the truck.

As he steadied himself, he sensed two heartbeats below him, both of them beating like jackhammers. He knew if he were inside, the smell of the women's fear would be overwhelming. No doubt it was tickling the nose of the driver and making him salivate, regardless of his blood type.

Before the jackass could swerve again, Campbell lunged for the front. When he saw it was the driver's-side door that was missing, he swung over the edge of the cab and slammed into the guy with his boots, knocking him halfway across the truck. Left unattended, the steering wheel veered sharply to the right as they approached the Brooklyn Bridge, sending Campbell swinging wildly by one hand again. Horns blared all around him, and headlights cut across his vision. The women in the back of the truck screamed.

His biceps strained as he pulled himself back to a safer two-handed position. But as he reached for the steering wheel, the other guy recovered, slid back into the driver's seat and punched Campbell hard in the face. He felt it to the root of his fangs.

"Wrong move, asshole!" Campbell yelled as he got in a good punch of his own, drawing blood from the guy's nose.

They traded a few more blows before the driver slammed on the brakes and the truck started to skid sideways. Campbell's grip slipped off the truck's side mirror and he fell to the pavement with a loud thud. He barely had time to roll to the side of the bridge before a car drove over the spot where he'd landed. Granted, there wasn't as much traffic as there had once been and all these cars were driven by his kind, but he'd still be every bit as flat if their tires rolled over him.

He jumped to his feet just as a horrible crunching noise filled the night. A car sat sideways in the lane with a gash down the side. The V Force truck had spun around and was hanging over the side of the bridge, the front wheels spinning in open air.

With a curse, he sped to the side of the truck and jerked the guy out of the cab. The vamp retaliated with a punch to Campbell's gut that tossed him back several feet. "Give up, loser."

Okay, this guy had officially pissed him off. "We'll see who the loser is."

Campbell lost count of how many times they slammed fists into each other, but he had to be dripping blood from half a dozen wounds, including one above his eye that was messing up his vision. He swiped at it as he ducked another blow and swept his leg in an arc that buckled the other guy at the knees.

The sound of metal on metal drew his attention. He looked toward the truck in time to see it tip a little more over the edge. Damn, he had to get those women out of there, and that meant ending this knockdown. The guy flashed his fangs and took another swing at Campbell, but he ducked out of the way.

"Just remember you brought this on yourself," Campbell said. With that, he slammed the full force of his fist against the guy's family jewels. Man or vampire, that always did the trick. When the guy doubled over, Campbell dragged him to the side of the bridge and tossed him over. He didn't wait to hear the splash but ran to the truck and leaped inside.

Both women screamed when they saw him.

"I'm not here to hurt you. You've got to get out."

The woman from earlier headed for the back door.

"No!" He moved to grab her but froze when the truck tilted again. Instead, he slowly extended his hand. "Give me your hand."

"Like hell." After everything she'd been through tonight, he was surprised to see she still had some gumption left. Even though it was stupid at the moment.

"Unless you want to end up in the East River with that vampire who was here before, give me your damned hand."

The younger woman who'd been in the blood den roused herself enough to scuttle toward the front and take his hand. Campbell grabbed her but didn't miss the look of betrayal and disbelief on the other woman's face. The former slave was so weak she couldn't manage to drag herself out of the truck, so he left the other one behind to move her to safety. Len and Colin pulled up in a black Camaro they'd *borrowed* from someone.

"Watch this one," he said as soon as Colin hopped out of the car.

The stubborn woman screamed. When he looked over his shoulder, the front of the damaged truck was tipping upward. He ran to the front bumper and grabbed it, keeping the truck from toppling over the side of the bridge.

"Len, hold this thing." When Len took his place, Campbell eased back into the truck.

Shock slammed into him. The back door had swung open and the woman had slipped out. She hung on for dear life, her feet dangling in thin air. Her slim fingers were white with the effort of holding up her weight, and her heart was pumping so fast that it momentarily distracted him.

He shook his head and edged into the back of the truck, trying in vain not to scare her even more. He didn't want his appearance to cause her grip to give way. Her eyes were huge when she spotted him. As he drew near, he extended one of his hands.

"Take my hand."

She simply stared at him. Even in her current state, she couldn't trust him. He saw the very real possibility that she would let go, choosing to drop into the frigid waters of the East River rather than accept his help.

"You won't survive the fall."

A shudder went through her and her hands slipped free. She screamed in that split second when she realized she was falling to her death, but that was all the time it took him to leap forward and grab her arm. He jerked her back into the truck and into his arms, trying to ignore the rich coppery scent of the blood trickling from a cut on her left cheek.

Good Lord, this woman was going to be the death of him.

It all happened so fast she barely had time to take a breath. She didn't, however, have time to exhale before the big bloody vampire yanked her back from certain death. He held her tight against his side, making it evident that his clothes were hiding plenty of muscles as hard as iron. She had to remind herself that he was a monster, and that those muscles didn't matter.

"What are you doing?" she managed to say.

"Saving your ass, again." This close, and without his fangs diving toward her neck, his voice was a sexy rumble that reverberated throughout her body, making a part of her tingle that hadn't in two long years.

Good grief, she must have cracked her head worse than she thought when the truck had shifted that last time.

Before she could attempt to free herself, he'd pulled her free of the truck and set her on her feet on the bridge. But he kept a firm grip on her shoulders. "You okay?" His eyes flicked to her forehead.

Her breathing stopped again as she realized he was looking at the spot that was stinging, a cut that was likely producing blood. His type of blood.

"Fine." It came out as a raspy whisper as she pulled against his hold.

"Camp," Colin said from where he was standing guard over the injured woman.

"I'm fine."

"You sure about that? You look as if you've gone a few rounds with Freddy Krueger."

"I said I'm fine. If I wasn't, you'd know."

He met Olivia's eyes and for the life of her she couldn't look away from that unnatural shade of blue. He finally broke eye contact and directed his attention to the other guys. She became aware of cars slowing down so the drivers could gawk, and she got the distinct feeling it wasn't the precarious position of the truck that had drawn their interest. He stepped to the side of the guy holding the truck in place. If she'd needed any more evidence of vampire strength, there it was staring her in the face.

Campbell helped his buddy, coworker, whatever the hell he was, pull the truck fully back onto the bridge. Then he glanced at Colin and the injured woman. "You two take her to the hospital then return that car to wherever you found it."

"How about you let one of us take her home?" Colin asked.

Olivia knew he was referring to her, and though she didn't fancy any more time in the presence of vampires, she'd much rather be with one who had no interest in feeding from her, one who hadn't already almost killed her today.

But he was one fantastic-looking man.

No, he wasn't a man. Hadn't been for who knew how long. Why couldn't being turned into a vampire make one butt ugly?

Campbell gestured toward the woman on the ground. "She's AB negative, too."

"Of course she is," Colin said with no little bit of sarcasm.

At the end of her mental rope, Olivia found the courage to speak to them as if they weren't deadly monsters. "I don't care who takes me home as long as I get there in one unbitten piece before I go for the trifecta of almost getting killed today."

"Your day has been a bit of a horror movie, hasn't it?" Colin asked.

Understatement of the century.

"Get in." Campbell gestured toward the truck.

Despite what she'd said, she hesitated.

"Or we can leave you standing on the Brooklyn Bridge all night and see how you fare." Campbell said it as though it didn't matter to him one way or the other.

She pressed her lips tightly together and managed to find enough courage to give him the stink eye before she turned and climbed into the passenger seat of the truck. Once inside she started to shiver, more because the reality of the day's events were crashing into her like hurricane-force waves than because of the cold night air. Not that the latter was helping any. She'd been running on adrenaline so long, she hadn't really noticed the cold of approaching winter since before she'd been attacked the first time. But she was pretty sure her body had burned up the final ounce of her adrenaline, and she was going to collapse the moment she stepped across the safety of her threshold.

Campbell took off his leather jacket and tossed it at her before he climbed in. She looked at him with genuine surprise. Yes, he'd technically saved her life twice today, but something about him offering her the comfort of his jacket seemed more surreal.

"Your teeth are chattering," he said. "They can probably hear you in Connecticut."

"In case you haven't noticed, it's not been my best day ever."

"Oh, I noticed," he said, sounding tired and a touch exasperated.

She wanted to refuse his gesture, but the cold was really seeping in now, down to her bones. As she slid her arms into the sleeves, she noticed the distinct lack of warmth that would have been there if a human man had been wearing it.

"Why do you wear a jacket, anyway? You can't need it."

"Habit. Plus I like it."

She admitted silently that she did, too. Despite the fact that he was a vampire, the jacket smelled as if it'd been worn by a man—in a good way. The scent of leather mixed with something woodsy, earthy. She pulled the too-big jacket close around her.

Out of the corner of her eye, she detected movement and glanced at him just as he pulled his shirt over his head.

"What are you doing?"

"I'm getting ready to have wicked vampire sex with you."

She gasped with pure, undiluted fear and reached for the door handle.

He laughed. It was so unexpected that she stopped and stared at him, at all that expanse of toned, well-sculpted chest, free of hair just the way she liked them.

"That's not even funny," she said.

"Just trying to break the tension."

She jerked her gaze away from his chest when it wandered there again, but unfortunately it caught his and the knowing smirk tugging at his lips. He lifted the shirt then proceeded to use it to wipe away the blood covering his face.

"Don't worry. Your precious human virtue is safe."

She didn't believe him for a second, and some part of her that evidently had a death wish was disappointed.

When he finished wiping away the majority of the blood, he tossed the shirt in the back and started the engine. "Where to?"

She opened her mouth but nothing came out. Did she really want him knowing where she lived?

"The sooner you tell me, the sooner you get to step beyond the point I can't cross. And it's not as if I couldn't find out anyway."

She gave him her address, hoping she hadn't just made the biggest mistake of her life. As he pulled back into traffic, she scooted as close to her door as she could. Not that the space between them afforded her any semblance of protection, but it was the best she could do in the current situation.

"You got a name?" he asked.

She didn't answer. Instead she counted the seconds, minutes until she could truly be safe from this most confusing and frightening of vampires. He'd almost killed her then saved her, all within the space of a couple of hours. Add to that the fact that he was the most gorgeous male specimen she'd seen in ages, and she felt as if her brain were going to short-circuit, sending sparks out her ears.

Unable to look away, she watched him. But he stayed on his side of the truck.

"Why aren't you attacking me?" What was she doing, inviting death now?

"Because I fed, nearly drank the blood bank dry of AB-negative."

"Oh."

He glanced at her as he made a turn. "Don't think that makes me any less dangerous."

"If you can control yourself, maybe other vampires can, too."

He gave her a hard stare. "Some don't want to." He pulled to the curb and turned off the engine.

When she looked out the window, she recognized the dark

street as where she'd been when the other vampire had stolen the truck with her in it. "This isn't where I live."

"No, but there's something you need to see."

"You said you were taking me home." Her heart rate picked up again. Had everything been an act to mess with her head? Was he going to kill her now, drain her body and leave her on the sidewalk?

"I will, but first you need to see this." He got out and rounded the truck, then opened her door. "Get out."

"No."

"Either you get out or I carry you."

With fear consuming every part of her, she got out of the truck and followed him through a door and up a darkened flight of stairs. "Where are we going?" Only she was afraid she knew.

"Before you start letting the fact that I'm not draining you make you think maybe vampires aren't dangerous, I'm going to show you how wrong you are."

Olivia stopped, frozen by his words. But when he kept climbing, the dark and what might follow her frightened her more than keeping up with Campbell.

When she entered a large high-ceilinged room behind him, the thick coppery scent of blood nearly overwhelmed her, causing bile to rise in her throat. Other unpleasant odors—those of unwashed bodies, rot, a dank wetness—mixed with the blood. She put her hand over her nose and mouth and tried not to gag. Her horror only increased as Campbell walked toward one brick wall and lifted a thick set of chains anchored there.

"This is what happens to humans who get caught by vampires if they're not immediately drained. You end up in a blood den, a living lunch for one vampire if you're lucky. Dozens, hundreds if you're not. It doesn't take long for you to start praying for death."

The stories weren't half as awful as the reality.

"That girl we just saved…she was chained in here, along with about a dozen others," he said. "You could've easily been headed to something similar if we hadn't happened upon you earlier."

It was all too much after everything she'd been through. She rushed to a corner and vomited. Cold sweat broke out all over her body, and she started shaking. Beyond the buzzing in her ears, she heard Campbell drop the chains and walk toward the door.

"I'll take you home now."

She lifted her head and looked at him. In that moment, she didn't know if she hated him for forcing her to see this evidence of vampire cruelty firsthand or was thankful to him for reminding her that her fear was well-founded.

He disappeared down the stairs, but she took a few seconds to make sure she wasn't going to heave again. Then she forced her shaky legs to carry her out of this room she was certain would show up in her nightmares.

Campbell didn't speak to her for the remainder of the drive to her apartment. When he pulled to a stop outside her building, she wasted no time slipping out of the truck and hurrying through the front door of her diner, which provided access to her second-floor apartment. Only when she was safely behind the protective barrier of the glass did she venture a look back at him and find him staring at her. Despite the space between them, she felt the intensity of that stare and wondered what it meant. Wondered if she really wanted to know.

Chapter 4

Campbell pulled away from the diner in Hell's Kitchen, hoping to leave not only the woman but also his dangerous thoughts behind. Because it'd been all he could do to not grab her and kiss her senseless. Too easily he could imagine stripping off her clothes and thrusting into her warm body. Just the thought had him hard as a stone pillar.

He shook his head as he headed back toward Tribeca, to the area where she'd been attacked earlier. If he was lucky, maybe the cold air barreling into the truck would knock some sense into him. Because as he'd watched the still-nameless woman step beyond the safety of her front door, he'd finally allowed himself to think about how beautiful she was. And not just physically. Though it put her in danger, he admired how she stood up for herself, how she fought back even when the odds were hopeless. He hoped it didn't get her killed after everything he'd done to keep her alive.

When he approached the area where the blood den had

been, he noticed some of his team heading for the door that
led to the stairs. He pulled over and hopped out of the truck.

"You get everything sorted out?" he asked.

"All the humans dropped at the hospital," Len said. "Colin
and Travis are questioning the vamps at Detention."

Detention was nothing but a big almost entirely underground room with white walls, but it still gave Campbell the
creeps every time he stepped foot into it. Maybe it was the
retractable door on the roof, the ever-present threat that those
in holding could be exposed to the sun if they didn't coop-
erate. He didn't know if anyone had ever suffered that sentence before going to trial, but the Imperium was very good at
spreading the word that they had. Keeping order through fear.

He followed the others up the stairs, his nose twitching at
the foul smell of old blood.

Kaja sniffed and scanned the room. "A human has been
here since we were," she said, sounding surprised.

"It was the woman we saved in Tribeca earlier," Campbell
said as he walked across the room.

"You brought her here?" Sophia looked at him as if he'd
lost his mind. "Why?"

"To impress on her how dangerous it was to get caught
out after dark."

"Harsh," Billy said, being his typical vampire-of-few-
words self.

"Oh, my God, Campbell," Sophia said. "You don't think
she'd already figured that out? And it's not as if she was deliberately walking the streets after dark."

If anyone else had spoken to him like that, he would have
told them to back off. But with Sophia it stung because she
was the most agreeable member of his team, a bit like their
mother hen.

"Way to kick her when she's down," Kaja said. "Why not
toss her out of the truck a couple of blocks from her apart-

ment and make her run for it while you're at it?" With an
eye roll she walked away with Len to investigate the scene.

Maybe he had gone too far. Sometimes it was hard to judge
and balance his vampire and human instincts.

"You owe her an apology," Sophia said.

"I think what she wants more than an apology is me to
stay the hell away."

"Then call her. Email. Text. Just don't become so damned
hard that you're not you anymore." With her words still hanging in the air, Sophia stalked off down the long room after
Len and Kaja.

Billy gave him an "I agree with her" look before returning his attention to the smartphone where he was no doubt
typing in details about the scene.

Seeing as how everyone else in the room was put out with
him, Campbell decided to put his investigative skills to work
somewhere else. He started to tell the others where he was
headed, but then thought, *Screw it,* and took the stairs back
down two at a time.

Sophia's words kept hitting his brain like a battering ram
as he drove the rest of the way to Tribeca. They kept up their
assault as he got out of the truck and started scanning the
area where he and his team had fought the other vampires.

He stopped walking and looked up at the sky, sighing. Sophia was right. He'd been a class A jerk. It was a wonder he
hadn't sent the woman into a nervous breakdown. Wasn't his
job to keep people safe, not scare them half to death?

He had to be honest with himself, if no one else. He'd
taken her to that blood den to ensure she was terrified of him
because once the red haze of his bloodlust had disappeared,
he'd noticed just how beautiful she was. Long blond hair. The
sense that she had wide eyes even when she wasn't afraid for
her life. Curves in all the right places. She was the type of
woman he'd have so gone after back in his NYPD days. And

someone off-limits to him now. He'd been damned lucky he hadn't killed her earlier.

But the fact that she was alive drew him as if she were a siren upon her seaside rock. Not because he wanted to drink from her. No, she tugged on the part of him that yearned to be human again, the part he tried to forget.

As he wandered up the side of the street where she'd been fleeing, something glinted in the reflected glow of a security lamp. He knelt down next to the curb and picked up a cell phone, the same kind the team carried. Had one of them lost it in the midst of the fight?

He palmed it and headed back for the truck. With this area now quiet and no vamps nearby, he wasn't going to find anything of any use in their ongoing investigation of the blood dens anyway.

When he slipped into the driver's seat, he plugged the phone into the charger. Then he started the engine and headed back to the cave.

The team didn't actually live in a cave, but they'd dubbed their underground facility the Bat Cave during one long day of watching—and making fun of—vampire movies. He actually smiled at the memory because it was the day when he'd felt them finally bond as something resembling a family unit. It was important for vamps to find support like that when they couldn't go back to their human families. It kept them from losing their humanity, as well, and becoming nothing more than animals with ravenous cravings.

He kept his eyes open for any illegal activity as he covered block after block. But after the craziness of the previous few hours, the night had settled into normalcy. The human-owned buildings sat quiet and locked up tight. When he crossed into the more commercial areas, the vamp establishments were bursting with activity. Vampires shopping, working, clubbing and dining out—just as humans did during the day.

When he pulled into the garage, he noticed Matt Callo-way, head of V Force Team 2, and another member of his team heading into the garage from the headquarters room.

"I see you're going for the air-conditioned look," Matt said with a teasing grin as Campbell slid out of his team's truck.

"At least we didn't turn ours upside down," Campbell said, poking fun at the time Matt had been in hot pursuit of some nasty blood thieves and took a corner a bit too fast and ended up rolling into the front of a store. The vampire woman who'd owned the clothing store had chewed him out for twenty minutes straight.

"Touché," Matt said as he saluted and headed for his own truck.

When Campbell stepped inside, he held up the phone he'd found. "Who lost their phone earlier tonight?"

Nobody claimed it, so he tossed it to Travis. "Figure out whose it is. Maybe we'll catch a lucky break and it'll hold something useful."

He stepped into his room, shoved off his jacket, which still held the woman's feminine scent, and pulled a clean T-shirt over his head. "Find anything at the den?" he asked as he came back into the main room.

"Squat," Colin said, leaning back in his desk chair. "Though Travis is trying to figure out who owns the building."

"That ought to be easy enough," Campbell said.

Travis looked up from his computer. "You'd think, right? But someone went to a lot of trouble to hide the owner's identity. The deed says PMG Inc., but that company doesn't seem to exist." Travis's computer dinged and he looked at the screen. "Looks like this phone belongs to an Olivia DaCosta."

When he read the address of the Comfort Food Diner, Campbell realized he now had a name to go with the beautiful face. And he had a sneaking suspicion that was going to make her even more difficult to forget.

Olivia kept waiting to wake up. But no matter how much she paced across her apartment on her twisted ankle, winced at the pain in her back or pinched herself, nothing changed. She really had been attacked by vampires and then been saved by the same species. A bubble of hysterical laughter threatened, but she tamped it down. If she was going crazy, she didn't want to acknowledge it quite yet.

She noticed the light blinking on her phone and hit the play button.

"Olivia, I just got your message. I was in the shower. Please call me as soon as you get this," Mindy's concerned voice said. "I called your cell, but you didn't answer."

When the machine beeped and the next message started, it was Mindy again, sounding even more scared this time. "Come on, Liv, call me. I'm freaking out here."

As Olivia made her way through the messages, they were all from her best friend, each one growing more frantic than the last. Her cell phone was who knew where. She'd lost it sometime between calling Mindy and the cascade of horrible events that followed. She picked up her cordless phone and dialed Mindy's number.

"Liv?" Mindy sounded on the verge of tears, very unusual for her.

"Yeah, it's me."

"Oh, thank God. You had me scared to death. What happened? How did you get home?"

Olivia let out a long breath. "You're never going to believe it."

"Try me. I've imagined just about everything waiting here by this phone, praying you were alive."

Olivia pressed her palm against her forehead as she continued to pace the floor of her living room, unable to sit still even though she ought to have her foot propped up on a cushion and ice packs on all the cuts and bruises. "Someone stole my car, and I got attacked as soon as the sun set."

Mindy gasped. "Attacked?"

Olivia heard the unasked question. "I wasn't bitten. Nearly, but I've still got a heartbeat."

"Were you able to get inside a safe building?"

"No. I couldn't find anyone willing to open their door."

Mindy cursed under her breath. "This new world has turned us into hardhearted bastards."

While there were still good people in the world, Mindy's assessment held enough truth that Olivia didn't contradict her.

"You know I don't believe in miracles, so how did you get away?" Mindy asked.

"This is the part you're not going to believe." She paused, thinking again about how crazy the truth was going to sound to her friend. "Vampires."

"Vampires?" There was no missing Mindy's disgust.

"Yeah, this black armored truck rolled up, and the next thing I knew, these commando-type vampires were fighting the other ones."

Mindy was quiet for several seconds. "Are you sure you're okay?"

Olivia didn't blame Mindy for sounding skeptical. She wouldn't believe it either if it hadn't happened to her. Part of her didn't believe it despite that fact.

The details of the rest of the night flowed out of Olivia, faster with each word. It felt as if she were draining her body of poison.

"Wait, let me get this straight," Mindy said, interrupting the flow. "The big vampire who attacked and almost killed you, he's the one who later pulled you to safety?"

"Yes." Olivia realized she was on the verge of sounding

hysterical. "It's all insane but one hundred percent true. And when I finally thought he was going to bring me home—" Her voice broke, and tears leaked out of her eyes to roll down her cheeks.

"What is it?" Mindy sounded worried, as if she wanted to help but was afraid to hear more.

"Never mind." She shouldn't be talking about this with Mindy, reminding her of how vile vampires were when she needed no reminding.

"No, it's okay."

Olivia took a deep, shaky breath. "He took me back to that blood den, made me go inside. Oh, Mindy, it was beyond horrible. It was like a castle dungeon and a slave ship all rolled into one. Chains." She sniffed and wiped at her tears. "They had them chained to the walls. My God, the smells." She felt as if she might throw up again at the mere memory.

"Don't think about it anymore. Try to push it from your mind."

Was that what Mindy had to tell herself each morning to survive the loss of her family? Olivia didn't think she'd ever forget that place if she scrubbed her brain with bleach.

"I know none of this makes any sense, but after that I swear he dropped me off at my front door and didn't leave until I was safely inside."

Mindy was quiet so long that Olivia wasn't sure she was still on the other end of the line. Finally, she spoke. "Had to be V Force. No other explanation."

"V Force?"

"Vampire cops, if you believe in such a thing. I've heard they attempt to keep the vamp population in line, but I always figured it was a myth or some propaganda put out to make the little humans feel better."

Well, didn't this night just get weirder by the moment?

"Damn fine job they're doing." Although they had saved her life, more than once.

Olivia spent the next few minutes answering more of Mindy's questions before the simple act of talking became too taxing.

"Listen, I'm exhausted. We'll talk more in the morning, okay?"

"Sure. You deserve a good night's rest."

But when Olivia ended the phone call, she wasn't sure she'd ever be able to sleep again. It'd been two hours since Campbell had brought her home, and she still couldn't calm down. Trying to focus her mind on anything but vampires, she planned the next day's restaurant menus, then the ones for the rest of the week. She followed that with a full inventory of the stock room. When sleep still seemed to be nowhere on the horizon, she even tried watching TV. Nothing stopped the anxiety that pulsed throughout her mind and body.

She desperately wanted to take a shower but couldn't make herself do it even though she knew no vampire could get inside without her inviting him in. Somehow fiction had managed to get that tidbit of lore right. The limitation didn't make sense, but it didn't make it any less true. She found she couldn't even force herself to change clothes, afraid to leave herself vulnerable for even a moment.

Though she was more exhausted than she could ever remember being, sleep would not come. She lay in bed and stared at the ceiling, her muscles tensed, ready to fight for her life yet again.

When daylight began to edge into her world again, she finally relaxed. But now she was faced with an entire day of work. If she were the only one who depended on the diner's income, she'd be tempted to stay closed for the day despite her need for the incoming cash. But Mindy's livelihood was tied to the diner, too, so Olivia dragged herself out of bed.

When she stood, she was careful about putting weight on

her injured ankle until she was sure it would support her. She was surprised to find it felt better than it had when she'd gone to bed. Evidently having it propped up during the long hours of the night had helped.

However, her back felt as if someone had hit her in the spine with a cannonball. Straightening her back brought tears to her eyes. She blinked them away, and when she could see clearly again, she eyed her bathroom door. Nothing sounded better in that moment than a long hot shower. With a full day of work in front of her, she needed something to help her get through it.

She winced her way to the bathroom. Her foot remembered it was injured and started throbbing in a rhythm opposite that of her back, a tennis match of pain. The idea of spending the entire day in bed beckoned to her, but she couldn't leave Mindy alone to handle the diner all day. She might not have the crowds she once did, but she needed to keep the customers who did come in happy so they'd return.

Besides, she needed to stay busy so she'd stop thinking about how she'd barely cheated death the night before.

She flipped on the bathroom light and caught sight of herself. In addition to her twisted ankle and sore back, more evidence of her nearmiss with death stared back at her. A bruise and cut on her cheek and assorted scrapes she didn't remember sustaining.

Olivia shook her head again and started removing her clothes. Instead of tossing them in the laundry basket, however, they went straight into the trash can. Despite some rips and stains, they were salvageable. But she didn't want any unnecessary reminders of how close she'd come to dying.

When she turned her back toward the mirror, she nearly gasped. The entire middle of her back was a massive bruise, the darkest part marking where she'd hit the rim of the fire hydrant's cap.

"That gives new meaning to *That'll leave a mark*," she said to her reflection. Considering a vampire's strength, she was lucky she hadn't broken her back.

Shoving all the could-have-beens from her mind, she turned on the shower and stepped under the flow of water. Her thoughts drifted to Jeremy and the familiar pang squeezed her heart. He'd been gone two years and she still missed him every day. The sorrow wasn't constant anymore, but she couldn't go out among the city's homeless without thinking of him. She'd wonder what he would have said to a homeless man who needed medical attention but had no money, what he'd think of her efforts to carry on his legacy, and how he would have reacted to the news that vampires were real and not anything like Kate Beckinsale in the *Underworld* movies.

That last thought made her smile. She remembered dumping an entire bowl of popcorn over his head when he'd gone on and on about how Kate did nice things for skintight leather. He'd laughed, she'd pretended to pout, and his tickling of her ribs led to a very nice lovemaking session on her couch as one of the movies played in the background.

Though the memory made her miss him even more, she was glad she could now look back and mainly remember the good times. In the months after his death, all she could think about were those horrible days of watching him die while she sat next to him. She'd hated herself for being one of the minority who were immune to the superdisease scientists had warned about for years.

A new kind of guilt swamped her as she rotated under the spray. Despite everything that had happened the night before, she couldn't deny the big vampire was attractive. At least he would be if he had a pulse. She'd loved Jeremy with all her heart and had intended to spend the rest of her life with him. It just seemed wrong to even be noticing another man so soon. Two years might seem like a long time to some, but it felt as if it had passed in the blink of an eye. Even telling herself the big guy wasn't really a man didn't help. Actually, it made her feel worse, as if her attraction to him was an even bigger betrayal of Jeremy's memory.

She stuck her face under the full force of the water, trying to wash away all the thoughts doing the dance of confusion in her head. Wanting to get downstairs before Mindy showed up for the day, she turned off the water and went about getting ready the way she did every morning. After yesterday she needed a boatload of normal today.

But as she started pulling bacon and eggs from the refrigerator a few minutes later, she realized every movement was going to be a reminder of her close calls. She popped a couple of ibuprofen and told herself that if she could just get through the day, she'd treat herself to a long hot soak in the tub with a good book and some relaxing music playing. And then an incredibly long night of sleep. She wasn't getting anywhere near outside once the sun started to set.

Her heart went out to all the homeless she wouldn't be able to help today. Hopefully the "I find stuff" vampire really would come through on locating her car before it got stripped down for parts. And if it didn't turn up soon, she'd have to figure out another way to resume the food deliveries. She could probably pick up another car on the cheap, but it wasn't as if she had much extra cash sitting around.

Mindy Kemp burst through the back door of the diner shortly after sunrise, her dark corkscrew curls highlighted with magenta streaks bouncing. She raced straight for Olivia and pulled her into a powerful hug. "I'm so glad to see you with my own eyes."

Olivia appreciated the gesture, but it made her cringe against the pain. She edged out of Mindy's embrace.

Mindy stepped back and examined Olivia's face. "You look like crap."

Olivia swatted her with a potholder. "You try getting attacked by vampires and then not sleeping all night and see if you end up looking like Miss New York."

Mindy's expression turned dark. "Are you sure you're okay?"

"Yes, considering. Though I feel as if I went a few rounds with a grizzly bear."

"I wish you could have killed the filthy bastards."

Olivia looked away and didn't remind her friend that one of those "filthy bastards" had actually seen her safely home. It still didn't make sense, and more than once as she'd lain awake she'd wondered if she'd imagined the entire thing. But each time she moved this morning, her battered body told her it hadn't been a nightmare. At least not the kind you had while sleeping.

They'd already gone through all the details the night before, so Mindy didn't make her repeat them. "Don't tell anyone, okay?" Olivia didn't want any looks of pity or to have to answer a million questions.

Mindy nodded. "Any word on your car?"

"Not yet."

"What are you going to do about delivering the meals?" Mindy asked, knowing that would be uppermost in Olivia's mind.

"I don't know." Mindy, like many New Yorkers, didn't have a car. And the subways had stopped running two years before, when it became widely known what really lurked down there in those tunnels. Now people walked, biked or drove everywhere, timing their commutes to minimize any chance of being stuck outside after dark. That meant shorter workdays and smaller paychecks, especially in the winter months. Life was leaner now, but everyone made do the best they could.

Cabs still ran during the day, but the fares were so high

that she couldn't afford to have a cabby drive her all over the city and to wait for her as she delivered meals.

"I'll figure out something," she said as she started cracking eggs into a mixing bowl. "But for now, we're going to have hungry customers in a few minutes."

Like clockwork, old Rusty Tangier walked through the front door and hung his cap and coat on the hooks on the wall. Rusty was a creature of habit, a retired high school biology teacher who went for a walk every morning as soon as the vamps retreated. The walk always ended up at the diner, where he had two scrambled egg whites, whole-wheat toast and a cup of whatever fruit was on the menu for the day.

"Morning, girlies," he said with a wave of his newspaper.

"Morning, Rusty," Olivia and Mindy called back.

They fell into the morning routine as more customers began to arrive. Olivia took a deep breath, thankful for the facade of normalcy even though deep down she wondered if her life would ever be the same again.

When the weekly food delivery showed up, Mindy hurried to handle it. That left Olivia to take out the prepared meals to Rusty and Jane Farmer, another regular, who always sat by the window and wrote on her laptop as she ate her breakfast.

"Lordy, girl, what happened to you?" Rusty asked when she approached his table.

Too late Olivia remembered the outward signs of her vamp encounter. She slid his plate in front of him as she tried to come up with a plausible story.

"Stupidity, that's what happened," she said as she noticed Jane and a couple of other customers looking her way. "I slipped on the stairs last night and took a nasty tumble."

"Honey, you've got to be careful." Rusty gave her a concerned, grandfatherly look.

She patted him on the shoulder. "Don't worry. There will be no more coming downstairs without turning on the light."

She felt bad for lying to him, but she didn't want to get into the real story with everyone who strolled into the diner throughout the day. Not many people lived to tell the tale of being attacked by vampires, and she wasn't interested in becoming the neighborhood celebrity.

She retreated to the kitchen and was glad to see Mindy had finished accepting the delivery and could take over the waitressing duties.

"For the record, I slipped and fell down the stairs last night," she said quietly to Mindy so no one in the dining room could hear.

"I work for a klutz. Got it."

Olivia stuck her tongue out at Mindy, grateful to her friend for setting aside her venomous hatred for vampires and instead acting as normal as possible. If she could fill her day with normality, maybe she could convince herself that the approaching night would be normal, too.

By the time she closed the diner and convinced Mindy to go home, Olivia was too tired for the long soak in the tub. Fatigue won over fear and she fell asleep almost the moment she crawled into bed, the light of dusk still illuminating her bedroom.

When she woke from a nightmare, her heart hammering, it was full dark, and panic surged through her at the memory of the vampire's teeth ripping out her throat. She lifted her hand to find her throat intact. She jumped from the bed, crying out when she put weight on her ankle. She blinked against tears but made herself walk through the apartment to make sure she was still alone and all the windows and doors were still locked. She knew a vampire couldn't be inside, but it still made her feel better to double-check.

She turned on the living room light and glanced at the clock. It read five minutes after four. She'd slept for ten much-needed hours. She made herself a cup of coffee and sank into the soft cushions of the couch to drink it.

The phone rang, causing her to jump and yelp in alarm. She placed her hand over her racing heart, wondering how much fear it could handle before it ceased to function. Phone calls at this time of night were never about anything good. She checked the caller ID and was shocked to see her cell number on the display. On the third ring, she picked up. "Hello."

"This is Campbell Raines."

Even more fear slammed into Olivia at the sound of that familiar voice. He knew her phone number. Did he know her name, too?

With her heart trying to beat a retreat in the opposite direction, she looked toward the window. Somehow she knew he was out there. How else would he know she'd be awake now?

"Olivia?"

Guess that answered that question. "How do you know my name?"

"I have your phone and a pretty good hacker on my team."

Her heart rate, which had only just begun to calm down, ratcheted up again. Bolstered by the fact she was safely inside and needing to not show her fear to him, she said, "Yeah, that doesn't sound stalkerish at all."

"Not my intent. I just need to talk to you."

She hesitated, not sure she wanted the answer to her next question. "You're outside, aren't you?"

"Yes. But you know I can't get to you, so you're safe."

Then why didn't she feel safe? A pane of glass seemed like such an insubstantial barrier for a being with that much strength. She'd felt that barely restrained strength a hair-breadth from snuffing out her life, and later pressing her next to him as he pulled her to safety. And yet a human bent on crime could more easily pass through that pane of glass than a vampire.

Olivia stood and limped slowly toward the window. Somehow she knew imagining him out there would be worse than actually seeing him. When she looked out, there he was staring up at her from the sidewalk. He waved and even smiled a bit awkwardly, as if he didn't do it often.

"Why—" Her voice broke, and she had to swallow against the invading dryness. "Why are you here?"

"To apologize for last night."

"That seems out of character." Well, hadn't she suddenly grown ballsy?

"Suppose I deserve that," he said. "Sometimes I get so wrapped up in the task at hand that I can be a jackass." He paused, as if this whole apology thing was a foreign language he was stumbling through. "I shouldn't have dragged you into that den. You'd already been through enough."

She'd heard stories about good vampires, but the vamps had always frightened her so much that she couldn't quite believe them. Now she wondered, especially if there was some sort of vampire police force patrolling the nights. This one, this Campbell Raines, really did seem as though he regretted attacking her.

Of course, it could all be a ploy to win her trust, to lull her into making a deadly move. That thought didn't ring true, though, not after he'd taken a pretty good beating in order to save her life. She couldn't believe she was giving a vampire credit for anything positive, but the truth was the truth.

And since he'd fed, he seemed in control, much more human than when he'd been staring down at her with those awful red eyes.

"You and your friends—are you V Force?"

Even with the distance between them, she thought he looked surprised that she'd heard of V Force. Of course, she wasn't going to tell him that she'd only heard the term within the past day.

"Yeah. How did you know about that?"

"I own a diner. You hear things." She took a shaky step forward and sat on the window seat before her legs totally gave out and dumped her on the floor. When she took the weight off her ankle, it throbbed worse than when she'd been walking. In fact, she felt as if she'd been body-slammed repeatedly. "Well, that explains a few things, I guess."

"The fact that a truckful of vamps dragged you around the city without killing you?"

"That and the whole black commando look you all have going." She motioned toward his clothing. Gone was the bare chest, and she wasn't quite sure if she was grateful or not.

He glanced down at his black boots, cargo pants, tee and flak vest. It struck her that they suited him, his dark hair, angular features and muscular build. When he looked back up at her, he was also wearing a crooked grin that was thankfully fang-free. And it made him oh-so-damn sexy.

That thought startled her enough that she squeezed the decorative pillow next to her.

"But there's not a cape in sight," he said.

She laughed at the unexpected joke. For a moment she feared she'd finally gone crazy. But then came the stunning realization that his comment had in fact alleviated more fear than her continually telling herself she was safe as long as she stayed inside.

"What's with the vest? Part of the look?"

He reached toward his waist and pulled a wooden stake from his belt. "So I don't get one of these to the chest and go poof."

She realized how little she really knew about vampires, what was fact and what fiction. The past two years had been a blur of work and grief. She didn't have time to think about vampires. She guessed a part of her wanted to pretend they didn't exist, and as long as she stayed indoors at night, she didn't have to think about them too much. Until last night.

"Is that what happens? You really go poof?"

He replaced the stake in its slot. "No. For whatever reason, wood in the heart is poisonous to vampires and we die in seconds."

"You don't know why?"

He shook his head. "I'm still working my way through the history, trying to figure out what's true and what's a load of crap."

"So you were turned recently?"

"About five years before the virus hit."

She'd swear she heard regret and loss in his response. Could vampires remember what it was like to be human? Did they miss it?

"What did you do back then, before?" She couldn't stop asking questions. Odd as it might seem, talking to him was better than being alone in her quiet apartment with only her thoughts and overactive imagination.

He laughed a little. "One of New York's Finest."

She felt herself smile and was fully aware of how surreal it was that the man who'd made her smile had tried to kill her only a short time ago. "Couldn't get away from it, huh?"

"Once a cop, always a cop, I guess."

"You like it still?" The idea that vamps would even have laws or law enforcement boggled her mind.

"Gotta do something good with eternity."

"And you're the head honcho?"

"Of Team 1. We cover Manhattan along with one other team. There are different teams in the other boroughs, other cities."

She stared at him for several ticks of the clock on her mantel. "So it's true? There are good vampires and bad ones?"

He leaned back against a car parked at the curb.

"Yeah. Well, as good as a vampire can be, anyway."

She shifted on the seat, leaning back against the wall. "What determines it? Free will like humans?"

"In a way. This is going to sound a bit woo-woo, something I would have laughed at before I was turned."

"We live in a world full of woo-woo now."

He nodded. "There are two kinds of vampires—Souled and Soulless. The Souled ones used to be good people and they brought that into their vampire lives. The Soulless were not so good—criminals, sociopaths, the kind of people we locked up. The Souled don't like being vampires any more than humans like the fact that we exist. The Soulless thrive on being immortal and powerful."

"So you believe we have souls?"

He shrugged. "It makes as much sense as anything else. Whatever the dividing line between good and evil is, it's what separates vampires."

Wow, she'd had no idea. She'd just assumed vamps were vamps, hungry and dangerous beasts one and all.

"Are the Souled vampires the ones who set up the deal with the blood banks?" She, like everyone else she knew, donated blood on a regular basis to help keep vampire attacks to a minimum.

"Yeah, at the direction of the Imperium, our ruling body. Humans might not believe it, but we have laws, too. For centuries vampires weren't supposed to feed any more than necessary for survival. Since the Bokor virus, it's been illegal to feed from humans at all. If they do and drain a human, they have to be eliminated."

Olivia swallowed hard at the idea that she might have been drained the previous night.

"That means…" For some reason she couldn't force the rest of her thought into words. Her eyes met Campbell's and held.

"Yes. If I'd killed you, I'd be dead now, too. My team

would have had no choice." He paused for a moment. "And that's as it should be."

Something had shifted about her perception of Campbell in the past few minutes, because the idea that he would have been killed didn't sit well. He was still a vampire, still deadly, and she was no less frightened of him. But as she stared down at him now, he seemed more like a man than a thirst-mad animal. He seemed…honorable.

But she didn't fool herself. The only reason he seemed sane and rational at the moment was because he had pints of human blood working their way through his system. She tried not to gag at that mental image and shifted her thoughts in a safer direction.

"Why don't we know about all this?" she asked. "Why don't you tell the world about the differences in vampires instead of having everyone think you're all evil?"

"Because it's too dangerous. Even Souled vampires have to fight their need to kill. You know that firsthand."

She shivered at the memory.

"It's safer for humans if they're frightened of all of us," he said. "Besides, do you honestly think they'd believe it if we suddenly said some of us were good guys?"

She understood the logic, was surprised any vampire would spare a thought for the safety of humans.

"So V Force enforces your laws?"

"Yeah. Just think of us as a SWAT team with fangs."

She laughed. When he wasn't trying to attack her, he had a nice sense of humor.

"What about you?" he asked. "Why were you out so late?"

She hesitated, not sure she wanted to reveal too much personal information even if he did seem harmless at the moment. Still, he hadn't tried to talk his way inside, had even told her how to kill a vamp. Not that she'd ever be fast or strong enough to do so, but it still showed some trust on his part.

"I take meals to the homeless. A lot of them hang out in the parks during the day. Some things haven't changed since before the virus."

"And you got your car stolen and were attacked by vampires for your trouble. Classic case of no good deed goes unpunished, huh?"

She couldn't help smiling at him, at his echoing of the very thought she'd had. "I guess."

A lull in the conversation had Olivia wondering what in the world she was doing having a friendly conversation with a vampire. And why it was so easy to talk to him.

A light came on in the apartment across the street—Dr. Stevens getting ready to go to work the moment the sun broke the eastern horizon.

"It's almost daybreak," she said, returning her gaze to Campbell. Twenty-four hours ago she couldn't have imagined giving a vampire any sort of warning. Would have instead been thankful that the sun had wiped another monster from the face of the earth.

"I know. I can feel it."

"You can?"

"Built-in self-preservation." He glanced over his shoulder before catching her gaze again. "Remember that. Even more than humans, vampires are all about self-preservation and taking out threats to that. So don't trust me or any other vampire. You were lucky last night. But luck can run out."

"Apology accepted." She wouldn't say what had happened was okay, because it wasn't. But she felt his sincerity down deep, too.

Campbell shoved away from the car. "Better get home before I turn into vamp barbecue. I'll leave your phone by the front door. I've added my number into your contacts so you can text me the VIN for your car. We'll let you know if we find it."

"Thanks." She watched as he gave her one last long look then headed back toward the center of Midtown. Even with darkness still hugging the street, she could appreciate the way he moved—all barely contained, graceful power. Why couldn't he be human?

She hadn't realized until that moment how lonely she was. She had a wonderful friend in Mindy, regulars at the diner, even her favorites among the homeless she helped each day. But none of those relationships reached the loneliest spot, the one that had started growing the day the virus had killed Jeremy. No one had tempted her to open up that part of herself again until tonight. And that man wasn't even a person anymore. Was he? What had always been clear lines before seemed a little blurrier after her conversation with Campbell.

Olivia watched him grow smaller, and a tinge of nervousness edged into her. If he didn't get off the street soon, the sun would kill him. Vamps had incredible speed to go with their strength. Why wasn't he using it? But then she blinked and he was gone.

And though it defied logic, she felt even lonelier than before.

Chapter 5

Campbell pushed his supernatural speed for all it was worth to cover the blocks between Olivia's apartment and Team 1's headquarters, the sun's deadly rays nipping at his heels as if they were the hounds of hell. When he finally reached home and ducked inside, he wasn't smoking or sprouting flames but his backside was definitely beginning to get uncomfortably warm.

"Cutting it a little close, don't you think?" Colin asked from where he lay sprawled out on the couch watching *SportsCenter*.

Campbell did a quick survey of himself to make sure he wasn't on fire. "Just took me longer to check on some things than I expected."

Colin snorted. "And how was the lovely Miss DaCosta?"

Campbell didn't answer. Instead he stalked to the other end of the large main living area, the rubber soles of his boots squeaking on the smoothly polished concrete floor. He rounded his desk and stared at the pile of paper work.

"You know, you're welcome to help me out with all this anytime instead of being a couch potato."

Colin spared him a raised-eyebrow glance. "Oh, no. I've done my time in that chair. You get paid the big bucks now."

It was Campbell's turn to snort. "Yeah, I think I'll take my piles of cash and retire to the Caribbean."

"Yeah, we'd go up like Roman candles in the Caribbean sun. It'd be the coolest Fourth of July ever!"

Campbell snorted again, then rifled through the previous night's reports from all the New York V Force teams, looking to see if anything out of the ordinary caught his eye. "I'm sure there are still bikini-clad women on the beaches at night."

Colin nodded. "You make an excellent point. I quit."

Campbell laughed. "You'd miss us."

"If there are babes in bikinis involved, I wouldn't even remember who you all are." Colin shifted to a sitting position on the end of the couch. "What's the retirement age for a vampire, anyway?"

"Thirty years shy of forever."

Campbell continued shuffling papers, also checking out reports from the New Jersey and Connecticut teams so he kept well informed about what was going on in the tri-state area.

And so he wouldn't think about how beautiful Olivia looked in that window, like a golden-haired princess in a tower, as unobtainable as a walk on a sunny beach. He still couldn't believe she'd even spoken to him after everything he'd put her through, let alone talked to him until nearly dawn.

"I don't need to tell you she's a bad idea," Colin said.

Campbell looked across the room, realizing he'd stopped reading reports at some point and drifted into daydreaming about Olivia's lips and how gorgeous she'd be with all that golden hair falling loose across her shoulders.

"You're right. You don't." Colin didn't know half of the

reason why, and Campbell wasn't about to share that dark part of his past.

Colin shook his head then returned his attention to the ESPN announcers as they commented on the latest Knicks game with the Magic. "Oh, nasty!" he said when they showed a replay of a particularly awesome dunk by the Knicks' newest player, Deangelo Bruce. "Damn, did you see that? Pretty good for a human."

The professional sports world was just now getting back on its wobbly feet after the dying from the Bokor virus had ended, though all of its games had to be played early in the day on the weekends, when people could actually attend. It made for fewer games and a shorter season, but at least it was another step toward humanity returning to normal. A new normal necessitated by the fact that vampires roamed the night.

Campbell was usually right there watching with Colin, making outrageous bets, but tonight all he could think about was Olivia. He'd always loved that name, and it suited her. When he'd seen her again after feeding, this time without the red haze of bloodlust half blinding him, the sight of her had stunned him. He'd thought she was beautiful, but he hadn't been prepared for just how gorgeous she was.

Wide blue eyes. Wavy blond hair that seemed infused with the sun he'd never see again. A body that was made to be held by a man's hands, that could give his body endless pleasure. And though he might no longer have a heartbeat, some things hadn't changed from when he did. His hands itched with the desire to explore all those luscious curves and that soft flesh. Her scent she'd left behind on his jacket revealed she smelled like flowers, a deliciously feminine scent. His mouth watered with the need to taste her—not her blood but her skin.

Campbell shook his head and sank into his chair to hide what fantasies of her were doing to his body. He picked up

the reports from the Bronx and Queens to give them a closer
look. The typical harassment crap perpetrated by pond-scum
vamps, real pain-in-the-ass stuff. One vamp dispatched to
the great nothingness beyond for killing a woman forced
outside because her home was on fire. An all-vamp melee
outside one of the Bronx blood banks when the blood supply
started running low.

The Caribbean was looking good right about now.

Colin clicked off the TV and sauntered over. "Team 2
found a vamp close to turning a homeless guy. They gave him
a good beating to get the message across. Too bad we couldn't
stake the bastard, but the guy he was feeding on will recover."

"Good. Last thing we need is another hungry vampire
roaming the city." Not for the first time, Campbell wished he
could roll back time. And if he couldn't recapture his human
life, he'd at least like to go back to before the pandemic, to
when there had been enough humans and enough blood to
go around. To when vampires had just been fiction to most
of the world.

Travis strode into the living area from his own room, one
of several personal living spaces located along the sides of the
main living-and-work area. "I might have something worse
than one more vamp looking for a vein."

"I'm afraid to ask," Campbell said as he leaned back in his
leather chair and propped his booted feet on the corner of the
desk. He rubbed his temples, wishing he still had the luxury
of sinking into the blessed oblivion of sleep.

"I've been tracking some online chatter, and it's looking
as if the black market has some new recruits."

"That's nothing new," Colin said.

"It is when those recruits are human."

Colin swore. Campbell agreed with every air-scorching word.

"Are you sure?" Campbell asked.

"Almost certain. I hacked into a couple of phone calls that

were suspicious. And I talked to Mickey over in Jersey, and he's been hearing rumblings of the same thing."

Colin cursed again. "So the night isn't enough for them anymore? They have to stake their claim on the daylight, too. Greedy bastards."

Campbell sat in silence. When he'd attacked Olivia, he'd thought that would be the worst moment of his week. He'd been wrong. This was so much worse. Huge.

They all looked at each other, the awful truth of what this meant sinking in and landing with a cold, awful thud.

Even the daylight wouldn't be safe for humans anymore.

Campbell's gut squeezed.

Olivia wasn't safe.

Travis's phone beeped with a text. After reading it, he slipped into his desk chair and started typing on his computer keyboard. A feeling of unexplained dread came over Campbell.

Travis turned in his chair and tapped the computer screen. "It just got even worse."

"How can it be worse than humans working for Soulless vamps?" Colin asked.

"When they have a kidnap list." Travis met Campbell's gaze. "And Olivia DaCosta's on it."

After Campbell left at dawn, Olivia continued staring out the window, still unable to process everything he'd told her. It had to be a trick, some ploy that would lead to her demise. Part of her mind kept asking what had gotten into her, why she'd spent the wee hours talking to a vampire. And not just any vampire, but the one who'd come within a moment of killing her. Dead, gone, forever.

But another part, what Mindy would call her softy tendency, had wanted to talk to him, had seen beyond the beast to the man he'd once been. The man who still seemed to re-side, at least partially, inside the vampire. She shook her head to try to knock loose her common sense. Why was she having such a hard time remembering he was a killer? Wasn't he?

She leaned her head back against the wall, wishing she could just go back to the way she'd thought the past two years. That vampires were animals, that nothing of the people they'd been remained. That belief was simpler, with no complications. Maybe it was too much to wish anything was that black-and-white, no matter how much she wanted it to be.

She'd lost track of how long she'd talked to Campbell, but her brain was still whirling with questions. What had his life been like before his turning? She knew he'd been a cop, but what had he done in his spare time? Did he have a family? Had he been married? She squirmed with discomfort over how much the thought of him having a wife out there somewhere bothered her.

She shook her head again, halfway convinced she'd lost her sanity somewhere in the course of the past couple of days. Maybe the shock of a vampire attack had scared her more than she realized. Was this some sort of weird post-traumatic stress? Stockholm syndrome?

In an effort to push away the crazy thought that she could be attracted to a vampire of all things, she shifted her legs off the window seat to the floor. Though she dreaded the thought of another day on her feet, she had no choice. But when she stood, pain shot up her leg. She squeezed her eyes against tears as she realized her ankle hurt worse than the day before. When she lifted her pajama leg, she saw how swollen her ankle was.

"Great," she muttered, then hobbled toward the shower. Through sheer force of will she managed to get showered, dressed and down the stairs. After retrieving her cell phone from where Campbell had left it outside the front door, she collapsed onto a stool in the kitchen. She was still sitting there recuperating when Mindy arrived.

"What's wrong?" Mindy asked as she came to stand in front of Olivia.

"My ankle is killing me." She lifted her pant leg.

"Well, no wonder. It looks like a melon. You need to be off that foot."

"Not really an option."

Mindy pulled out her mutinous look.

"You're going to run the diner all by yourself?" Olivia asked.

"It's possible."

Olivia rolled her eyes. "I'll sit while I'm at the grill, okay?"

"And keep the foot elevated and iced."

Olivia gave her best friend a crisp salute.

While Mindy prepped an ice pack, Olivia dragged the stool to the grill and started the morning prep. Mindy placed a chair next to the stool for Olivia's leg and taped the ice pack around Olivia's ankle.

"Damn, that's cold," Olivia said.

"Thus the name ice pack."

"Smartass."

"Better than being a dumbass."

Olivia sighed and started placing strips of bacon on the grill.

"How did you sleep last night?" Mindy asked as she brought eggs, sausage and thick slices of bread to Olivia.

"Surprisingly well. I think my body finally just shut down." She wasn't about to tell Mindy about the nightmare or the talk with Campbell. Mindy had enough nightmares of her own when it came to vampires. Even thinking of Campbell in a remotely positive light felt like a betrayal of her friend.

"Good. You pushed yourself too much yesterday."

"I needed to." She didn't have to explain about needing to

work to occupy her mind after a traumatic event. Mindy had personal knowledge of that tactic.

Mindy simply nodded and headed to the dining room to unlock the front door.

As Olivia cooked, the phone rang. She flipped omelets while reaching for the receiver on the wall.

"Comfort Food Diner," she said as she cracked more eggs.

"Olivia?"

She fumbled and dropped an egg on the floor and cursed. That voice. She hadn't expected to hear that deep, sexy rumble during daylight hours. But she guessed as long as Campbell was underground or safely protected from the sunlight, he could talk freely. It wasn't as if he was ensconced in a coffin somewhere. Even in this crazy new world, that piece of fiction was too goofy to be believed.

But why was he calling her now? She couldn't handle this, not so soon. Not with Mindy nearby. Not when her own thoughts about him were as scrambled as the eggs she was dishing up.

"Are you okay?" he asked.

"Yes. You...just surprised me." She wished he'd stop sounding so concerned, so damned human.

Mindy gave her a curious look as she stepped up to the pickup window, but Olivia waved her away, irrationally afraid the fact she was talking to a vampire would be written across her face.

"Listen, do you have a gun?" he asked.

"What?"

"A gun?" he repeated.

"Uh, yeah." She pictured the Glock in her nightstand. It hadn't been out since she'd last gone to the shooting range a year ago. "Why?"

"Because my kind are not your only concern now."

"I feel as if I'm getting more lost by the moment here."

And they might as well start prepping her room in the nearest mental ward.

She listened to what sounded like him pulling out a chair and sitting down.

"Travis intercepted some information that indicates the Nefari is employing humans to do their bidding during the daylight hours."

"The Nefari?" Did vampires have their own freakish language?

"Basically the vampire equivalent of the Mob."

Olivia focused on a spot on the grill and took a couple of deep breaths. She didn't know which part of Campbell's words surprised her more, that there were humans who would willingly work for vampires or that there was a vampire Mafia. Wasn't there a band by that name at one time?

"Olivia?"

"Yeah, still here."

"This means you're not safe, even in your own home. Even during the daytime at the restaurant."

She did her best to keep a sudden rush of anxiety at bay. "The world has been a dangerous place for a while now."

"But it's never had humans kidnapping other humans for the vampire black market," he said.

A chill went down her back, but she quickly reined in her fear. She was tired of being afraid. "I'm always careful, but I don't want to live looking over my shoulder all the time. That's not living at all."

"Neither is being chained up in a feeding den."

There went that chill down her back again, accompanied by some stomach churning thrown in for good measure. She hugged herself against the image his words brought to mind. If he and his team hadn't arrived when they had, she might be living it right now, chained up as if she were an animal and slowly going insane. She hated the idea that no place, no time of day, was safe from the vampire threat anymore.

"Do you know who these people are? What they look like?"

"Not yet. We'll get to the bottom of this, though. When I find out who is behind this, you won't have to worry about them anymore."

She envisioned him taking the culprit and ripping him apart, and it oddly didn't bother her. Though she wouldn't be inviting him in for a nightcap, her gut instinct told her he was a good guy, good vampire, whatever.

"Take every precaution you can," he said. "And if someone or something looks suspicious and it's daylight, call the NYPD. If it's night, call me."

Despite the gravity of the situation he was describing, she smiled a little at his tone. It was easy to see why he was in charge of his team, but it wasn't the commanding edge that got to her. It was how he sounded every inch the protector.

Vampire, vampire, vampire. She shouldn't even be talking to him. But should she be denying the protection he offered as long as he was no threat to her? *Yes,* her instinct screamed. *He's a vampire!*

This man, this vampire, had her feeling a bit like a teenage girl who'd just been noticed by the hottest boy in school. But teenage girls were ruled more by emotion and hormones than common sense, weren't they? She was a grown woman now, one who lived in a dangerous world where common sense was often the dividing line between life and death.

"Campbell?"

"Yeah."

"Why are you telling me this?"

"You're at a greater risk because of your blood type."

"Me and everyone else in the city with AB-negative. Are you calling all of them, too?"

He hesitated before speaking. "There's a list of targets,

and your name is on it along with a few others in your neighborhood. Those vampires who were trying to take you, that was no random attack. And if vampires can't get you at night, whoever is behind this is going to try again with human lackeys during the day."

Cold dread settled in Olivia's stomach. "I'd thank you for warning me, but I'm kind of wishing for an ignorance-is-bliss moment right now," she said, trying to make light of a situation that held not one iota of light.

"I'm sorry."

"I think maybe you've apologized to me enough already."

He didn't respond for several seconds, ones in which she realized she was close to burning the omelets. "Crap!" She scooped them onto plates and refused to make eye contact with Mindy when she zipped by to pick them up.

"I've caught you at a bad time, haven't I?" he asked.

"Just the busy morning rush. And I'm not paying attention."

"I distract you that much?" His voice held some teasing she knew was meant to lessen her tension, but it also had the effect of making her skin warm all over. Did the man have any idea how sexy his voice was? A vision of him naked, rolling around with her in tangled sheets, caused her body to tingle in interesting places. Thank goodness vampires didn't have the ability to read minds. At least she hoped they didn't.

"You could say that." Damn, she'd said that out loud while wishing he was still human. She wished she could recall the words because they were definitely the least wise ones she'd uttered in a long time. This was not the time to be playing with fire, even if it had been a long time since she'd felt these kinds of sexual sparks. She let herself fantasize about what it'd be like to take Campbell to bed if he didn't pose such a threat to her.

"Be careful," he said, his voice deepening more. He

sounded…aroused. And that sent a thrill through her. A very unwise thrill but a thrill nonetheless.

"Why?" Hell, why couldn't she shut up?

"Because as much as I'd love to go there with you, it's not safe. For either of us."

He'd love to go there with her? Lord, their conversation had taken an unexpected and way-too-honest-for-comfort turn. She let her breath out slowly, wondering what had possessed her. "I know. I'm sorry."

"No need to be sorry. It's my fault." He sighed, and something about it sounded so forlorn. "Listen, I'll let you get back to work. Just be careful. You might not want to be delivering meals, at least until we can round up these lowlifes."

"Right now I don't have the means anyway."

After they both hung up, Olivia couldn't stop thinking about him. She'd never been the kind of person who wanted to live dangerously, so her attraction to Campbell didn't make the first bit of sense. But how could she see him and not be attracted? The man was sex on two very long legs.

"Okay, I'm dying to know," Mindy said from where she now stood at the entrance to the kitchen. "Who is he?"

"Who?"

Mindy crossed her arms and lifted her eyebrow. "Don't play that game with me. I know what a woman looks like when she's thinking about doing naughty things with a man."

"I'm not thinking about doing naughty things with a man."

"I don't believe you."

"It's true."

"Then what are you thinking about that has you smiling like a fool and nearly burning half a dozen omelets?"

Olivia looked her best friend in the eye and knew she should keep her crazy feelings to herself. After all, Mindy loathed vampires and with good reason. They'd killed her mother and sister, and she'd had to see the horrible result to identify their bodies. Olivia's nerves fired at what Mindy might think of her if she told her the truth. Would she think she'd gone bonkers? Well, that was an obvious yes. What she couldn't handle was if Mindy felt betrayed.

But she and Mindy had always had an open and honest friendship, hanging on to each other even more when the virus and the subsequent emergence of vampires had robbed them of those closest to them. What if Mindy had no idea good vampires were real? Could she possibly believe that after what the vamps had done to her family? Once you saw that kind of viciousness, could you ever look beyond it? How could Olivia expect her to?

"I'm afraid to tell you."

"Afraid? Good grief, do you have a kinky side I don't know about?"

Olivia stared at her friend, not knowing how to answer that question. For a moment she considered shooing Mindy back into the dining room and avoiding the admission altogether. But she wasn't used to holding things in. And maybe Mindy could talk some sense into her.

With a deep breath, she met Mindy's eyes. "I'm thinking about doing naughty things with a vampire."

Chapter 6

Mindy's eyes went wide and her mouth dropped partially open before she spoke again. The color drained from her face. "Are you crazy? Did they do something to you? Please don't tell me they have mind-control abilities, because that will just take the world to a new level of hellish."

Olivia dropped her gaze toward the floor for a moment. She'd known telling Mindy was a bad idea. Why hadn't she listened to her common sense screaming at her?

She lifted her head but turned her attention back to the grill, where she flipped a few slices of bacon. "Never mind. Pretend I didn't say anything."

"Oh, no, you don't." Mindy moved to stand next to Olivia, propping her hip against the edge of the metal countertop adjacent to the grill. "You can't drop that bombshell, then not tell me what is going on. Seriously, did they do something to you?"

Olivia sighed and wished with all her might she'd kept

her mouth shut. "No, I'm pretty sure they don't have mind-control abilities. Even in the world we now live in, that's a bit too unrealistic."

"Is it?"

Olivia met Mindy's gaze. "I think if they had that ability, they would have used it to calm me down when I was freaking the hell out."

Mindy considered that tidbit for a moment before giving a curt nod. "So, then, what is going on? You know they're monsters."

Olivia eyed the front door when a young couple came in. They looked like tourists. Though the city might never recover to the point where it was a tourist mecca again, amazingly people were beginning to trickle back in. The economy, including her own personal one, sure could use their dollars.

"Customers," she said to Mindy.

Mindy didn't even glance through the order window. "They can wait." This wasn't the fun, joking Mindy Olivia normally spent her days with. In her place was the hard, cold Mindy from the days after her family was killed. The Mindy who'd wanted nothing more than to go on a merciless vampire-killing spree.

"It's nothing really. Just crazy thoughts brought on by too much stress."

"I've never heard of attraction being caused by stress. Insanity maybe."

Olivia shook her head. "I'm sorry I said anything."

Mindy gripped Olivia's arm, forcing Olivia to look at her. "Out with it. I'm not letting this go until I know what made you say it in the first place."

Olivia sighed, trying to figure a way out of this conversation. "You don't have anything to worry about, okay? One of them was just good-looking, enough that if he still had a pulse, I might be interested. But he doesn't, so that's the end of that."

"Is it?"

"Of course. Why would you ask that?" *Because you're acting nuts, Olivia.*

"Because I've been trying to get you to even look at another guy for months. Not once have you been receptive until now when it will get you killed."

"I'm not going to act on the attraction. I'm not a fool." She had to convince Mindy of that even if she wasn't so sure herself.

Remembering the long phone conversation she'd had with Campbell the night before and feeling like a teen lying to her mom, Olivia couldn't meet Mindy's eyes anymore and returned her attention to removing the bacon from the grill.

"What are you not telling me?" When Olivia didn't immediately answer, Mindy pressed. "Liv?"

"I...I talked to him on the phone."

"You talked on the phone, with a vampire?" The volume of Mindy's voice went up with each word.

Olivia motioned for her to be quiet. "Keep it down. I don't need to lose what little business I have. And speaking of which, that couple has been waiting long enough." She motioned toward the dining room, where the newcomers had taken seats at a window table behind Jane's.

Mindy looked about to protest, but instead she stalked into the dining room, not happy in the least. And Olivia couldn't blame her. Despite her assertion otherwise, Olivia knew she was ten kinds a fool.

As Mindy took the couple's orders and did a round of the room to check on the other customers and top off coffee cups, Olivia took the moments to try to bring her racing thoughts under control. She eyed the back door, for a split second considering making a run for it despite her injured ankle. But then she remembered the news Campbell had shared with her and resisted the urge to shove a large appliance in front of the door.

Mindy blew back into the kitchen and slammed a dirty plate down on the prep table. "Okay, duty done. Who is this vampire and what on earth did you find to talk about?"

"Min, please let it go. It's not important."

"No, I'm interested." She didn't sound interested, more as if she was compiling information for when she called the guys with a straitjacket to haul Olivia away.

"You don't really want to hear this."

"No. But I need to know where your common sense went."

An irrational anger rose up in Olivia at Mindy's tone, but she took several breaths to calm down. The sooner she just spilled everything, the sooner they could move on and forget about it.

"His name is Campbell Raines." She hesitated, wondering at the wisdom of a full confession. "I was as surprised as anyone that we actually found a lot to talk about."

"Such as?" Mindy's voice cracked like a whip.

Olivia looked at the order form Mindy had slid onto the counter and went about pouring pancakes onto the grill. "For instance, did you know there are different kinds of vampires? Souled and Soulless?"

At Mindy's confused look, Olivia relayed all that Campbell had told her about the "good" and "bad" of the vampire world.

Mindy stood with her arms crossed and her expression full of doubt. "Sounds like a story concocted to make you think he's a good guy."

"He is." Olivia was surprised by how much force she put behind her words then felt the need to backtrack. "I mean, he seems as if he might have been despite some rough edges." She glanced at Mindy, wondering if she should go on or quit before she made things worse. But she had no one else to talk to about what Campbell had told her, no one with whom to ponder if any of it could possibly be true. "I know how crazy this sounds, but I got the feeling he missed being human, that if he could undo being a vampire that he would."

"Listen, no one knows better than me that the vampire mystique can be alluring. At least it was when we didn't know they were real, life-sucking monsters. But this vamp is playing you...." Mindy's voice trailed off in such a way that Olivia made the mistake of making eye contact. "Just which one of the vampires is this?"

Olivia knew what Mindy was asking, and there was no use in trying to hide the answer. "He's the head of the V Force team that saved me."

Certainty slid into place on Mindy's face. "The one who attacked you."

Olivia lowered her gaze and flipped the pancakes. Her stomach grumbled at the smell, and she realized how long it'd been since she'd eaten anything.

"The AB-negative monster who nearly *killed* you?"

It sounded so awful when she said it like that. Who was Olivia kidding? It was awful. He *had* almost killed her, and given the chance, he might again. Might succeed the next time. Had said so himself.

"Yeah."

"Well, that's taking Stockholm syndrome a bit too far, don't you think?"

Olivia flinched at how Mindy's words echoed her own thoughts. She scooped the pancakes onto two plates and placed them on the counter next to Mindy. "It was one conversation. I was safely inside my apartment, and he was on the other side of the glass, unable to get to me."

"He was here?"

Crap, how did she manage to step even deeper into this uncomfortable conversation?

"He found my cell phone, so he brought it by. And…he apologized for what happened."

"For almost munching on you."

Olivia's nerves finally snapped. "Yes, Mindy. We've established he was a victim of bloodlust and just about did me in. I was there, remember?"

"A victim? Now, there's a term I've never heard used to refer to vamps."

Olivia stared at her friend, not wanting to hurt her but needing to make sense of the past thirty-six hours. "What would you call it when your life is ripped away and you're condemned to roam the earth forever drinking human blood and never being able to see the sun again?"

Silence fell on the kitchen. Mindy looked as if Olivia had slapped her.

"Vampires don't have feelings," Mindy said. "They are predators, and you are the prey he's very, very good at luring in. You know the AB-neg vamps are the most aggressive because that blood supply is the lowest."

"I know. Really, I do. And I'm not going to do anything stupid like invite him in." Beyond talking on the phone with a vampire who made her pulse quicken and wishing he was a flesh-and-blood man.

The sound of more people coming in the front door drew Olivia's attention away from her thoughts.

Mindy threw up her hands and moved toward the dining room. "I can't listen to this anymore."

"Mindy."

She stopped and looked back toward Olivia, though she seemed reluctant.

"I'm sorry I brought it up."

A momentary look of pain flitted across Mindy's face before she turned without a word and walked away.

For several seconds, Olivia sat staring at the spot where

her best friend had been standing. She couldn't help but feel she'd made a colossal mistake in confiding to Mindy. The irony of Mindy's situation was that she'd once been the biggest fan of the vampire genre you'd ever meet. *Buffy, True Blood, The Vampire Diaries,* every book series she could get her hands on. But that was before she'd come home to find her mother and younger sister drained and left on the front porch steps of their house.

The cruelest part? The fact that they had survived the global virus outbreak only to die one day before the official word went out that vampires were real and that people should stay indoors after sunset. Mindy's mother and sister hadn't even known they needed to protect themselves.

Throughout the rest of the morning rush, Mindy refused to meet Olivia's gaze. Olivia hated that she'd brought back bad memories. And if Mindy was that worried over a phone conversation with a vampire who couldn't even come inside, how was she going to take the news of the new human threat? Because Olivia had to tell her so she'd know to protect herself. As a type O, she might not be in as much danger, but any danger at all was too much.

But maybe that information would be what convinced Mindy that Campbell wasn't like any vampire she'd imagined. He'd have no reason to warn her about daylight dangers if he weren't truly trying to keep her safe, right?

Doubt warred with a need to believe in something good until a headache started forming between her eyes. She silently cursed whoever had stolen her car. If the thief had kept his grubby fingers to himself, she would have arrived home safely before dark as she always did. She wouldn't have been attacked, kidnapped and terrified to within an inch of her life. She wouldn't have met Campbell Raines and spent the dark predawn hours talking to him about the nature of vampires.

And she wouldn't be having thoughts that could lead to her death.

Campbell threw the dart with enough force to impale it halfway through the dartboard.

"Dude, you know you don't get extra points for doing that, right?" Billy said.

Campbell gave him a hard stare.

"Be careful, Puppy," Colin said, using the nickname they'd given Billy because of his relative youth. "He'll impale you with the power of his mind."

"He's just feeling cooped up," Len said as he sat shaving new wooden stakes to a fine point. "I can relate. Sometimes I want to go out and dare the sun to burn me up."

"Another of your spectacularly smart ideas," Kaja said as she strolled by wearing a new black skirt and heels.

"Yeah, about as smart as buying clothes like that."

"At least I care what I look like."

"My clothes were fine when I was alive, so I don't see any reason to change now."

"Ditto."

Campbell left the familiar bickering behind as he retreated to his room. Privacy didn't alleviate his caged-up, edgy feeling, though. The smaller, windowless room just made it worse. He'd never liked windowless rooms when he'd been human, and having to exist with them all the time now was his own private torture.

He eyed the phone but resisted the urge to call Olivia. Sure, he was worried about her, but he didn't want her to think he was a crazy stalker. He flopped onto the bed that was there mainly for rest, though he had no need for sleep anymore.

That was another thing he missed, the oblivion of sleep. Those few hours when he didn't have to think or plan or be in charge.

But he was in charge, and he was going to make the most of it. If it helped Olivia in the process, so much the better.

He picked up his cell phone and dialed the number he always dialed when he needed to know what was going on down in the dregs of vampire society.

"Yo," came the Italian-accented male voice on the other end of the line.

"Rico."

"Oh, man, you have the worst timing in the world. I'm in the middle of something." Rico Bovari was always in the middle of something. That was what made him such a valuable confidential informant.

"Then wrap it up."

Rico cursed and by the sound of things, what he'd been preoccupied with was decidedly female. After a few moments and one door slam, Rico came back on the line. "Man, you so owe me."

"I repay you every day by not arresting you."

"For what?"

"I'm sure I could find something."

"Hey, hey. I'm one of the good guys, remember? I have a soul and everything."

"Just because you have a soul doesn't mean you're perfect. Just means you're not evil to the core."

"Glad to hear you think so highly of me."

"You'll do in a pinch." Truth was Campbell actually sort of liked the guy. Despite having been active with the Mob prior to growing a conscience, he didn't really seem like a bad sort. At least not Mob-level bad. More of an opportunist who liked living on the edge a little. Of course, that living on the edge had been what had gotten him turned. The walk home after an illegal game of poker had been his last with a heartbeat. Why he hadn't been drained instead, Campbell didn't know and Rico wasn't telling.

"Have you heard anything about the Nefari enlisting humans to work for them during daylight hours?"

"Humans? What kind of crazy person would do that?"

"Maybe ones who like the looks of the money involved, no matter where it's coming from."

"No, haven't heard anything. Sounds like just a rumor to me."

"Rico, you paint yourself as a man in the know. I can't believe you've heard nothing."

"I've been a little busy with other things."

"The female I heard."

"Used to be a yoga instructor. Very limber."

"Classy."

"Don't get me wrong, man. I love her. I just appreciate her abilities, too."

"Love? Did you cross someone one too many times and they dropped you on your head?"

"Now who's being classy? Man, forever's a long damn time to be alone, don't ya think?"

What the hell was going on? First he couldn't stop thinking about a human woman who was off-limits to him. Now his informant was going all lovey-dovey. The world was surely coming to a vile and bitter end.

"Listen, just keep your ear to the ground, okay? It's very important we know immediately if you hear anything, anything at all, about the Nefari using humans to abduct other humans."

"You think they're doing that to get past the only two defenses humans have?"

"I hope not, but there's chatter. And if it's true, daylight and buildings will no longer help humans."

"They'll be sitting ducks." Rico drew in a deep breath he

didn't need. He could no longer be part of the living crime families, and the Nefari wouldn't accept him because he had a soul. The only reason he hadn't been taken out was because he'd saved the life of one of the Nefari's big bosses. They allowed him to coexist in the same section of Little Italy because they didn't consider him a threat. Little did they know he'd been an informant even when he'd been alive.

He'd reached out to the NYPD, to Campbell, after seeing his higher-ups wipe out an innocent family because the father refused to pay protection money. Because of Rico, who was never going to be the guy you suspected of ratting you out, the NYPD had put away half a dozen mobsters for all manner of crimes. By tapping him in this instance, Campbell hoped that good fortune would continue and they could wipe up this using-humans-as-fetchers mess before it got out of hand.

"I'll let you know if I hear anything," Rico finally said.

"Thanks."

Just as Campbell disconnected the call, someone knocked loudly on his door.

"Hey, man," Travis said through the door. "Got something you're gonna want to look at."

Campbell stood, determined to flood his mind with work so he'd stop imagining greasy humans snatching Olivia and dragging her off where he'd never see her again.

He shook his head and tried to convince himself that it didn't matter if he never saw her again as long as she was safe, from vampires and her own kind alike.

"Be right there." He made the mistake of closing his eyes for a moment, and a vision of Olivia immediately materialized against his eyelids, her hair dancing in the breeze and sunlight glinting off those golden waves. He had to forcibly yank himself from that daydream and head out into the work area.

"Find something new?" he asked, in command.

Travis slid behind his desk. It was loaded with two computers and four monitors and all kinds of other high-tech gizmos Campbell couldn't even begin to name. Travis had garnered the nickname Wizard not because he looked a thing like Gandalf or Harry Potter but rather because the dude could do magic with computers. It was hard to believe he'd been a stockbroker instead of some tech wonder boy out in Silicon Valley.

"I was checking security cameras around the city and spotted this from a couple of hours ago." Travis pulled up a video recording and pointed at the screen. "Watch this building here."

It looked like the back entrance to a high-rise apartment building. After a few seconds a van with Dan's Carpets written on the side pulled into the parking lot close to the large garbage bin. Travis hit a button to skip ahead a couple of minutes to when a woman carrying a garbage bag stepped out the door.

Campbell realized whoever was in the carpet van hadn't gotten out. Just as the woman tossed her garbage into the bin, the van's sliding side door opened behind her. Before she could scream, a masked man clamped his hand over her mouth and dragged her backward into the van. The door slid closed before a total of five seconds had elapsed.

"Think that's our guys?" Colin asked from where he stood with his arm propped on top of one of Travis's four-drawer filing cabinets.

"I'd be willing to bet a week's supply of blood on it. The abductee is Jennifer Watson." Travis looked up at Campbell. "She's on the list and type AB negative. They all are. We hadn't been able to reach her to tell her about the danger."

The muscles in Campbell's crossed arms bunched. "They've taken her for a blood slave."

Travis nodded. "She'll bring top dollar. All of them will if the slavers get their hands on them."

What happened to the days when picking up the odd human who wandered out at night had satisfied the blood slavers?

Campbell pointed at the computer monitor. "Find out everything you can about Dan's Carpets and Jennifer Watson. I want these guys stopped, and stopped yesterday."

He had to put an end to this newest threat before the trail to AB-negative humans led them to Olivia's front door. And if they even attempted to touch her, he would rip them apart limb by limb and not be the least bit sorry about it.

Chapter 7

Olivia tied the garbage bag as she glanced toward where Mindy was adding up the receipts for the day and reconciling it with the cash and credit card slips. "Go on home," she said. "I can finish that up."

Mindy gave her a suspicious look. "I do this every day."

"After everything that's happened, I'm a little jumpy. I want to make sure you get home before sunset."

Mindy returned her attention to her work. "I'm almost done."

Truth was that Olivia wanted to be alone. Well, no, that wasn't exactly true. The idea of being here alone when kidnappers might break in at any moment frightened her near senseless, but trying to ignore all the looks Mindy had been shooting her all day was exhausting. She'd felt as if she had to play at normal when her life felt as if it had left normal far in the rearview mirror.

She picked up the trash bag and headed for the back door.

She stopped halfway there, overrun with a not totally irrational fear of stepping foot outside despite blue skies and plenty of sunshine left in the day.

"Olivia, what's wrong?"

Olivia dropped the bag and leaned against the center worktable. "Don't get mad. Just listen."

Mindy's expression hardened, but she stayed quiet.

"I've talked to Campbell more than once. He was who called this morning."

Mindy cursed and took a couple of angry steps to her right.

Olivia pressed on. "He told me something you need to know."

"I doubt he has anything to say I want to hear."

"He said his team had heard that something called the Nefari—I can't believe I'm saying this—the vampire Mafia, has employed humans to work for them during daylight hours."

Mindy jerked, startled. "Humans? Working for vampires? That seems unlikely."

"Is it? Think back to before we knew vampires existed. There were always people who would do anything for money. Maybe they're even doing it for guaranteed protection."

Mindy paced across the room and then back. Her face was scrunched up as if she was thinking hard.

"I wondered the same thing, you know," Olivia said.

Mindy stopped pacing and met her gaze. "What?"

"If he had some ulterior motive for telling me that, but I can't think of a single reason it would benefit him."

"Maybe scare you so you trust him more?"

"Scare me into staying inside? That doesn't exactly put me within his grasp."

Mindy seemed genuinely stumped, and she wasn't happy to be left without a quick vampires-are-evil answer.

"Trust me. This doesn't make any sense to me either, especially after seeing what vampires can do up close and way too personal. Either he and his team are different or I'm the world's biggest fool."

"I'm leaning toward the latter," Mindy said. She stood silently in the middle of the kitchen for several seconds, biting her lip as if debating with herself. "What did he say these humans were doing? Stealing from blood banks or something?"

Olivia eyed the back door again and imagined replacing it with a metal blast door that would keep out a nuclear bomb, not to mention people with a nefarious purpose.

"They think they're kidnapping people for blood slaves."

Mindy cursed again then eyed the door with as much suspicion as Olivia had. "Bastards." She returned her attention to Olivia. "What else did he say?"

"That his team discovered a list of names of people the slavers are evidently after." She swallowed, trying to keep a new wave of fear at bay. "I'm on it."

"No." Mindy sounded pained by that revelation. It was the first time since Olivia had revealed her attraction to Campbell that Mindy had shown her anything other than anger and disbelief.

"He asked if I had a gun."

Mindy stared at Olivia for a few seconds before slowly shaking her head. "I feel as if the world just got turned upside down again."

"Welcome to my past twenty-four hours." Olivia glanced out the front window. "You really better get going."

"The hell with that. I'm not going anywhere. I'm staying here tonight. If bad dudes show up, two chicks with weapons are better than one." She stared hard at Olivia. "And I'm not comfortable leaving you alone when you're not thinking clearly."

Olivia didn't even bother to argue. Once Mindy made up

her mind about something, there was no changing it. Plus, she was right.

They were both single and lived alone with no other family in the city. That made them easier targets. And if Olivia's name was on a list for her neighborhood, Mindy's might very well be on one for hers.

After they finished all the closing tasks and locked up for the night, checking both doors about three times each, they headed upstairs.

When they reached Olivia's apartment, an odd awkwardness settled between them. Mindy looked around the main room, antsy and appearing as if she wished she were somewhere else. But it was too late now.

"What do you want to do?" Mindy asked.

"Honestly, I want to take a long hot soak in the tub. I'm feeling every one of my bruises tenfold."

Mindy waved toward the bathroom. "Go on. I'll scrounge up something to eat. I'm in the mood for something with no nutritional value whatsoever."

Olivia sighed. "Man, I miss just ordering pizza or Chinese food."

"Yeah, the filthy vamps robbed us of a lot of stuff."

Olivia sighed, unsure whether she could handle Mindy's attitude all night. Her friend was entitled to her opinion, but Olivia was tired and confused and wanted to sleep for a week. She headed for the bubble bath that was calling her name.

When she sank into the tub of warm water, it was nothing short of heavenly. She didn't read as she thought she might, instead laying her head back and closing her eyes. As the warmth soaked through her, relieving her aches and pains, she drifted into a state of semiconsciousness. Her thoughts drifted, as well, and ended up settling on one Campbell Raines, all six-plus muscular feet of him.

Somehow her mind knew this wasn't real and so it was

safe to go where she wanted. He stood in the middle of her living room, and she stared at him in confusion.

"How did you get in here?" she asked.

"You invited me in, remember?"

"I did?"

"Yes, Olivia. You wanted me here, where I could touch you."

"Bite me?"

"Only if you want me to."

Did she want that? No, of course not. But something else? She walked closer and looked up at his handsome face. Yes, she definitely wanted something else. "Kiss me."

He smiled and she was glad to see his fangs were safely tucked away. His mouth lowered toward hers, and her heart rate picked up in anticipation of the feel of his lips on hers. When their lips met, her entire body started to vibrate with need, with wanting him. He seemed to feel the same, and the kiss deepened. Why hadn't she invited him in sooner? Why had she been so afraid?

She was so caught up in the kiss that she didn't notice the change in him at first. A low growl, an animal sound, had started in his throat. Fear leaped inside her and she tried to push away. He didn't let her.

"Campbell, let me go." She pushed at his chest, but it was no use.

"Never," he growled next to her ear. He pulled back enough for her to see his fully descended fangs a moment before he plunged them into her neck.

Olivia gasped and sat up so quickly she sloshed water over the side of the tub. Her heart was beating so fast she wondered if it would ever slow.

"Liv, you okay?" Mindy asked from the other side of the bathroom door.

Olivia stared at the door for a few seconds as reality fell

a little more into place. She was fine. She hadn't invited any vampires into her home. She lifted her hand to her neck and found it free from puncture marks.

"Yeah, fine. I just drifted off."

"Well, don't drown yourself. I can't eat all this food by myself."

Olivia smiled a little, thankful her friend sounded a bit more like herself. No doubt she'd pulled out every bit of junk food in the apartment and made a smorgasbord of it. When Mindy was working out a problem, she fueled her brain with chips, dip and snack cakes—enough salt and sugar to freak out every cardiologist in Manhattan.

"I'll be out in a minute."

When she heard Mindy walk away from the door, Olivia sank back into the cooling water for a moment to let the rest of her scrambled thoughts sort themselves out between reality and dream. And then between the parts of the dream she liked and the part that was pure terror. Maybe it was her subconscious reminding her that no matter how nice Campbell seemed, no matter how attractive, he was still basically a killing machine.

But that kiss. She had no idea if that was how it would really feel, but it made for a mighty fine dream kiss. She lifted her hand out of the water and touched her lips, realized just how much she missed being held, being made to feel desirable and loved.

"Oh, Jeremy," she whispered. "Why did you have to leave me?"

She pushed thoughts of Jeremy and Campbell away as she got out of the tub, toweled off and put on her most comfortable cotton pajamas. If the bath didn't set her troubled mind at ease, maybe a night of TV and junk food would do the trick. She walked out to find Mindy had baked a sausage pizza and some mozzarella cheese sticks, held a bag of barbecue potato chips in her hands and by the smell of things had a pan of brownies in the oven.

"How long was I in there?" Olivia asked.

Mindy shrugged. "Awhile."

Olivia swiped a slice of pizza and a soda and headed for the couch. The buzzer went off on the stove, sending Mindy toward the kitchen to retrieve the brownies.

"Turn on something," Mindy said. "It's too damn quiet in here."

Olivia flipped channels until she found *Leap Year* just starting, then sat back to enjoy her pizza. It was so good to have something escapist to watch again instead of the nonstop news coverage during the virus outbreak and the revelation of the vampire threat. Worse had been when so many media people died that TV broadcasts were intermittent. Gradually, on-air time had returned to a normal schedule with something other than all gloom all the time.

Mindy slid the pan of wonderful-smelling brownies onto the coffee table and sat down with her own plate of pizza.

They ate in what could only be called a tense silence. Olivia cursed herself for revealing anything about Campbell and ruining the friendly ease between her and Mindy.

"You didn't have to babysit me tonight," Olivia said.

"You're in danger and already injured. Of course I had to stay."

"*Had* to?"

"You know what I mean."

Olivia was afraid she did. She'd committed the one unforgivable sin—thinking anything remotely positive about a vampire.

Mindy motioned toward Olivia's ankle. "How's it feeling?"

"Better."

They fell into silence again and watched some more of the movie. Olivia set her plate on the coffee table, her appetite gone. She stopped paying attention to the movie even though it was one of her favorites. Instead she started thinking about how to protect herself against the latest threat. "Min, when my ankle heals, will you teach me self-defense?"

Mindy had taken karate, Tae Kwon Do, kickboxing and who knew how many other classes meant to ensure she was never an easy target. She nodded. "Good idea, on one condition."

"What?"

Mindy turned toward her and met her gaze. "You promise me you'll never talk to this vampire again."

Olivia hesitated a moment but realized this was for the best—for her relationship with her best friend, not to mention her own safety and sanity. She nodded. "I promise." Why did those words feel wrong?

"One other thing."

"What?"

"Find someone to date, someone with a heartbeat."

Olivia shook her head. "I'm too busy for a relationship. I have the restaurant to run, and I've got to figure out a way to start delivering meals again."

"If you've got time to talk to a vampire on the phone, you've got time for a relationship."

"I don't think I'm ready."

"It's been two years. You know I loved Jeremy, but he's gone. And if the past few years have taught us anything, it's that we don't know how much time we have."

"We never knew that."

"No, but doesn't the distant possibility of heart disease or being hit by a crazy-ass cabdriver seem so minor now compared to global pandemics and vampires?"

She had a very good point. Still, it was a huge step to move from being in mourning to trying to find romantic happiness again. She wasn't sure she was ready or able to take it.

"Well, I obviously have time to think about it with no viable prospects on the horizon. And what about you? I don't see you pairing up."

"Oh, honey, I've been looking. Just haven't found the right guy yet."

"And what would Mr. Right look like to you?"

"I'll know when I see him." Mindy sounded surprisingly serious in her answer.

The phone rang, startling Olivia and causing Mindy's jaw to tense. Olivia forced herself not to say anything as Mindy answered.

"No. This is Mindy, her best friend. Who is this?"

Olivia knew it was Campbell even without hearing his voice.

"She doesn't want to talk to you, so don't ever call back. And if you show up here, I will find a way to stake your ass deader than dead." Mindy slammed down the phone. "There, that takes care of your vampire-caller problem."

Olivia forced herself to nod and return her attention to the movie. She tried not to focus on how much she wanted to call Campbell back and apologize. This was for the best. Then why didn't it feel like it?

Chapter 8

To cover more ground and to make the most of the night hours at their disposal, Campbell and his team split up. Sophia, Billy, Len and Colin worked on getting more information on Jennifer Watson and beating the streets for anything else about humans working for vampires. Kaja, Travis and he headed for Dan's Carpets. He needed the work to occupy his mind so he'd stop thinking about how Olivia didn't want to talk to him. Hell, it shouldn't be a surprise. Just showed she had more sense than he did.

No surprise, Dan's Carpets was closed up tight for the night, but there was no sign of any human captives on the property.

"This not being able to break down doors and have a look around sure makes things difficult," Kaja said.

Travis laughed.

"What?"

"Sorry. It's just funny thinking of a skinny little model kicking down doors."

"Models are tougher than you think. They have to be. Didn't you see *Kill Bill?*"

Travis retreated into his laptop as Campbell pulled out of the parking lot and headed for Little Italy. After a lot of key punching, Travis cursed.

"That doesn't sound like good news," Kaja said from where she was touching up her fingernail polish in the back of the truck.

"Looks as if the delivery van used to kidnap Jennifer Watson had been reported stolen two days before."

"Convenient," Campbell said.

"It looks legit." Travis stared out the windshield. "What if they're stealing vehicles, using them in one abduction and then dumping them?"

"Covering their tracks." Campbell squeezed the steering wheel even tighter.

"Well, that just made catching these cretins harder," Kaja said.

"Don't worry, we'll catch them," Campbell said. And the perps weren't going to like it when they did. He pulled his phone from his pocket and checked for messages.

"You expecting a call?" Kaja asked.

Campbell made the mistake of meeting Kaja's eyes in the rearview mirror. Kaja might seem vain and frivolous, but she was also supersharp and didn't miss anything, either overt or subtext.

"Just seeing if the others have found out anything."

"Uh-huh."

He ignored her disbelieving tone, but it did him no good.

"It's the human woman—you like her."

He forced a shrug. "She seems like a nice person."

"Don't be deliberately dense, Campbell. You know what I mean."

"I'm sure I don't."

She made a disgusted sound. "Too bad the turning process doesn't make men smarter."

Travis looked up from his computer and back at Kaja. "Hey, what's with the generalizations?"

"You were already smart. Though I've never seen you around women. I'll reserve judgment on that until I see you in action."

"And when do any of us have time to date? We work non-stop."

"Now, that's just not true," Campbell said. "What is this, National Pick on Your Boss Night?"

"No, but I like the sound of that," Kaja said. "But stop avoiding the topic. You know you can't be with her, right?"

He sighed. "Yes, I'm abundantly aware. Not that it's any of your business."

"Excuse me? It is my business if I end up having to stake you because you've killed her."

An icy chill went down Campbell's spine. At Kaja's words, a flash of Olivia cold and lifeless in his arms, blood trickling down from bite marks on her neck, hit him and turned his stomach. He didn't have to imagine it. He'd seen it all too vividly before.

"You okay, man?" Travis said.

"Yeah." Not in the slightest, but he would be as soon as he purged Olivia DaCosta from his thoughts.

Olivia's exhaustion made her sleep so hard that Mindy had to wake her the next morning.

"Come on, sleepyhead," Mindy said. "You forgot to set your alarm."

Olivia blinked her eyes, trying to alleviate the ripped-from-sleep confusion. She looked at the clock, which did more to wake her up than Mindy's words. "Good grief!" She threw off the covers and raced for the bathroom as fast as her healing but still-tender ankle would let her.

"I'm going on downstairs, get things started," Mindy said.

"Okay, be down in a minute."

She flew through her toothbrushing, changed clothes and ran a brush through her hair before hurrying downstairs. Rusty was already out front when she hit the bottom step, so she veered toward the door to unlock it.

"Is something wrong?" he asked as he stepped inside.

"No, nothing. We just overslept this morning. Too many brownies last night and not enough setting of alarm clocks."

Rusty shook his head. "Girl, you can't scare an old man like that."

"Well, if I see an old man, I'll try not to scare him."

Rusty planted a kiss on her forehead and headed toward his usual table. "You're good for my ego."

"We aim to please, serving up ego stroking with your bacon and eggs."

"You know, life is short and I'm feeling a bit adventurous today. I think I'll have some French toast."

Olivia's mouth dropped open. "Who are you and what have you done with Rusty?"

He laughed. "Guess I'm just tired of the same thing day after day. Where's the fun in that?"

It hit Olivia that she could say the same about herself. Her days didn't differ much from one another, unless, of course, you included a vampire attack and phone calls from a tall, sexy vampire who was so off-limits it was painful. She glanced at Mindy, hoping she couldn't magically read her thoughts.

As more of the morning regulars and a few new faces started arriving, Olivia headed to the kitchen to start another of her carbon-copy days. The sense of dissatisfaction surprised her. She loved her diner and the customers. Cooking for them made her happy. So why did she suddenly feel as though her life wasn't complete?

Because she was alone, surrounded by people but still alone. Except she hadn't felt that way when she was talking to Campbell. Maybe Mindy had been right about staying with her the night before. Maybe she did need babysitting.

She shook her head and focused her attention on filling orders.

"Did you all see this?" Rusty asked as he thumped a story in that morning's *New York Times*. "Leila Russell is reporting that she's come across evidence that humans are working for vampires, that there have been kidnappings in the past week."

Olivia's heart slammed against her rib cage and she had to grab the edge of the countertop to steady herself. She'd hoped that Campbell had been wrong, but having the same story in black and white, reported by a human journalist who covered the vampire beat, made it even more real. She resisted the very real urge to be sick.

"Guess it was just a matter of time before some lowlife got that idea," said Barney Bretton, a retired cop. "Bottom-feeders in every species."

"How could a person even think about working for one of those animals?" Barney's wife, Cheryl, asked. "I can't stomach the idea of even speaking to one, let alone going into business together. I hope they all get their heads chopped off."

Olivia jerked at the hatred in Cheryl's voice and had to turn away. She went to the large walk-in freezer, where she couldn't hear the continuing conversation. Once inside, she took slow, deep breaths.

"You okay?"

Olivia gasped and took an involuntary step backward before it clicked that it was only Mindy. "Yeah." She grabbed a box. "Just needed some more cheese."

Mindy didn't look convinced, but she didn't press the point and left Olivia alone.

Olivia took another moment to calm down, reminding herself that people had very good reasons to hate vampires. Two days ago she likely would have agreed wholeheartedly. Now her head hurt every time she wondered if the world actually had a lot more shades of gray instead of being all black-and-white when it came to vampires. Thankfully the dining room conversation had shifted to the more usual griping about politicians when she returned to the kitchen, and she fell into her normal rhythm as the morning progressed.

When the breakfast crowd left and they found themselves in the morning lull, Mindy came into the kitchen and took off her apron. "The first rule of self-defense is to always be aware of your surroundings. Look people in the eye. If something feels wrong, don't do it. I'm a firm believer in gut instinct."

Over the next hour, Mindy showed Olivia the location of pressure points, how to disable an attacker by kicking the side of his knee and how to make a fist and use the other hand to help make an elbow strike more effective.

Olivia glanced at the clock. "I need to get started on the lunch prep."

"One more thing. Palm strikes to the nose can be effective because they're painful and can knock your attacker off balance, giving you a chance to get away." Mindy showed her how to hold her palm forward, bring back her arm then shove the heel of her hand up into someone's nose. "You ram them with as much force as you can."

Olivia performed a few practice jabs, wondering if any of this would have the slightest effect on a vampire. Not that she planned to be in a situation to have to protect herself against a vampire again. But all of this was good to know because there were plenty of lowlife humans still walking the streets of New York.

Now that Mindy had assumed the role of self-defense teacher, she went all in. Any downtime at the diner was spent practicing jabs and kicks. She even spent the next two nights at Olivia's apartment, and they practiced until Olivia's muscles were screaming from the atypical use. But it felt good to do something proactive to ensure her own safety. Mindy even found her practicing some moves when she got out of the shower the morning after their second night practice.

"Addictive, isn't it?" Mindy asked as she toweled her hair dry.

"Yeah. Just call me Ninja Olivia."

Mindy snorted and walked toward the coffeepot as Olivia headed for her own shower.

Around ten o'clock, right when they would normally be starting another self-defense session, two guys ambled through the front door and immediately set Olivia's nerves on edge. They didn't get many customers who weren't locals, and these didn't look like tourists either. Big, muscled, the type who looked as though they might work for vampires. As Mindy headed toward their table, Olivia wrapped her hand around one of her large kitchen knives. She didn't take her eyes off them as Mindy took their orders then headed toward the kitchen.

When Mindy saw Olivia's grip on the knife, she whispered, "I see you got the same vibe I did."

Just then the bigger of the two met Olivia's gaze, and her blood frosted. She swallowed hard. "What do they want?"

"Two BLTs and coffee."

Olivia moved out of their view before speaking again. "Keep an eye on them."

Mindy nodded as she turned back toward the dining room.

Olivia placed bacon on the grill with one hand while she reached for the phone with the other. When it rang, she jumped. She answered, but it was a wrong number. She used the phone's ring to cover up the fact she then dialed Campbell's number.

"Raines," he answered.

"Campbell, it's Olivia DaCosta."

At first she thought he wasn't going to respond. "Olivia." His voice was toneless, distant, as if he didn't know her. Not the time to worry about that now.

"Listen, this may be nothing, but there are two big guys who just came in the diner and they're giving Mindy and me a weird feeling. I know you can't do anything, but—"

"Don't apologize. I'm glad you called me." He didn't sound glad. He sounded worried. And yes, odd timing, but that made her feel a warmth inside she hadn't felt in a long time, the warmth of mattering to someone. "If you get too scared, call the police. Doesn't matter if it's a false alarm."

"Better safe than sorry, I know."

"Describe them to me," he said.

"They're both tall, over six feet, though one is probably two to three inches taller than the other. Blue-collar dress. Jeans, work boots. One's wearing a denim jacket and the other black leather. The taller one has dark curly hair, dark complexion."

"He look Italian?"

"Maybe some, though I'd say not totally."

"What about the other one?"

"Sandy hair, little scruffy. Looks maybe of Eastern European descent."

"What are they doing?"

Olivia casually moved so she could glance through the pass-through window. "Just sitting there talking, waiting for their BLTs. But…"

"But what?"

"I don't know if I'm just freaking myself out or what, but when one of them looked at me, I swear my blood went cold."

Campbell cursed, and she heard him moving around, as if he was pacing. "I hate this."

She knew he was talking about being trapped by the daylight. He didn't have to say the words for her to know that if he could, he'd be there in a flash to stand between her and the two spooky dudes. Did that make sense? No. Did she feel the absolute truth of it? Yes.

"It's okay. Just talking helps."

He was quiet for a moment, and she wondered if she'd sounded as goofy to him as she did to herself. "I'm surprised."

"I'm sorry about the other night. I can't believe I'm apologizing to a vampire, but there you go."

"Your friend is probably right. You shouldn't be."

As she finished putting the sandwiches together, Mindy came back into the kitchen.

"No, we already have a supplier," Olivia said, unwilling to let Mindy know she'd broken her promise by calling Campbell. She wouldn't be able to explain how just talking to him made her feel safer. She didn't understand it herself.

"What?" Campbell asked.

"Sure, you can send us some material in case we ever decide to switch."

"Your friend is there and she doesn't know you're talking to me."

"That's right."

Mindy grabbed the plates, but Olivia stopped her by grasping her wrist. "Wait." She slid one of the smaller, less conspicuous knives out of the butcher block and into the pocket of Mindy's apron. "Be careful," she whispered. Mindy nodded then headed for the dining room.

"What's going on?" Campbell asked.

"Mindy's taking them their food," she said softly so Mindy wouldn't hear her.

"She lost someone, didn't she?"

"How did you know that?" If what he said was true, he was a cop. Had he been running checks on her and Mindy?

"I can always tell. There's a hostility in human voices when they've lost someone to vamps. Otherwise, it's usually just fear."

Olivia glanced toward the dining room to make sure Mindy was still out of hearing range. "Her mother and sister were drained and left on the front steps of their house the night before the announcement was made about vampires being real and to stay indoors at night."

Campbell cursed.

"It was a horrible time for her. You won't find anyone who hates vampires more."

"I don't blame her."

Olivia watched as Mindy delivered the food to the guys and nothing out of the ordinary happened.

"Everything okay?" Campbell asked.

"Yeah, they're just eating."

"I'll stay on here as long as you want me to," he said.

"I appreciate it. I feel sort of silly."

"Don't."

Needing to talk about something else until there was a reason to return to the topic of their unsettling customers, Olivia asked, "So, what were you doing before I called? Sleeping?"

"I don't require sleep anymore."

"Really?"

"We rest, but no sleep."

"Wow, I could get so much done if I didn't have to sleep," she said, trying to relieve some of the tension knotting her muscles and making her nerves spark.

"Trust me, I wish I could sleep. I miss it."

"You miss a lot of things, don't you?"

"What makes you say that?"

Why had she? "Just a feeling. But I'm right, aren't I?"

"Yes." He didn't elaborate.

She tried just letting his presence on the other end of the line be enough, but the silence started grating on her nerves. So she filled it with whatever questions came to mind. "Do you still have family?"

"Some distant cousins. No one close."

"Oh."

"They didn't die in the pandemic. I was an only child, and my parents died in a car crash when I was a kid. I grew up in foster care."

"I'm sorry."

"It was a long time ago. What about you?"

Was he really interested, or was Mindy right and he had some well-concealed ulterior motive? For the life of her, she couldn't figure out what it might be. He'd had his chance to kill her several times and hadn't.

"Just my mom. She lives upstate with my uncle. He never married, and he's glad to have someone cook for him."

"Your dad?"

"Never knew him. He skipped out when I was still in diapers."

"Sorry."

She didn't know why she laughed, but she did. "Aren't we the tragic pair?"

He made a sort of snuffing noise, the meaning of which she couldn't identify. "I guess everyone has a tragic story now."

Wasn't that the truth? She couldn't think of a single pandemic survivor who hadn't lost someone, either to the ravages of the disease or to the vampires who'd emerged in its wake. That last part sobered her.

"Do any other humans know about the differences in vampires? For example, does our president talk to whoever is in charge of the Imperium?"

"Maybe. That's above my pay grade."

"I know what you said about if everyone fears vampires, it helps keep humans safe, but maybe the Imperium and world leaders could work together somehow for our mutual benefit."

"They did, on the blood banks."

"That's one thing. There's got to be something else."

"Let it go, Olivia. The world is what it is, no matter how much we wish we could change it."

Campbell fell silent again for several seconds, and she watched as the two guys ate their sandwiches slowly while Mindy took a to-go order from a bike messenger at the front counter.

"What made you become a cop?" she asked, taking them down a different path.

"In the blood, I guess. My dad and my grandfather were both with NYPD. Even though I lost them both when I was young, I never forgot that. What makes you run a diner?"

"I like to cook. Take care of people, I guess."

"I can see that."

"How? You barely know me."

"I didn't see anyone else out delivering meals to the homeless," he said. "Most people are so wrapped up in their own lives that they don't even see them."

"That unfortunately is nothing new. And it's why I need to get my car back, so I can start delivering meals again. The idea that people are out there hungry makes me sick."

"It's too dangerous now," Campbell said.

"You'll eventually catch whoever is working with the Soulless vampires."

"I'm glad you have so much faith in us, but I'm afraid that even when we shut down this particular operation, there's just going to be another. That door's been opened, and there's always going to be someone to exploit it."

"That sounds so hopeless. How do you keep going out and fighting it every night?"

"Because if we don't, no one will. And because…" His words trailed off as if he'd forgotten what he was about to say. But when he started to speak again, Olivia thought maybe he'd just gotten lost in a memory. "We can all remember what it was like to be human, and we fight to allow as many people to keep that type of life as possible."

"So the vampires don't run out of food."

"No. So at least someone can feel what it's like to breathe, to feel their heart beat, to be warm."

Olivia didn't have time to really soak in Campbell's words, because one of the big guys suddenly scooted his chair back and stood as Mindy slid the bike messenger's order slip through the window. Olivia's eyes met Mindy's and she saw her friend's hand slide toward the knife in her pocket.

Olivia must have made a sound of distress, because Campbell asked, "What's happening?"

"They're standing."

"Do you have your gun?"

"No, but I have a really big knife."

"I don't want you that close to them," he said. "They'll be able to overpower you."

Olivia's pulse skyrocketed as she considered she might have to fight these two brutes off with only a knife and her wits to save her. They looked at her again as they stepped up to the counter and paid. And then they simply left.

"Olivia?" Campbell said on the other end of the line.

"They just left." She relaxed and Mindy visibly did the same. "I feel really dumb now for calling you."

"The danger might not be over. They could be checking out the lay of the land before coming back later."

"Or they could just be two hungry guys who contributed to my bank account. I don't want to live in a constant state of fear, suspicious of everyone who walks through the front door."

She braced herself for an argument because she could feel the disagreement cross the miles between her and Campbell.

"I think you might be right," he finally said. "Maybe it is time for the Souled vampires to reach out to human officials about working together. It's time I contact my former brethren at the NYPD. You need protection. Keep your eyes open until I can arrange it." And then he hung up.

Olivia pulled the phone away from her ear and stared at it. Evidently, the male sex's tendency to take charge without asking didn't go away when they turned into vampires.

"Who was that?" Mindy asked.

"A really pushy salesman." She didn't like lying to Mindy, but it was better than losing her.

"I guess some things never change."

Olivia looked toward the table where the two guys had sat. Despite what she'd told Campbell, she still had the heebies.

Mindy noticed where she was looking. "You ready for some more self-defense lessons?"

"More than ready." She needed to rely on herself for protection, not her friend, not the overworked cops and definitely not a vampire.

Chapter 9

Campbell felt like cussing until the walls melted around him. The first time he'd called his old NYPD precinct to ask for protection for Olivia, the officer on the other end had told him to stop prank calling and hung up. The next time, he'd asked for a supervisor and had gotten an earful about how the day the officer did something for a vampire was the day hell froze over.

They had to know the kidnapping threat was real. It had already hit the news outlets. Why wouldn't they listen? Because they had their hands full and probably received at least a dozen prank calls a day. And he'd made the mistake of telling them he was a vampire.

He rubbed his hand over his face. How was he supposed to protect Olivia if he couldn't go out during the day and the cops who patrolled then wouldn't listen to him? Why the hell did he think he could bridge the gap even the Imperium didn't attempt to bridge?

He paced his private quarters and ran his hand over his face. At least he wasn't out in the main room, where his team members could hear every word and shake their heads at his involvement with a human.

He wasn't involved, not really.

But he'd like to be.

He sank onto his bed and propped his back against the wall. Here, in the privacy of his own space, he allowed himself to fantasize about what it would be like to be with her. To touch her soft skin, inhale her scent, run his fingers through all that lovely blond hair, join with her body and lose himself.

The thought of her being hurt or worse ate at him. He knew if the Nefari got hold of her, he'd tear Manhattan apart brick by brick, as well as anybody, vampire or human, who got in the way of finding her.

The power of that image jolted him. Olivia was right—he barely knew her. There was no reasonable explanation for why he felt such a pull toward her, why keeping her safe consumed him. In some moments it felt a little as though he was losing touch with reality.

And sitting in this little room alone wasn't helping.

He stood and headed out to the fridge for a bag of blood from a supply he'd picked up the night before from the blood bank on the Upper West Side. He popped it in the microwave for a few seconds then drank it as he headed toward his desk. If he didn't occupy his mind with something besides Olivia and his inability to protect her how he wanted to, he was going to go stark raving mad. And forever was a long damn time to be crazy.

"You okay?" Sophia asked when she looked up from her own desk. She said it quietly, with a glance toward where Len and Colin were watching a football game.

"I'd say yes, but you'd know I was lying."

"Is it Olivia?"

He liked how Sophia used Olivia's name and didn't just call her *the human woman* like some of the others did. Of all his team members, he and Sophia probably missed being human the most. Though she certainly had more reason than he did and was more open about it.

"I tried to get her protection during the day, but let's just say the NYPD wasn't keen on listening."

"Maybe a delegate could speak for you."

The last thing he wanted was to bring the Imperium into this. "Not sure they'd be thrilled with my being so concerned about one human."

"I doubt you talked to the NYPD just about her."

"No. I mentioned the list, but they thought I was pranking them."

Sophia nodded. "Have you talked to Olivia about this? What does she say?"

"That she doesn't want to live in fear of every person who walks through her front door."

"Understandable. Goodness knows there's plenty to be afraid of without one more thing."

Campbell stared at the TV for several seconds, then at how relaxed Len and Colin looked on the couch with their feet propped on the coffee table. He envied them.

"Do you think I'm off my rocker?" he asked.

"No," Sophia said simply.

He shifted his gaze to her. "Why not?"

"Because I don't think there's anything crazy about caring about someone."

"Even someone I barely know?"

Sophia placed her forearms on top of her desk and leaned forward. "That's what makes you a good team leader," she said. "You care about justice, about truth, about keeping both vampires and humans safe, helping us coexist the best that we can."

If she'd claimed to be the reincarnation of Cleopatra, he wouldn't have been more surprised. That was how she viewed him? He was one part humbled and one part embarrassed.

"Plus, this can be a lonely existence," she said. "I'd venture that everyone on the team yearns for someone to be with. Of course, some of them wouldn't admit it if you had a stake pointed at their hearts."

"But she's human. Why her?"

"Maybe because she's human. I think we're all still human deep down. We just have a condition that doesn't allow us to live alongside them anymore."

He heard the sadness creep into her words and knew she was missing her family, the husband and children she'd lost when she'd been turned.

But then she smiled a little. "Plus, she's really pretty."

He found himself smiling back. "That she is."

Sophia went back to working on her computer, and Campbell sat back and tried to read the latest news from the Imperium's headquarters in Bucharest. When he realized he'd read the same paragraph three times without having any idea what he'd read, he tossed the paper onto his desk and leaned back in his chair.

"I know the others will disagree with me, but I think maybe it's a good thing if you befriend Olivia," Sophia said. "You may not be able to be any more than that, but friendship is better than nothing. It's a link that none of us have anymore."

"I don't want to use her just so I can feel human again."

"That's not what I meant. It's more…maybe there's a reason the two of you met."

"I'm not a big believer in destiny or fate or whatever you want to call it." And if it did exist, it had a cruel, morbid sense of humor.

"I am. And who knows? Maybe it'll be the start of our two species understanding each other better."

"Now I know you're giving me way too much credit."

"Hey, guys, switch to Channel 2," Travis said as he shoved his rolling chair back from his desk and spun toward Len and Colin.

"Like hell," Colin said. "The Jets are inches from the goal line."

"Just do it."

Colin grumbled under his breath as he snatched the remote control and switched the channel.

"If you're just joining us, a recap of our top story," said the familiar voice of local news anchor Joe Finnion. "*New York Times* reporter Leila Russell was abducted by unknown assailants this afternoon as she was leaving the paper to conduct an interview. Russell has covered the vampire beat since it was revealed that vampires were indeed real. Police are investigating the possibility that her abduction was tied to her coverage."

"Tell me the paper has video surveillance outside," Campbell said.

"Computer's looking for it now," Travis said. Just then the computer dinged that it had completed its search. Travis punched a couple of buttons and pulled up the video. He advanced it slowly to the approximate time the news report had said Leila Russell had been taken. And there it was, a wedding-catering van pulling up to the curb next to her. Someone grabbed her and dragged her inside with little effort, and then the driver sped away.

"What do you want to bet that van was reported stolen?" Len said from where he'd come to stand behind Travis with the rest of the team.

A few clicks on the keyboard, and Travis was in the NYPD report database. "Yep, five days ago."

"Generate a list of all the vehicles reported stolen in the past month," Campbell said.

"You think whoever is behind this is who took Olivia's car?" Sophia asked.

"Possible, but I doubt it," Campbell said. "Looks as though they prefer vans. Easier to nab a person and make a quick getaway. Hard to stuff an unwilling victim in a compact car."

He didn't have to look at a clock to know they had about an hour before they could go topside. But they would make the most of that time.

"We need information, everything we can get our hands on. Cross-reference to see if the two victims we know about have anything in common other than being women. Hack their medical records to see if they have the same blood type. Find out if there have been any more missing persons reported in the past month."

Campbell divvied up the tasks, then started searching the *Times'* archives for Leila's articles to see if she'd written anything to fire up the Nefari or anyone else in the vampire community. Her recent coverage of humans working for vamps seemed the most likely catalyst. The moment he felt the sun hit the horizon, he stood and started gearing up. When it was safe to emerge, he headed for the stairs that led up to the street level.

"I'll be back in an hour," he said without looking back at the rest of the team. He headed straight for Hell's Kitchen and the Comfort Food Diner. The team could think what they wanted, but he needed to know Olivia was safe, see it with his own eyes.

The hardest part would be not caving in to the need to talk to her. Because if he started, he didn't know if he could walk away. And he had work to do, work that would hopefully keep her and the rest of Manhattan's human population safe from the very ugly side of his species.

* * *

It took a lot of effort, but Olivia finally got Mindy to go home. Once she was alone, however, she started jumping at every little sound, things that she wouldn't have even noticed before. After rubbing the muscles she'd put through the ringer that afternoon with karate lessons in the diner's kitchen, she tried to watch TV. But she kept worrying that the noise of it would prevent her from hearing if an intruder was climbing the stairs from the restaurant below. Seeing the report that Leila Russell had been abducted didn't help.

"Dang it, DaCosta, stop driving yourself batty."

Reading didn't help with her anxiety, so she headed downstairs to check the door locks for what must have been the hundredth time. With that completed, she went to the diner's fridge and stared at the contents. Lots of leftovers.

Needing to reclaim a semblance of power over her own life, she started pulling out pork loin and mashed potatoes, three-bean salad and chocolate pudding. Maybe assembling a few meals to take to Central Park the next day would settle her nerves.

It did feel good to think she could venture out and help people again. If she left Mindy in charge of the restaurant during the morning lull, she could either walk to the park or take a cab. She couldn't afford to do the latter every day, but one day of feeding the hungry was better than none.

In the middle of scooping potatoes onto several paper plates, a chill skittered over Olivia's skin. She got the distinct impression that someone was watching her. She spun with the serving spoon in her hand, as if that would do her any good as a weapon. As she moved slowly toward the butcher block, she scanned the darkness outside the front windows but saw nothing. But there was someone out there. She was as certain of that as she was her own name.

Her cell phone buzzed in her pocket, making her yelp and

drop the potato-covered spoon on the floor. It slid far back underneath the metal prep table, but it was just going to have to stay there until morning. When she checked the display on her phone, she recognized Campbell's number.

"Please tell me you're outside," she said when she answered after the third ring.

"Well, I have to say I've never heard that from a human before," he said.

"Are you?"

"Yes. Are you okay?"

She let out a long breath. "You scared me half to death."

"By calling you?"

"No. I felt someone watching me, and my hyped-up imagination was not being kind to me."

"I'm sorry. I didn't mean to frighten you."

As she watched out the front window, Campbell stepped into view, though he remained partially shadowed. "Why are you here?"

"I wanted to make sure you were okay."

"A phone call would have done that." She sounded snappish, and she realized it was because she was unable to tell him to stay away. And each time she talked to him, she betrayed Mindy even more.

"I believe I'm on the phone with you right now."

"Pretty sure your phone will work from anywhere in Manhattan."

He met her eyes, and even though he was several yards away, she felt their intensity. "Do you want me to go?"

Say yes! "I didn't say that."

"Then you want me to stay."

She sighed in frustration. "I don't know. Maybe."

He smiled a little. "I'll try not to get a big head from the enthusiasm."

She laughed. "Who knew vampires had a sense of humor?"

"Oh, yes, we're regular stand-up comedy material."

"You could get your own late-night talk show and interview all your vamp friends. Hey, maybe your own network. VTV."

"Somehow I don't think we'd get very good ratings."

"Vampires have TVs. I've seen them in the shop windows in the vampire shopping districts."

"Have to have something to do all day."

She thought about how TV and movies used to have a fascination with vampires. While she and everyone else knew they were no longer fiction, she realized there was a lot she didn't know, more information the vampire world kept hidden in the name of self-preservation.

"You look as if you're thinking hard," he said.

"Just curious how much of the vampire lore is real and how much is a bunch of bunk."

"What do you want to know?"

"I know stakes can kill you. What about crosses and holy water?"

"Crosses only affect the Soulless. They burn their skin, very painfully, from what I've witnessed. Holy water will burn them, too. And as you've seen, if any of us wear silver bracelets or cuffs soaked in holy water, it prevents our fangs from descending."

"I feel the sudden need to wear a cross all the time and to go to St. Patrick's for some holy water."

"Not a bad idea," he said. "Though those won't help against the humans."

A chill raced down her back.

"Do you think Leila Russell was taken by the same people who took that other girl?" she asked.

He shrugged. "We don't know, but that's the theory we're working right now. Did you see any more of those two guys?"

"No. They just ate, freaked us out and left."

"I still don't like it." He leaned against the post for the streetlight, which drew her attention to his long legs. "What are you still doing down in the restaurant? You're too easily seen."

She forced her attention up from where it was roaming over his body back to his eyes. "I tried going upstairs, but I kept spooking myself at every little sound. So I came down here to make some lunches to take to the park tomorrow."

"Olivia."

She held up her hand to halt his objection. "If it's humans I have to worry about now, they could just as easily stroll in and get me here."

"But it'd be easier to grab you on the street. The two women we know have been abducted have been grabbed outside."

"I'll be very careful. But, Campbell, there are people out there who are hungry, who don't have homes, who the world has forgotten about. I can't sit here and do nothing while that is going on when I could make a difference. Maybe it's a small dent in the problem, but it's something."

"I'm not going to talk you out of this, am I?"

"No. It means too much to me."

"Why?"

"I just told you."

"I know, you care about the people. But it's more than that. There's caring, and then there's passion."

She turned her back on him and started wrapping the prepared plates with plastic wrap and placing them in the refrigerator. "Someone close to me started this program, someone who isn't around to do it anymore." She turned back to face him again. "Listen, I'm going upstairs. There's a small balcony on the back side of the apartment. You're welcome to sit out there if you'd like."

"I need to get back to work and patrol the area."

"Oh, okay." She was surprised by how much she wanted him to stay, but she wasn't about to admit that just because she didn't want to be alone.

"But I can stay a bit longer."

She climbed the stairs, calling herself a fool all the way up. By the time she reached the top one, he was already seated outside on the balcony.

"Now, that's just annoying," she said, causing him to smile. The sight of it, fang-free, took her breath away.

He glanced toward the darkened building behind hers. "Aren't you afraid someone will see me up here? Word is spreading that there are humans working with vampires. Your neighbors might get the wrong idea about you."

"That building is empty. Everyone either wiped out by the virus or they moved away from the city. Even the owners died, so I don't know if it's even safe now. Ownership may be wrapped up in court."

She crossed the room to the door next to the tiny balcony, knowing she was safe from Campbell as long as she didn't invite him inside. She gestured toward the brick building. "It's things like all those empty apartments that make me so angry. After humanity took a bigger hit than it ever has, there's plenty of space for the homeless. But either the buildings are not safe or the owners are greedy and won't allow anyone to live in the space for free." She shook her head at the waste. "There are some shelters, but not enough and they don't have enough funding. They're crowded, dangerous, run low on food and supplies."

"Maybe things will change," he said. "It really hasn't been that long since the world got turned on its head. People are still in shock."

Being this close to him should have scared her, but it didn't. He couldn't hurt her. And if it weren't for the bright blue of his eyes in the half-light, she wouldn't have been able to tell he was a vampire. Feeling silly talking on the phone to him when he was only a few feet away, she started to open the balcony door.

"Olivia, no!"

She halted and met his gaze. "You can't come in unless I invite you, right?"

He hesitated, staring at the crack in the door as if it might lead to eternal damnation. Finally, he nodded.

Her heart beating faster, a fact of which he was most certainly aware, she opened the door a little wider and pulled one of her dining chairs up next to it. She ended the call and slipped the phone into her pocket.

"You'll get cold," he said.

She smiled. "I have blankets. I'd offer you one, but I know you don't need it." His gorgeous expanse of chest that first night had shown her that. Her skin flushed at that memory, and she had to shove away a fantasy about running her hands over all that taut, muscled skin.

He shook his head and looked out into the night when a metallic bang sounded in the distance, most likely an animal scavenging in the alleys for food. She watched as he assessed any potential threat then relaxed.

"Are you always cold?" she asked.

"I would be to the human touch. We don't really notice it after a while."

"But you do at first?"

He nodded, and she didn't think he would elaborate.

"That's the oddest part of the transition, feeling the heat slowly drain out of your body. That and feeling your heart slow until it finally just stops."

"You felt yourself dying and were awake for it all?"

"Yeah."

"That's horrible."

He shrugged. "What's done is done. Just have to make

the best of it." He stared at her for a long moment. "Why are you talking to me?"

She held his gaze as she thought for a moment. "I like you. Despite the fact I know you could kill me in the blink of an eye, my instinct tells me you're a good guy. At least as much as you can be. A few days ago I would have never believed that was possible."

"What changed your mind?"

"When you came back to apologize, how concerned you've been for my safety and that of the other people on that list. You probably don't even realize how many times you've scanned the area for danger just since you've been sitting on the balcony. I don't care what superpowers vampires have—I don't think that can be faked that well."

He stared at her for so long that she grew uncomfortable. "What?"

"No one ever sees that. Granted, humans being killed by vampires and left in the streets made it impossible to believe that some of us aren't all bad."

"You all are so powerful. How did you stay hidden so long?"

He received a text and replied before answering her.

"Centuries ago we weren't. That's how all the stories about vampires got started. But the Imperium eventually set up strict laws about feeding and revealing ourselves. That's when V Force, or the Guard, as it was called then, was started, the enforcement arm of the Imperium. It's how we ensured our survival."

"Did the Imperium change the laws when Bokor hit?"

"Not about revelation. But when you have a limited food supply and too many vampires falling into bloodlust, it became impossible to keep them all in check. The feeding laws did change after the blood banks were established. It's illegal to feed from a human now."

"And your job got a lot more difficult."

He nodded. "Staying fed and keeping ourselves under control became a lot harder." He glanced at her before looking away with what looked like shame on his face. "Still is sometimes, despite the blood banks."

"None of us knows what we'd do if we were starving until it happens," she said. "Humans have killed for food, too." The full force of that truth didn't hit her until she said the words, making her realize that on that one thing humans and vampires were similar.

"That's different."

"Is it? There's brutality in survival, for every species."

He was quiet again for several seconds before finally saying, "I guess."

They fell into silence and she glanced up at the rising full moon. Though the city that used to never sleep lay quiet, it was nice to know some things never changed. The sun still rose each morning. The wind still blew. And the moon still made its way through its phases month after month.

"Who did you lose?" Campbell asked, his voice quiet.

She shifted her gaze back to him.

"The person who started the food delivery to the homeless," he said.

The old pain that never entirely went away stabbed at her. She would have guessed she wouldn't have wanted to share that information with him, but she found she wanted to talk about Jeremy. He'd been on her mind even more the past couple of days. Maybe it was her too-close brush with death, or the fact that for the first time since he'd been gone she was feeling attraction toward another man. And to her, no matter what Mindy said, Campbell was a man. He was no longer just a mindless animal.

She took a deep fortifying breath. "His name was Jeremy. He ran a charity that accepted donated meals from restaurants all over Manhattan, food that would have likely been thrown away at the end of the day, and delivered it to the homeless all over the city." She bit her bottom lip when she felt it tremble, then met Campbell's eyes. "He was my fiancé."

Chapter 10

Fiancé. Olivia could have been married by now. It shouldn't bother him, but it did. And then he hated himself for thinking it because she'd obviously lost someone she loved. He had a hard time getting the next question out.

"Vampires?"

She shook her head. "The virus." She blinked against the tears shining in her eyes.

Why had he mentioned it, this memory that brought her pain?

"He died the day before our original wedding date. He was so upset we had to change it, but I told him it was okay. We'd get married after he got better." She grew quiet, lost in the past.

"But you knew he wasn't going to get better."

She nodded. "He couldn't see what I did, that the disease was ravaging his body. But it was important to let him believe he'd get better. He was always such a positive person, and I couldn't stand the thought of seeing that die, too."

"I'm sorry, Livvi."

She looked up at him with a confused expression. "What did you call me?"

He had to think about it for a minute. "Livvi."

"No one has ever called me that. Liv, yes, but not Livvi."

"I won't if you don't like it. I didn't even think about it, but it fits you."

"No, I like it." She smiled a little, and it made his unbeating heart swell. He could sit here and just look at her all night. Each time she smiled, it transformed her from beautiful to breathtaking. He wanted to tell her that but kept his mouth closed. No matter how open-minded she was becoming, he doubted she wanted to hear such a thing from a vampire.

"You and Jeremy, you were together a long time?" He didn't really want to know the answer, but he remembered Sophia's words. He and Olivia could never be more, but they might be able to be friends. He hadn't realized until that moment what having a friend who was still human would mean to him. He felt an unusual ease with her, as if he could say things he could never share with his team. Things he'd never realized he wanted to share.

"Only a year. It was one of those things where you just know it's right almost from the moment you meet."

Campbell forced down the thought that he knew exactly what she was talking about. He and Olivia, that wasn't right at all, no matter how much he might like to see if it could be otherwise.

"For a long time, I couldn't believe he was gone," she said. "I kept thinking I'd wake up and it would have all been a long horrible dream." She clasped her hands together in her lap, making him wish he could reach through the doorway and hold them in his own. But that invisible barrier of nonconsent was stronger than steel and concrete as far as he was concerned.

"The day after he died, I sat on my couch with my wedding dress in my arms and stared out the window for hours. Part of me wonders if I wouldn't still be sitting there if Mindy hadn't forced me back into the land of the living. So I hung my wedding dress in my closet, unable to give it up. I know this sounds silly, but I still take it out sometimes and stand in front of the mirror with it. Imagine what my life would have been like if the pandemic had never happened."

His heart broke for her. "I don't think it's silly at all. After my parents died, I thought everyone was lying to me, that Mom and Dad were going to walk in and tell me it'd all been a misunderstanding. But they never did."

"But one day you realized that they were really gone and not coming back," she said, verbalizing like no one ever had how it had felt.

"I can't even remember when their deaths went from being impossible to reality." He picked at the chipped paint on the balcony railing. "Sometimes I'm glad they're not here. They didn't have to see what I became, what the world turned into."

She didn't give him false assurances that they would have been okay with his turning, and he was thankful for that.

"Listen to us," she said with a little half laugh. "We're beginning to sound like a therapy session."

"Nobody'd believe it even if they saw it with their own eyes."

She glanced at him before lowering her gaze to where she was now picking at a cuticle on her thumb. "It's nice, isn't it? Talking like this."

He hesitated for a moment. "Yeah." It was more than nice, but he kept the extra feelings, ones he didn't quite understand or trust, to himself. He didn't think it was the vampire within him trying to cultivate a food source, but even after the years he'd lived as a creature of the night he wasn't sure he fully understood that side of himself.

Whatever the reason, being near Olivia calmed the edge that was his constant companion while also exciting the man who still existed within the vampire. He imagined lying next to her, doing nothing but feeling her warmth soak into him. He longed to be human more than he had in a long time. Wished he could go back, undo so many things.

His phone buzzed in his pocket, no doubt the team wondering where in the hell he was and if he planned to work tonight. He looked at the display and noticed it was Colin calling. "Excuse me. Duty calls."

"No problem," Olivia said. She stood and headed toward the little apartment kitchen.

He barely kept himself from calling her back. Instead he put the phone up to his ear and stared out across the surrounding neighborhood. "Yeah?" he said in answer.

"Are you babysitting diner babe?"

"Don't call her that."

"Oh, touchy."

"Did you have an actual reason for calling?"

"We just ran into your buddy Rico. He said he might be onto something and that he'd let you know soon."

"He say what?" Campbell asked.

"We weren't exactly in a spot where he could talk freely and not seal his fate for being a snitch."

"Where are you?"

"Blood bank. Kaja was getting snappy, and Len threatened to toss her out of the back of the truck if she bit his head off one more time."

"Where are you headed next?"

"As soon as she's done feeding, Kaja is going to get all dolled up and work the crowd at the new club in Tribeca, some swanky place. Travis is going with her. Word is it might be Nefari owned. Puppy's going to the skate park, see what the other puppies are saying. Rest of us are patrolling."

Campbell glanced at Olivia's back where she stood at her sink, drinking a glass of water. He imagined stepping up behind her, nuzzling her neck, nibbling her ear, leading her to bed.

"Hello, you still there?" Colin said.

"Yeah. I've got a couple of places I want to check out. I'll meet you guys back at the cave in the morning."

"You okay, man?"

"Yeah. Good."

Colin was silent for several beats, enough to drag Campbell's attention away from Olivia.

"Whatever you're doing, whatever you're thinking, just remember there's more at stake than your undead life if you make a mistake," Colin said.

"I know."

Which was exactly why he needed to get off this balcony and stay away. But despite what his common sense was telling him to do, he didn't move. After hanging up the phone, he sat and waited for Olivia to return to her seat, to where he could talk to her, watch her graceful movements and imagine he wasn't her worst nightmare.

Olivia knew she needed to go to sleep or she'd be dead on her feet the next day, but she couldn't find the strength to end the conversation with Campbell. Sitting and talking to him made the night not seem so long or lonely. She realized that she'd been fooling herself for a long time, telling herself that she was fine living alone, that she had plenty of enjoyable things to fill her time. So many good books to read, movies to watch, sweaters to knit for the same people to whom she delivered meals.

But it'd all been a lie. She did enjoy those things, but they also were a way to trick herself into believing she wasn't desperately lonely. Not lonely for friends but for romance, for someone to hold her, for love.

She swallowed hard at the thought that she couldn't have that with Campbell either, not if she valued her life. Not if she valued his.

When she returned to the balcony doors, he was gone. But then she noticed him atop the opposite building. His attention was focused on something she couldn't see, and chills scurried down her arms at the thought of vampires prowling the streets right outside her home.

She sank into her chair just as he dropped out of sight on the other side of the building. He hadn't even said goodbye. Well, what did she expect?

She sighed and closed her eyes. Without him to talk to, fatigue tugged at her with more insistence. She forced herself to stand and reached for the sliding glass door to close it. Campbell landed on her balcony, causing her to yelp in surprise.

"Sorry," he said. "Thought I'd be back before you were."

She glanced past him. "Where did you go?"

"To take care of some business."

She noticed a rip in his shirt and figured that business had included a few fists being thrown.

"Are you okay?" he asked.

She looked up and saw him watching her. "Yeah, just tired."

He shifted as though he was going to leave again. "Go to bed. I have to get back to work anyway."

"Okay." She paused, wondering what else and how much to say. "I've enjoyed talking with you."

His expression changed to one of disbelief, but he hid it quickly.

"Sorry if my chattering on has kept you from your work," she said.

He smiled, making her go a little gooey inside. "We keep apologizing to each other."

"Sorry." The moment after she said it, she laughed. "I think I'm getting punchy."

"Perhaps a little," he said, teasing.

Maybe it was her fatigue, or maybe it was the way he was looking at her, but all kinds of images of the two of them together flooded her mind and caused her body to warm.

His eyes widened almost imperceptibly. She still didn't believe vampires could read minds, but she suddenly realized that he could probably read every little change in her body. Heart rate, scent, temperature.

"You have another long day tomorrow," he said as he shifted his gaze to somewhere beyond her. "Close and lock the door, and get some sleep."

She wanted to ask if he would come back the next night, but that sounded too needy. So she just smiled and grasped the edge of the door. But she couldn't close it when her eyes met his. He took a step toward her then stopped.

"Lock the door so I can go," he said.

She knew he was watching out for her safety, but instinct told her there was more to his words. And she wanted to see what it was. With her heart beating fast, she stepped through the doorway onto the balcony.

"Olivia, stop," he said as he took a step backward. "Go back inside."

"I don't want to."

"You're not safe out here. Please go back inside."

"Kiss me and I will."

She saw the war going on inside him reflected on his face.

"You don't know what you're saying," he said.

"You're wrong."

He closed his eyes for a moment, but then he pulled her to him and lowered his mouth to hers. The intensity of the kiss, the hunger fueling it, stole her breath. A momentary shot of fear was swept aside by a swell of desire. She ran her hands up his back and let him deepen the kiss. Her body flooded with warmth in the same moment he growled and broke the kiss. He set her away from him.

"This is crazy," he said.

She noticed he was breathing hard despite the fact he didn't have to.

He wasn't the only one whose lungs were working extra hard.

Before she could catch her breath and speak, he stepped toward the edge of the balcony and gripped the railing. "Good night, Olivia," he said in a strangled voice without looking at her. And then he bounded over the side effortlessly and disappeared.

She gasped and peered over the edge. He stood on the street below staring up at her. What was she thinking, exposing herself like this? He could have killed her instead of kissing her until her knees went weak. He could still attack her before she got back inside. But he didn't move. He simply looked up at her until she understood that he wasn't going anywhere until she went inside and locked the door.

Though it was surprisingly hard to do so, she turned and went back inside, locking the balcony door behind her. And then to help keep her from retracing her steps back outside into vulnerable territory, she closed the blinds. She had to stop this before she got in over her head. Between now and the next time she saw him, if she ever saw him again, she had to figure out a way to think of him as nothing more than an unlikely friend. For both of their sakes, she had to chase away the wild attraction that only seemed to build with each moment they spent together. That had exploded with that kiss.

Oh, God, she'd kissed him, a vampire. She touched her lips,

remembering the feel of his cool mouth on hers. She dropped her head back against the glass door and shook her head.

She tried focusing on the terror she'd felt when he'd attacked her, but that freaked her out so much now that she was alone in her apartment that she had to shove that memory away. Part of her wanted to talk to Mindy about this, but she couldn't. She couldn't tell anyone. No, it was best she had to keep it all to herself. She could relive the glances, the conversations, the sight of him and that kiss in every tiny detail. If no one else knew, no one could tell her what an idiot she was being, that she'd lost her mind.

A glance at the clock revealed it was almost one in the morning, and dawn was going to come way too soon. So she headed for the bedroom, changed into her pajamas and slid into bed. But no matter how tired she was, she couldn't shut off her brain and fall asleep. She rolled onto her side and ran her hand down the other half of the mattress. For the first time since Jeremy's death, she imagined another man lying there, pulling her close, kissing her. Another man's skin touching hers as he slid inside her and made her gasp with pleasure.

She evidently fell asleep with that image playing in her mind, because she had dreams hot enough to burn the building down. Campbell's gorgeous body spread out next to hers, moving along and within her, giving her a pleasure indescribable outside of the dream. When she woke to the barest hint of dawn, she was panting.

Embarrassed, she placed her hands over her burning cheeks and grasped on to every image before it faded away the way dreams tended to do. She closed her eyes and let herself float on the sensations those memories had caused. It took only moments for her to grow truly hot and bothered again. She really should go take a cold shower and get her mind on the day ahead instead of something that hadn't really happened.

But it'd been so long since she'd felt like that, so long that she wasn't going to deny herself. Pushing embarrassment away, she let her hand slide lower under the covers and finished what Campbell had started in her dream.

When she finally made her way on shaky legs to the bathroom, she flicked on the light and looked at herself in the mirror, wondering if she looked different.

And she did. It took the image staring back at her to realize that until this morning, she hadn't been truly happy in two years. A part of her that had been dormant was coming alive again. Heartache came on the heels of that revelation. She couldn't put herself at risk like that again. It was too dangerous. Campbell might not want to hurt her, but he wasn't always in control of his actions.

As she stared in the mirror and replayed the details of her dream, she wondered how she was ever going to convince herself that dreams would be enough.

Campbell met back up with the team at the cave just before dawn and sat on the edge of his desk as everyone gave reports of the night's activities.

"What about you?" Kaja asked. "Where were you all night?" She raised a perfectly shaped eyebrow as if she knew exactly where he'd been.

"I went to check on Olivia DaCosta. She had two suspicious men come into her diner yesterday. Scared her and her best friend."

The not-very-well-hidden smiles and snickers of his team faded at his news.

"It's possible they were the guys who have been kidnapping other women. Could have been scouts. Could have been nothing more than a couple of grunts who needed some food. But it's worth keeping an eye on the place when we can. I patrolled by the homes of the others on the list but saw nothing but a vamp snooping around."

"But these kidnappers hit during the daytime," Sophia said. "We can't protect her or any of them then."

And that fact tore him totally to shreds inside. "I have a call in to the Imperium representative here, see if he can make the NYPD listen. Until I hear back, we concentrate all our efforts on finding out who is behind this and shutting them down, hard."

From the nods around the room, the team was in total agreement.

Campbell nodded toward Travis's computer. "Do we have any shots at all clear enough to identify the abductors? Height, hair color, anything?"

"No. It's as though they know exactly where the security cameras are and are very good at shielding themselves from them."

"No demands have been made, so we know these aren't your typical kidnappings," Kaja said. "Those girls have been taken into the blood-slave trade. I'd bet my immortality on it."

"Monsters," Sophia said under her breath.

Campbell met the eyes of every member of his team. "If it takes us kicking down every vampire's door in Manhattan to find those girls, we're going to do it. We monitor every police report, every security camera in the city, every whispered rumor on the street. We get help from other teams if we need it. But I'm not having this happen in my own backyard."

After forceful expressions of agreement, his team went to their respective desks and got to work, a renewed fervor in their efforts. The vampires behind these abductions had no idea what level of hurt was coming their way.

When he tried to work, his thoughts kept straying back to Olivia, hoping she was safe. His hand itched to grab the phone and call her, but it was too early. He'd already kept her up too late talking, kissing. God, that kiss had been even more amazing than he'd imagined. And stupid. Really, really stupid. Even after he'd jumped from her balcony, it'd been so difficult to leave. He hadn't felt that human in a very long time. He'd been afraid if he left, he'd never feel it again.

And if he truly cared about her, it would be the last time he got anywhere near her. Each time he saw her, it got harder and harder to walk away, to not ask her to invite him in.

That last thought was what frightened him more than anything. If he ever lost control with her again and the worst happened, his team wouldn't have the chance to take him out, because he would do it for them. He needed to assign one of the others to the patrol of her neighborhood and figure out how to ensure her safety during the day while he waited for the Imperium member to take his good sweet time getting back to him.

"Seriously?" Kaja said as she looked up to find Len walking back to his desk after warming up some B-positive in her mug. "Now I'm never going to be able to use that mug again."

"We have this thing called water. You use it to wash dishes," Len replied, then took a long drink just to further irk her.

Kaja wrinkled her nose. "I could use the entire New York City water supply and never get the stench of that vile stuff you drink out of there."

Len just chuckled and went back to work. Kaja gave him another hard stare before resuming her work, as well.

Campbell shook his head. He didn't know why those two were like a case of sibling rivalry on steroids, but they'd been that way from the day they'd met. He shifted his attention back to the computer screen, where he was looking through the business records for both of the companies whose vehicles had been used in the abductions. He wanted to see if someone at either place had a reason for wanting to go into business with vampires or faking the reports of stolen vehicles.

But the more he tried to concentrate on the task at hand,

the more his thoughts diverted back to Olivia and how she'd felt in his arms. The way she'd talked to him as if he were just a normal guy, how she'd put herself at risk by coming out onto the balcony. She'd been so beautiful, and he'd found himself wishing he'd met her before he'd been turned, before she'd met her fiancé.

He also remembered the meals she'd been preparing the night before and how he wasn't able to talk her out of delivering them. As his gaze wandered the room, it lit on the wall full of weapons and blessed cuffs. An idea popped into his head. Not a perfect one by any means, but something that might prevent Olivia from going out alone. Unwilling to make the necessary call in front of the others, he got up and went to his room.

He picked up the phone and dialed.

"St. Patrick's Cathedral," came the bright and cheery voice on the other end of the line.

"Hey, Chloe. It's Campbell."

"Hey there. What's shaking in the Bat Cave?"

"Kaja and Len snapping at each other again. You know, business as usual."

Chloe chuckled. "I swear those two are either going to kill each other or fall head over heels for each other."

This time it was Campbell's turn to laugh. The idea of those two together just didn't compute. "If ever there was a story of oil and water," he said.

"So what can I do for you this bright and sunny day?"

"That's right, rub it in."

"Sorry. Just trying to help you live vicariously. So do you all need more holy water?"

Chloe Ferris, the younger sister of Ethan "Doc" Ferris at the blood bank, was basically a dealer for V Force. They needed holy water to do their jobs, and her job as secretary for St. Patrick's Cathedral put her in the position to get it for them.

"No, we're good for now, thanks. I... Listen, I need a favor."

"Sure, if I can help."

Campbell stared at the ceiling and tried to convince himself he was doing this for all the people Olivia helped and not just her.

"We helped a woman a couple of days ago whose car was stolen. She was out delivering food to the homeless, which I guess is something she does on a regular basis. Travis is trying to find her car, but until then she has no transportation."

"And you want me to provide the wheels for her meals."

"Is that too much to ask?"

"No. I think it's a great idea. I just wish people could see this side to you guys."

"Maybe someday." But again, he wasn't sure if it was a good idea for humanity's safety.

Chloe sighed, and he knew the look of frustration she likely wore. She'd tried, unsuccessfully, to get the church to consider the possibility that all vampires weren't bad. To them her brother was one of the damned, a demon who should be burning in hell. Though she was one of the perkiest, happiest people he'd ever met, that particular fact weighed heavily on her.

"Before you agree too quickly, I need to tell you something else," he said. "You've seen the stories of the abductions on the news?"

"Yeah. It's awful."

"We have information that makes us believe that vampires are behind it."

"So this is what they've been talking about on the news, the humans working with vamps?"

"Yes. We suspect the Nefari, or at least someone who knows he can make a nice income off selling humans to the blood-slave trade."

"Oh, no."

"It gets worse. There is a list of targets and the woman who delivers the meals is on it. So she's in danger until we catch these people. You would be, too."

He felt awful for asking Chloe, the one human before Olivia who didn't think they were a pack of ravenous beasts, to put herself at risk.

"Stop it," she said.

"Stop what?"

"You're feeling guilty for asking me when it makes perfect sense that two people are safer than one. We can watch out for each other."

"How do you know what I'm thinking?"

"I'm an intuitive genius?" she said, a smile evident in her voice. "Now, what's the lady's name and number?"

Campbell gave her Olivia's contact information and told her how to get to the diner. "I want you both armed when you go out, no exceptions," he said. "And be aware of everything and everyone going on around you. Don't go too far from your car."

"Okay, Dad."

"I'm not old enough to be your dad."

"You will be before long."

"I don't age, remember?"

"On the outside."

"Remind me why I like you," he said.

"Because I'm impossible not to like."

"Oh, yeah, that."

She laughed, and he thought some guy would be very lucky to win her heart. In a world that was full of too much darkness, she was like a bright ray of happy sunshine.

"I'll help her as much as I can," she said.

"Thanks. You're the best."

"I know. If only some hot guy with a pulse would notice."

Five minutes after the call ended, Campbell was still staring at the same spot on the ceiling and still thinking about Olivia. What had gotten into him? She wasn't the only beautiful woman he'd ever seen, not even the only one since he'd been turned. He should be directing his attention toward a female vampire if anywhere, but something unnamed was pulling him toward Olivia. And it wasn't just her blood type. Wasn't even the fact that she was stunning. What the hell was it?

Chapter 11

Olivia burned with guilt all morning as she and Mindy worked to feed the breakfast crowd. She hated that she'd broken her promise to her friend, hated that she couldn't talk to her about what had happened.

She glanced through the pass-through and saw a young redheaded woman approach the front counter. Mindy stopped clearing tables to help her.

"What can I get for you?" Mindy asked.

"I'm here to see Olivia DaCosta."

Olivia froze for a moment before telling herself that this woman looked about as likely to be a kidnapper as Bugs Bunny. She wiped her hands and went to stand next to Mindy.

"I'm Olivia. How can I help you?"

The pretty redhead smiled. "Of course you are." Before Olivia could ask what that meant, the other woman glanced over to where a few older guys were in the corner drinking coffee and shooting the bull. When she looked back at Olivia, she said, "I'm Chloe Ferris, a friend of Campbell's. He sent me to help you."

"Help me?"

"I understand you need to deliver some meals and are without wheels." She gestured to where she'd parked outside. "I happen to have wheels."

Mindy made a sound of disgust and stalked toward the kitchen.

"Excuse me," Olivia said to Chloe then raced after Mindy, who was headed toward the back door. "Min, wait." She grabbed Mindy's arm, but she shook her off.

"You're still in contact with that vampire, aren't you?" The look on her face was one of wounded disbelief.

Olivia hesitated for a moment. "Yes."

"You promised me you wouldn't."

"I tried. But he really is different."

"I'll remember to say that at your funeral." Mindy grabbed her jacket and left, slamming the door in her wake.

Olivia stared at the door for several seconds, her heart breaking. She didn't have many friends left, and she'd done the one thing Mindy might never be able to forgive. Slowly, she forced herself to turn and retrace her steps to the dining room. She noticed the coffee drinkers had left their money on the table and vacated the premises.

"I take it she's not a fan of Campbell's," Chloe said.

Olivia shook her head. "No. Her mother and sister were killed by vampires."

"Ah. I understand, then."

Trying to get her mind off Mindy and how she might have just walked out for good, Olivia asked, "How do you know Campbell?"

"I work at St. Patrick's Cathedral. I provide V Force with the holy water they need to do their jobs."

"Are you…a nun?"

Chloe shook her head, her riot of beautiful copper curls bouncing around her face, and laughed. "That's the funniest thing I've heard in a long time. No, I'm just the church secretary."

"Oh."

"But I like to think of myself as a covert operative." Chloe shot Olivia a wide smile. "I sneak holy water out when the priests aren't around. The church doesn't do shades of gray well. It's all good or evil, and vampires are firmly ensconced in the evil column. But I know better. My brother was turned, and he's the same guy he always was unless he's hungry. Luckily he doesn't get hungry since he works at the blood bank."

Olivia scanned the empty diner. "We'll have to make the deliveries quickly so I can get back before lunch. Looks as if I'll be running things by myself." Suddenly, she wondered if talking to Campbell, kissing him, had come at much too high a price.

"Quick we can do. I have to get back to work, too."

Olivia went to the kitchen and boxed up the dinners.

"Here, let me take that," Chloe said, and reached for the box when Olivia returned to the front. "Campbell wants us to be armed when we go out. You got something?"

The idea of a church secretary with a weapon struck Olivia as really out of place, but she guessed over the past two years lots of people had started taking precautions they'd have never considered before.

"Yeah. Be right back."

She made quick work of running upstairs and slipping her Glock into the back waistband of her jeans and covering it with her shirt and wool peacoat since the temperature had taken a dip overnight.

Olivia changed the sign on the door to show when she'd be

back, then locked the door before hurrying outside and into the passenger seat of Chloe's little blue SUV.

"Where to?" Chloe asked.

"Central Park."

As Chloe zipped out of the parking space, turned the corner and dodged a garbage truck, Olivia realized how cooped up she'd felt the past couple of days and how freeing it was to be outside of her building.

"So have you done this for a long time?" Chloe asked.

"About three years."

"Like I told Campbell, I think it's awesome. There's just not enough kindness and selflessness in the world anymore. People have let the fear replace them."

"You don't seem afraid."

Chloe shrugged. "Don't much see the point. As long as I don't go out at night and don't do something stupid, things are pretty normal."

"Until now."

"We just have to be cautious. Doesn't mean we have to go around afraid all the time. That's not the kind of life I want to lead, especially after it was spared during the Bokor outbreak."

Olivia decided she liked Chloe a lot, really admired her attitude and outlook on life. "So how did you start working with V Force?"

"My brother was turned toward the tail end of the pandemic, and Campbell's team found him and helped him through his transition. Now he's sort of their unofficial doctor. Ethan told me about them and how they did their work. When he told me that their source for holy water at St. Patrick's had died, I went the next day and made a very successful argument for the church to hire me so I could help V Force. Of course, I didn't tell the church officials that last part."

"If you don't mind my saying, you have a very different attitude toward vampires than I'd say pretty much everyone."

Chloe glanced toward her. "Except you."

"Oh, no, I held the prevailing attitude until a few days ago."

"Really? What changed then?"

"Campbell showed up outside my building to apologize for almost killing me."

Chloe jerked her attention to Olivia, a wide-eyed look of surprise on her face. "What?"

"He didn't tell you how we met?" Olivia said.

"Um, no. Wait, Ethan told me Campbell came into the blood bank recently in full-on bloodlust. Is that when it happened?"

Olivia pushed down the remembered terror. "Yeah. I've never been so frightened in my life."

"And an apology changed that?"

"Sounds insane, doesn't it?"

"Or fate."

"I think it's more likely I've gone completely loony."

Chloe made another turn and headed along the edge of the park. "Maybe not. He's attractive. A good guy."

"A vampire who shares my blood type."

"Okay, I'll grant you it's problematic."

"Try impossible."

Chloe didn't have anything to say in response. Her inability to claim that there was a way Olivia and Campbell could maybe see where things would go caused a fresh sadness to wash through Olivia.

When they reached the area of the park where Olivia normally distributed the meals, Olivia directed Chloe to a pull-off. With the box of food in hand, Olivia made her way toward the group of people sitting on the benches passing the time, Chloe beside her.

"Olivia," an older man said as he stood and toddled toward her.

"Hey, Herbie. Your arthritis bothering you today?"

"Oh, you know it. Weather changes and my old bones feel they have to protest. Where you been? We were worried."

"Have had a little trouble with my car." No need to concern Herbie and his friends any more than they already were. They had enough to worry about surviving day to day.

Attitudes toward the homeless hadn't changed after the pandemic, so their lives certainly weren't any easier. People in power were still more likely to hire and rent to the people coming to New York from other cities, states and countries than those who'd lived here their entire lives but who called the streets their home.

Herbie gestured toward Chloe. "You have a mighty pretty chauffeur."

"Why, thank you," Chloe said. "You're a handsome devil yourself."

Herbie got a good laugh out of that, as did the rest of his buddies.

The guys tried not to show it, but they were obviously glad to get a meal. Olivia couldn't help wondering if they'd eaten since she'd seen them last, if the shelters that provided food had been full. Though it wasn't her fault, guilt nevertheless swamped her at the thought that they'd been hungry all that time. Chloe endeared herself to her even more when she sat down next to Herbie's best friend, Roscoe, who was trying in vain to get a splinter out of his finger. She pulled out her tweezers and made quick work of it.

"I think I'm in love," Roscoe said, earning himself a kiss on the cheek from Chloe.

When they got ready to leave to head to another part of the park, Herbie grabbed her hand, then Chloe's. "You girls be careful. We've been hearing awful stories about girls being stolen right off the street."

"We're being careful," Chloe assured him.

Olivia squeezed his hand. "What have you heard?" Maybe he'd know something that could help Campbell and his team.

"These girls get taken, and nobody sees them again. Get taken underground. Permanent blood supply for big-shot vampires, the ones with money."

"What else?"

Herbie shook his head. "That's all I know."

As Chloe drove away from Herbie and his friends, something about what he'd said was tickling the back of Olivia's brain.

"You okay?" Chloe asked.

"Yeah."

But she remained unsettled throughout the rest of their deliveries and all the way back to the diner. "You want to come in for some pie? I have fresh lemon meringue."

"That sounds wonderful, but I'll take a rain check. Got to get back to work."

"Thank you for doing this. It means a lot. And thank Campbell for me, too."

Chloe smiled. "I think I'll let you take care of that last part yourself." She glanced at the diner. "I hope you and your friend patch things up."

"Me, too."

By the time Olivia got inside, she had to race to get ready for the midday rush.

"Where's Mindy?" asked Faye Jarvis, who worked down the street at a chiropractic clinic.

"She had something she had to do today." Like be furious at Olivia.

When the last of the lunch customers left, Olivia collapsed into a chair, exhausted. The quiet began to weigh on her, making her realize how alone she was. Though he was the reason she was alone, she called Campbell since she knew he wouldn't be asleep.

"Raines," he said, sounding distracted.

"Hey. I called to thank you for sending Chloe over to help with the food deliveries."

"No problems?" He sounded less distracted but still not totally like himself.

"No. We're both back at work."

"Good."

"Campbell?"

"Yes?"

"Why are you helping me?" She felt as if she was treading into dangerous territory but that she had to know the answer to the questions uppermost in her mind—was he experiencing the same types of feelings she was? Was that kiss playing over and over in his mind? Did he think it was a mistake? Did he think about it at all?

He was quiet for several moments before saying, "Atonement. For what happened that first day."

"Oh." Her heart sank, and she chided herself for caring so much when she knew nothing could come of it. What a fool she was.

"Why did you want to know?"

"Curiosity." She tried to sound casual and hoped she'd pulled it off. How had she totally misread the look in his eyes the night before? The urgency of the kiss? Had she simply seen what she wanted to see? "By the way, I don't know if this helps at all, but when I was talking to one of the guys in the park today, he said he'd heard that the girls who are being taken are being kept underground. For vampires who are wealthy enough to pay big bucks for them."

"That's not a surprise."

Though he didn't sound derogatory at all, his comment

felt like a slap. Maybe it was just that she wanted to be able to help and had offered up nothing useful.

"Okay, I...I don't know what I thought. Listen, it's busy, so I need to get back to work. Thanks again."

"You're welcome."

She hung up as his last word still hung in the air, the only sound in the emptiness around her. She scolded herself for being such an idiot, but that still didn't prevent tears from blurring her vision as she sliced a large piece of lemon pie. When she got through the rest of this day, she was taking what was left of this pie upstairs and eating every single bite. She'd eat her way back to sanity.

Chapter 12

For three days, Campbell stayed away from Olivia, didn't even call her. They were the three longest days of his immortal existence.

During the past seven years, he'd done nothing but work, keep his sexual encounters limited to vampires and remind himself of Bridget Jameson every time he was tempted by the human world. Then Olivia ran into his life and turned everything on its head.

When Kaja stopped on the sidewalk in front of him and placed her hands on her hips, he realized she was waiting for a response from him.

"Honestly, have you heard a word I've said?" she asked as she spun to face him.

"No."

"Will you please just go see her?"

"Who?" he said, looking past Kaja to the dark street beyond her.

"Don't play dim. I know you're smarter than that, your attraction to a human notwithstanding. You have been half here at best since you last talked to Olivia. If it takes regular visits to her for you to keep your head in the game, then by all means, do it."

"I thought you believed it was a bad idea."

"I do. For her, at least."

"Thanks."

"You know what I mean."

He sighed. "I do. That's why I'm staying away."

"So you don't get any more attached?"

He didn't respond to that question. Rather, he walked past her down the street they were searching for any signs of the missing women or evidence of illegal vampire activities.

"You know you just answered the question by not answering it, right?" Kaja asked as she fell into step beside him.

"Why is everyone suddenly so interested in my love life or lack thereof?"

"Vicarious thrill?"

He glanced at her and laughed. "Sorry you're not getting much of a thrill."

"Why her?"

He stopped again and looked up at the top of the Empire State Building. "I can't explain it. I never believed in this sort of thing, this kind of attraction, until it hit me square in the chest. It doesn't make any sense."

"Once upon a time none of us believed in vampires either."

He glanced at her, shook his head and started walking again. "It doesn't matter. You were right. I can't be with her. It's too dangerous."

Kaja was quiet for the space of a block. "I can't believe I'm saying this, but you could make it work. You could wear blessed bracelets like Ethan."

"And be useless in my job. That's unacceptable."

"You'd only have to wear them when you're with her."

"I'd still be a danger to her with nothing more than my strength. And the bracelets wouldn't control the hunger, just my ability to act on it. I don't want her to see me like that again. Damn it, I already almost ripped her throat out once."

This time Kaja didn't have any response. They fell back into their search on their way to a designated meeting spot with Rico, who'd texted with a short message earlier that he had some information.

It was almost 1:00 a.m. when they entered the warehouse district that was well away from the hotbeds of nighttime activity and thus prying eyes. As they rounded a corner, they both stopped abruptly, having both caught the scent of death. With a glance at each other, they pulled out stakes and edged forward as quietly as they could.

When they rounded the front of a big box-style delivery truck, they found Rico, a stake in his heart and way too far gone to save. He was stone-still, his eyes now totally devoid of color, and his body was as white as chalk. No matter how many times he saw staked vampires, it always sent a shock through him. It was so final, even more so than human death.

Campbell cursed, then stood still and slowly did a sensory check in every direction. There was nothing more than a stray dog three buildings closer to the river.

He stared down at Rico. The guy might have been on the sketchy end of the Souled spectrum, but he'd been basically a decent sort and a good informant. He didn't deserve to go this way. Hating that he had to do it, Campbell lowered himself to his knees and searched Rico's clothing for any evidence, any indication of what he might have been going to share with them. When he found nothing, he sat back. To be so close to maybe cracking open this case, only to have the answers ripped away along with Rico's life caused his anger to flare like roaring flames.

"Call Travis. Have him see if he can figure out where Rico was when he sent that message," he said. "I'll call for the disposal team."

Kaja walked away while dialing Travis. Campbell hit the number on his phone that always caused his stomach to heave.

"Blake, it's Campbell. We need a pickup in the warehouse area off of Water."

"The dead human male or female?" Blake always contacted the human authorities about where to find bodies when there was a vampire kill.

"None. Just one of our own this time, a Souled vamp."

Blake cursed. "We'll be there in ten."

It actually took only nine minutes for the disposal team to arrive. When Blake Sands stepped out of the black van, it struck Campbell as it always did how big the man was. Campbell wasn't small by any stretch, but Blake had been a professional wrestler once upon a time. Add vampire strength to that, and Campbell doubted anyone dared to mess with him. He'd actually tried to recruit Blake for V Force, but the guy had said he'd rather work in a job where people didn't talk back and he wasn't tempted to break their necks.

"A friend of yours?" Blake asked as he and Vaughn Styles made quick work of covering and loading up Rico's body.

"An informant."

"Think that's what got him killed?"

Campbell stared at the sheet-covered body on the stretcher. "Probably."

Blake cursed again. He was actually quite fond of colorful words. "As if we don't have enough problems. We have to go around killing each other."

As Blake and Vaughn got in the van and drove away, Kaja came back. "Travis said he'd have to go back to the cave to do that kind of search. He'll call when he's got something."

Campbell was struck with the oddest sense of not knowing what to do next.

"I'm going to head over to a friend's place, see if she's heard anything in the wind," Kaja said.

"Vampire model gossip?"

"None better. See if you can find something to do with the rest of the night." She gave him a significant look, and he knew exactly what she was thinking.

He had every intention of spending the rest of the night making his way through known Nefari hangouts, and he did for a couple of hours before he found himself patrolling Olivia's neighborhood. Everything appeared quiet, so he took time to pause outside her apartment. He kept to the shadows so she wouldn't see him if she happened to look outside, but she didn't seem to be awake. His senses told him that she was sleeping and no one else was in her building. That relieved the anxiety he hadn't realized he'd been carrying around like a heavy weight since he'd last talked to her.

He hated the idea that he might have hurt her feelings by disappearing, but maybe he was assigning more caring on her part than was really there. But he kept coming back to the night he'd spent on her balcony, how easily they'd been able to talk to each other, how she'd felt so right in his arms.

He sat on the hood of a car and watched her window, lit only by what was probably a single bulb, maybe a lamp or light in the kitchen. He wondered if that was new, her leaving on a light at night. How ironic that she was probably safer at night now than in the daytime. Vampires couldn't get to her, and even the humans working for vamps weren't stupid enough to venture forth after nightfall.

The night passed as he watched, silent and still. He could sense the rotation of the planet, knew exactly where the sun was and how much time he had to sit here wishing things were different, that he couldn't easily imagine how lifeless Olivia would look in his arms if he killed her. Part of him wished he'd never met Olivia DaCosta, but a bigger part didn't want to imagine his life without her in it. He had given himself headache after headache trying to figure out why he felt so drawn to her. He couldn't explain it away simply because she was beautiful. It was something deeper, something he wasn't equipped to understand.

His phone buzzed in his pocket, drawing his attention away from Olivia's window and his never-ending search for answers.

"Hello," he said after noting it was Travis calling.

"Hey, I ran the phone trace and I can only narrow it down to about a six-block area in Tribeca."

"Any video pick him up?"

"You're not going to like the answer to that."

"Why am I not surprised?"

"Every security camera in that entire area mysteriously went out tonight."

"Of course they did." Campbell resisted the urge to throw his phone as hard as he could. The thing might end up in Queens.

He did a quick calculation of the sun's location. "We'll have to check there tomorrow night."

After the call ended, he sat for a few more minutes, hoping to catch a glimpse of Olivia. When he didn't, he told himself it was for the best. Seeing her would only make it harder to leave. It was enough that she was safe, asleep in her bed.

He imagined lying beside her, watching her sleep, holding her close. The reality that such a scene would never happen hit him as hard as any bout with bloodlust ever had, like a sucker punch to the gut.

He slid from the hood of the car to stand firmly on his booted feet and stared hard at Olivia's window. This would be the last time he came here, because each time he did, it got more difficult to leave.

With one final glance, he turned his back and started walking away, each step taking him deeper into his vampire eternity and farther away from the glimpse he'd had of the life he'd once lived.

As Olivia dragged herself through the preparations for another day of solo work, the sound of a motor in the alley behind the diner surprised her. When it stopped right outside her door, her heart started thudding extra hard. She tried to force the fear down and remember all the self-defense techniques Mindy had taught her. She grabbed a heavy wooden rolling pin in one hand and the cordless phone in the other then hid next to the refrigerator. If someone broke in the back door, they were in for a rude welcome.

The doorknob rattled as someone slid a key in the lock. No one besides her had a key but Mindy. She was trying to tie Mindy to the sound of the motor when the door opened. Olivia raised the rolling pin, ready to strike with full force as Mindy had taught her.

Mindy stepped into view and yelped when she spotted Olivia. She put her hand over her heart as if she could stop it from racing. "Damn, you scared me half to death."

Olivia lowered the rolling pin and felt like collapsing after the spike of adrenaline. "Ditto. I heard a motor and then the door rattling."

"I got a scooter."

Olivia crossed to the door, opened it and looked out. There chained to the drainpipe was a black scooter. "Is that a Vespa?"

"Yeah. Guy in my building is moving to the middle of nowhere, Oklahoma, where they drive pickup trucks and not scooters. I got a good deal on it. Wanted something a little faster than my feet."

Olivia closed the door, hating that the world was changing again to one where even Mindy didn't feel safe walking the streets alone in broad daylight. "It's cute."

Mindy didn't acknowledge her compliment, instead taking off her jacket and slipping into the familiar morning routine.

"I didn't know you were coming back today," Olivia ventured, hoping she wasn't swatting a hornet's nest.

"Gotta make a living."

Olivia sighed as she placed the rolling pin back on the prep table. Mindy obviously didn't want to talk about why there was a boatload of tension between them. Honestly, Olivia didn't either. After all, it might all be a moot point now anyway.

Mindy interacted with the customers throughout the morning the same as she always did. It was only when she stepped into the kitchen that she grew quiet. By the time the breakfast customers vacated for work, school and whatever else filled their days, the tension had Olivia wanting to be the one to flee through the back door.

She stopped scraping the grill when Mindy came into the kitchen with the last of the dirty dishes. "I really am sorry."

Mindy kept walking and didn't say anything until she'd loaded the dishes in the washer and started the cycle. When she finally turned around, Olivia saw how tired she looked. She wondered if Mindy hadn't slept well since she'd stormed out of the diner.

"I know you are. I just don't understand what you're thinking. I've never known you to be so careless."

"I can't explain it beyond saying I've just gone with my gut feeling."

Mindy looked away, obviously wishing Olivia had said something different, that maybe she'd finally cut ties with Campbell while Mindy had stayed at home.

Screams suddenly filled the silence. Olivia stared toward the back door as the frantic sound increased. She and Mindy made eye contact a moment before they each grabbed the nearest weapon—the rolling pin for Mindy and a butcher knife for Olivia—and raced for the door.

When they reached the alley, Olivia saw a white van at the far end. A guy in dark clothes was trying to force a young woman into the back. When the woman screamed again, he punched her in the face.

"Oh, hell no," Mindy said, and started running.

Totally agreeing with the sentiment, Olivia pointed the knife behind her and followed Mindy. The guy looked up at the sound of their approach and reached for his waistband.

"Gun!" Olivia yelled, and raced past Mindy. She stopped and threw the knife with as much force as she could. She didn't have perfect aim, but it did cut his upper arm enough to halt his reaching for his gun. It was enough time for Mindy to reach him and get in a kick to the side of his knee.

He roared in pain, but he still managed to wrap his hand in Mindy's hair and yank hard. Mindy cried out and struggled to free herself.

All of the lessons Mindy had given Olivia clicked into place in her head. While Mindy kicked and clawed, Olivia saw her chance. She grabbed the rolling pin Mindy had dropped and brought it down hard on the guy's arm. When he released Mindy, Olivia rammed the heel of her hand up into his nose. This time he was the one to go down as blood flowed from his broken nose.

Mindy gave him a swift kick in the ribs for good measure.

By then all the noise had brought other business owners out the backs of their shops. "Call 911," Olivia yelled at Han, the guy who owned the Chinese place at the end of the block.

"Already did," he said.

When the attacker tried to get to his feet, Mindy gave him another jab to the nose. He howled but stayed down.

Olivia lowered herself next to the woman who'd nearly been the city's latest kidnapping victim and realized it was the granddaughter of the old lady who lived above the dry cleaner's. She was dazed and her mouth was bleeding, but she was alive. When she spotted the guy on the ground, she started crying and turned her face into Olivia's chest. Olivia wrapped her arms around her and rubbed her hand over the girl's long hair. "It's okay. It's over. He can't hurt you now."

Sirens approached, and it didn't take long for the alley to be filled with medical and police personnel.

"What happened?" a police officer asked.

"This bastard tried to kidnap this girl," Mindy said, and kicked the guy in the side again.

The officer guided Mindy away from the guy before she could do more damage.

The girl in Olivia's arms flinched when the paramedic tried to examine her. "It's okay. They're here to help you."

Reluctantly, the girl let the paramedic help her stand and walk toward the ambulance at the end of the alley. She stopped in her tracks and looked back at Mindy and Olivia. "Thank you."

Olivia smiled. "You're welcome."

For the next half hour, Mindy and Olivia answered the police officer's questions and told him exactly what they'd done when they heard the screams.

"You should have called the police," he said.

Olivia got the impression that he had to say it but that he was actually impressed with what they'd done. "If we'd waited, that girl would be on her way to a blood den now."

He nodded.

"What was she doing out here?" Mindy asked. "Shouldn't she be in school?"

The officer nodded to where the paramedics were headed up to the grandmother's apartment. "She said her grandmother was sick last night and wouldn't answer the phone this morning, so she skipped school to come check on her. She noticed the van following her about a block before she got here."

"Her grandmother okay?" Olivia asked.

"Looks as if she has pneumonia, so they're taking her to the hospital."

Once the officer headed back to his car, Olivia and Mindy walked to the end of the alley to check on the girl and her grandmother. The older woman gripped Olivia's hand in hers. "Thank you for saving my granddaughter." Tears streamed from the woman's eyes.

"We were happy to do it. Now you just concentrate on getting better."

She nodded. "I will. And then Tracey and I will come down and have lunch at your diner."

"Sounds like a good plan. Speaking of, we better get back to work." She smiled at Tracey and her grandmother and turned to head back to the diner.

But when they turned, they found their way blocked by a gaggle of reporters with microphones and television cameras pointed their way. They answered a few questions before insisting they had to get back to work.

On the way back up the alley, Olivia flexed her hand. "You know what? That felt good."

For the first time in what felt like forever, Mindy smiled at her. "It did, didn't it? We make a pretty good ninja team."

Olivia laughed as they stepped through the back door to find the diner full of curious customers.

"Looks as if we'll be serving up a tale with lunch," Mindy said.

"As it happens, we have one to tell."

* * *

"Hey, Campbell," Travis called from his spot in front of the TV. "You might want to see this."

He was up for anything to get him away from his desk, so he wandered across the room. What he saw stopped him in his tracks. There on the TV screen were Olivia and Mindy.

"Two women are being hailed as heroes today after they thwarted the attempted kidnapping of a teenage girl," the studio anchor said. "Olivia DaCosta and Mindy Kemp heard the girl screaming and raced to her aid. Our Sierra Carnes has more."

Campbell was vaguely aware of the rest of the team filtering into the room as he watched the reporter interview Olivia and Mindy.

"We couldn't just do nothing," Olivia said. "We knew what might happen to her if the guy got her into the van."

"Damn, I knew she was a fighter, but evidently the girl's got skills, too," Billy said.

"Both of them," Colin said.

"Yeah, and they just painted huge bull's-eyes on themselves," Campbell said. He spun and stalked back to his desk and picked up the phone.

"Comfort Food Diner," Olivia said when she answered. "How can I help you?"

"You can start by not taunting the Nefari on the news," he said.

"Campbell?"

"Yes. What were you thinking?"

He heard a loud thump and wondered if she'd just slammed something down.

"I was thinking I was saving a girl's life," she said.

"And you had to talk to the reporters about it?"

"It wouldn't have made a difference if we'd said no comment. They already knew who we were and what we'd done."

He growled in frustration. "So you decided to just bask in your fifteen minutes of fame?"

"You know, last time I checked, you weren't the boss of me. In fact, I got the distinct impression you didn't even want to talk to me. So I'd appreciate it if you'd keep your opinions to yourself." With that, she hung up on him.

He slammed his own phone down. Damn fool woman.

When he looked up, he noticed everyone had left the room. Good move.

He stared at the door that led to the street and cursed the fact he couldn't go over to Olivia's right now. As he paced the length of the room and slowly calmed down, he realized that it was a good thing he couldn't go outside at the moment. Instead of racing to the diner to try to continue his tirade, the truth had time to soak through the crevices of his brain.

Olivia was right. He didn't have the right to tell her what to do, even if he only wanted to make sure she stayed safe.

Chapter 13

As he normally did when he wanted to push something from his mind, Campbell focused his energies on work. It didn't totally keep his argument with Olivia from his mind, but at least he had something to do besides pace the Bat Cave like a caged panther.

He and the rest of the team spent the night scouring nearly all of the six-block radius to which Travis had traced Rico's phone call, both inside and out. Not surprisingly, no one seemed to have seen anything. Chances were one of the people standing in line for one of the trendy vampire clubs had seen Rico, but they knew what the Nefari did to vamps who were a little too loose with information. Rico was proof enough of that.

He spotted Kaja and Travis going into yet another club across the street and Billy keeping watch from a nearby rooftop, gun and stakes at the ready. Campbell and Colin stepped to the front of the line at Universal Donor.

"The names of these places get more stupid every time I come down here," Campbell said as they approached the beefy bouncer.

"Hey, stop cutting!" someone yelled from somewhere back in the line that stretched to the end of the block.

"Pig!" Yeah, that one never got old.

The bouncer pointed behind Campbell and Colin. "Back of the line."

Campbell wasn't in the mood for attitude. He stepped into the guy's personal space. "You want to try that again?"

Colin stepped up beside them. "Official V Force business."

The guy didn't look happy, but he nodded toward the inside of the club. When they stepped through the entrance, it was almost comical how many pairs of eyes looked in their direction, narrowed then went back to whatever had held their attention before. Campbell scanned the interior. As expected, there were lots of reds and blacks, and the walls were frosted glass lit from behind. Red liquid had been made to look as though blood ran in a constant stream behind the glass.

"You'd think one of these places would try something a little out of the box. You know, bright colors or something," Colin said.

"At the moment, I don't give a flying rat's ass about the decor. I'm more in the mood to knock heads until someone talks about Rico, about the abductions, something."

Colin nodded, linked his fingers and popped them. "I can do that."

Movement at the back of the club caught Campbell's attention. His gaze landed on a familiar face just before the guy darted into the crowd. Campbell smiled.

"I think we're about to get some answers. That little weasel Charlie Benson doesn't look as if he wants to talk to me." Charlie was the type of vampire who would do anything for a buck, or a pint. He had expensive tastes, ones that a legal job wasn't likely to fund. If bad crap was going down in the vampire community, chances were Charlie had at least heard about it.

Campbell ignored the yelps and objections as he pushed his way through the crowd. Charlie glanced back over his shoulder, saw Campbell and Colin in pursuit and made a run for it.

They caught him a few steps into the alley that separated the line of clubs from the row of buildings behind them. He stood staring up at where Billy was aiming a gun modified to shoot stakes.

"Good thing you stopped when you did," Billy said with a crooked grin. "I'm pretty good with this." He waved the barrel of the gun. "Lots of hours of video games as a kid."

"Stopped in your tracks by a puppy," Colin said to Charlie as he shook his head. "The shame of it all."

Campbell slammed the pimped-out vampire against the wall of the opposing building.

"Where you going in such a hurry, Charlie? Aren't you glad to see me?"

"No one's ever glad to see you guys."

"Now, that's just rude," Colin said from where he lounged against the club's wall, one booted foot propped against it.

"I can't be seen with you," Charlie said.

"Why not? Are we hazardous to your health?" Campbell asked. "Like Rico, perhaps."

"I don't know what you're talking about."

Campbell stepped closer to Charlie and spoke so close to his face that Charlie would have felt his breath if he'd had any. "Now, see, Charlie, I just don't believe you. You wear lies like you do that slick suit. You're going to tell me everything you know, and you're going to tell me now."

"I'd listen to him, dude," Colin said.

"I don't know what you think I'm supposed to tell you. I'm not a mind reader."

"How about you start with who killed Rico and why."

"How the hell am I supposed to know?"

Campbell growled low in his throat. "Don't mess with me. I am not in the mood. I doubt there's anything going on around here that you don't know about. You like to keep your fingers in a lot of lucrative pies."

Charlie tried to squirm loose with no luck. When he couldn't break free, his attitude changed from innocent and clueless to defiant.

"I'm not telling you anything," the slimy bastard spit back at Campbell. "They'll kill me."

Campbell knew who "they" were—the Nefari, kings of the black market in blood slaves and every other nasty business in Manhattan.

"I will kill you if you don't."

The guy's mouth stretched in a taunting smile. "You can't do that, break your own laws."

Campbell leaned in even closer to the guy's face and tightened his fingers around his throat. "Then I'll make you wish you could die."

The harder he squeezed, the purpler the scumbag's face grew, the wider his eyes. He'd fed recently to have any color. And though he didn't have to breathe, having his throat crushed wasn't pleasant. Instincts held over from his human existence told him that throat crushing meant death.

"Okay, okay," he managed to squeak out through his constricted windpipe.

Campbell slammed him against the wall again just for good measure, causing mortar between the bricks to break loose and hit the pavement at their feet.

"What did Rico know?"

"I knew that guy was a rat."

Campbell reached for the guy's throat again, and Charlie held up his hands, palms out. "Wait. Give me a minute."

"You've got five seconds."

"And that's generous," Colin added.

Charlie looked up and down the alley, nervousness making him twitchy. "I might have heard that he had stumbled upon some information that the Nefari didn't want shared."

"What kind of information?"

"About some new project."

Questioning Charlie was like pulling fangs. He decided to get more specific.

"Is it true the Nefari is employing humans to do their dirty work during the day?"

Charlie winced that he was stuck with telling the truth if he wanted to get out of this alley in one piece. "Yes."

"Who are these humans?"

"I don't know."

"Charlie, I'm at the end of my very limited patience."

"I swear! All I know is they are all O-positives, so it won't matter as much if they get killed."

Damn it, the guy appeared to be telling the truth. "What are they doing? Looking for?"

"I think you know that already." The guy swallowed and rubbed his neck. "Blood slaves, sex slaves."

Anger surged through Campbell. "Sex slaves? They're pimping the humans out?"

"Yes. Certain vampires have a thing about wanting to keep a warm body around, always at the ready."

Campbell's stomach knotted. He understood wanting a warm body, Olivia's, to be exact, but he couldn't imagine keeping a human slave for his amusement and satisfaction. He'd never force Olivia or keep her against her will.

Unless he let the bloodlust take over again.

"Do you know how many people they're targeting?" He needed to know if there were other lists of names, if he needed to call in more V Force teams for protection detail.

"I don't know," Charlie said.

Campbell's eyes narrowed. "You're holding out, weasel. Be very careful that the next words that come out of your mouth are the truth and useful to me." Campbell's fangs descended to emphasize his threat. In that moment, he was more vampire than man.

Charlie swallowed hard. "I might have heard they wanted to get back at that chick who messed up things for them earlier today."

Olivia. Dread settled in Campbell's stomach.

"When? What's their plan?"

"That I don't know. But they were talking about it inside the club only an hour ago."

Cold washed over Campbell, and it had nothing to do with the brutal November wind whipping through New York's concrete canyons. He backed away, and if he had a heartbeat, it would've been going crazy. He started to turn down the alley, but Colin clamped down on his arm.

"We don't have time." He nodded to the east, at the approaching sunrise.

"I have to make sure she's safe." He jerked away from Colin and left him behind, engaging his top speed. He didn't know if God answered or even heard the prayers of vampires, but he prayed nonetheless that Olivia was safe.

If anyone tried to hurt Olivia, he'd kill him. And he wouldn't feel even an ounce of remorse. He'd take them out for good then face the punishment. He might cease to exist, but Olivia would be safe. That was all that was important.

Mindy had been right. Olivia had lost her mind. Desiring a vampire was the height of insanity. Especially when he refused to admit he wanted her just as much. She'd suspected it after the kiss. But his anger and concern over her appearance on the news confirmed it. Despite that knowledge, she wasn't about to beg him to come back. The next move was his. And if he didn't make one, well, she'd find a way to get over him.

Unable to get anything resembling restful sleep, she got up before sunrise. Maybe today she'd figure out how to get on with her life without thinking of him nearly every moment. As she descended the stairs from her apartment to the restaurant, her mind went back over the dreams she'd had when she had managed to sleep last night. They alternated between Campbell ripping her neck open with a frightening savagery and his making love to her with a strength and skill that had her panting and crying out his name.

When she flipped on the kitchen's overhead lights, she gasped. Two men stood across the room. They weren't vampires, but the term *unsavory* fit perfectly. All of Campbell's warnings came back to her, and she cursed herself for leaving her gun upstairs, loaded beside her bed. Which was where she'd thought she might need it during the night.

As sleep receded more, she realized who they were—the two customers who had made her so uncomfortable that day she'd called Campbell.

"We hear we can get a free meal here," the taller one said.

She wasn't fooled. These weren't the kinds of lost and forgotten faces she fed each day. And did they honestly think she didn't remember that they'd already been here once as paying customers? "How did you get in here?" She wondered if she could make it up the stairs before they caught her.

She didn't get the chance. The man nearest her was across the room before she could make the first step. Bastard moved fast for a big guy. He pulled her arms behind her, and she winced. She struggled, determined to free herself, to get upstairs to that gun. She'd never seriously considered killing anyone before. But if it came down to it, she would shoot them before she let them drag her away to some fate worse than death.

Olivia kicked and bucked, but she couldn't connect with her captor's legs. The other guy moved close and ran his awful fingers down her cheek, over her neck, coming to rest just above her breasts. Her skin crawled in an attempt to get away from his touch.

"You are a pretty thing. I'd love to have you myself, but I wouldn't live long after that. Still," he said as he licked his lips, "it'd almost be worth it."

She didn't know where she got the strength, but she spit in his face.

His expression transformed to a portrait of anger just before he slapped her.

"Olivia!"

She blinked away the stars, would swear she'd heard Campbell's voice.

"Olivia, let me in!"

She looked toward the front of the restaurant, and there he was standing on the sidewalk, his hands pressed against the glass of the front door. He looked desperate to get to her, to help, but he couldn't pass that barrier without her inviting him in. Could she do it? Give a vampire free access to the only place she was truly safe from his kind? These creeps holding her were human, like her, so she had a chance of getting free. But if she invited Campbell in, she'd either have to move or live knowing that when he got hungry, he might come for her.

Campbell's gaze caught hers, and his eyes blazed a brighter blue than she'd ever seen. Some instinct told her it had nothing to do with bloodlust.

Before she could utter a word, the man behind her clamped a hand over her mouth. She struggled again, but she couldn't move her mouth enough to bite his hand.

The tall man cupped one of her breasts and looked straight at Campbell. "It must really eat you that you can't help her, that you have to watch. Maybe I'll just have my way with her and take my chances."

Campbell's face hardened and his eyes narrowed. He was the epitome of dangerous, and knowing that it was out of some protective instinct toward her made Olivia's heart warm.

"I will kill you," Campbell said very slowly, deliberately.

"Not if the sun kills you first."

Oh, God! The sun. Olivia looked beyond Campbell and saw a hint of daylight working its way toward him. She widened her eyes, trying to tell him to go, to save himself. But even though he met her gaze, he didn't move. As she watched in horror, smoke began to drift up from his back. Still, he didn't move, not even when the increasing daylight became painful. She saw it on his face even though he tried to hide it. She closed her eyes, unable to watch him burst into flames.

Struggling did no good, but what if…? She went limp, and her captor lost his grip on her mouth just long enough.

"Campbell, come in!"

He moved so fast, she hadn't even taken a breath before he had both of the men by the throats and was shoving them out the back door. She didn't want to know what he did to them. All her worry was for the vampire who was risking his own existence to protect her. Campbell Raines knocked a hole in everything she'd ever believed about vampires. Good and evil, they weren't so black-and-white as she'd always thought.

The first ray of sun hit her shoulder right as Campbell stumbled back inside, his body burned and smoking, unsteady on his feet.

"Oh, my God!" She grabbed his arm and shoved him away from the windows and into the large walk-in freezer and closed the door behind them. She fumbled in the dark for the light switch as he collapsed at her feet.

When she finally turned on the light, she gasped. Campbell looked as though he'd walked through a fire.

Chapter 14

Campbell didn't dare think about how many layers of skin he'd lost or the pain he'd go through as it regenerated. What he had to concentrate all his strength on was not attacking Olivia, not after she'd decided to trust him. He craved fresh blood so his body would heal faster, but he couldn't give in.

"Pull the cuffs off my belt," he said as he met Olivia's wide eyes. He could tell how bad he looked from the horror on her face.

"Why?"

"I need you to cuff me so my fangs won't descend."

"You...you need to feed?" She took a step backward, the memory of that first day they'd met plainly written on her face. He didn't think she even realized it.

"The craving is there, to help with the healing." He winced when he tried to sit up.

Olivia stood frozen, and he hated the idea that maybe she was doubting her decision to invite him inside.

"Please."

She inched forward.

"The quicker, the better. I don't want to hurt you."

Olivia took a deep breath and met his eyes. "You won't."

"While your confidence in me is flattering, it's not wise. I may be a Souled vampire, but I'm still a vampire. You know what I'm capable of."

She knelt beside him and unhooked the handcuffs that had been dipped in holy water, her hands shaking. "I see a lot of people every day who nobody believes in, so I've become a good judge of character." She snapped the handcuffs gently around his wrists in front of him then met his eyes. She lifted her hand to his burned face and gently caressed the outer edge of the damaged area. "Anyone who is willing to face a horrible death to protect someone else is the very best kind of person."

He tried to smile but stopped when it pulled his tender skin too much. "But I'm not a person."

She touched his shoulder, hoping it wasn't burned beneath his shirt. "Yes, you are."

Something moved in his chest. His heart hadn't beat in years, but he'd swear he felt it do exactly that.

"Olivia!"

She jerked at the sound of another woman's frantic voice. "Stay here," she said as she jumped to her feet and headed for the freezer door.

As if he had any choice.

The moment Olivia emerged from the freezer and quickly shut it behind her, Mindy screamed and pointed a gun at her.

Olivia threw up her hands. "It's me!"

Mindy lowered the gun and pulled her into a one-armed embrace. "Oh, thank God you're okay!" Mindy was shaking as she stepped back, dropped the gun into her purse and grasped Olivia's upper arms. "There are two dead bodies outside the back door."

Nausea and dizziness hit Olivia simultaneously, and Mindy guided her toward a chair. Once she was seated and out of danger of falling on her face, she took a long, deep breath. "They broke in this morning. They…" Her voice faltered and she had to stop to collect herself and try to bring her shaking under control. "They were trying to take me."

"God, humans working with vampires. Just when you thought life couldn't go down the crapper any more."

Mindy marched to the refrigerator, pulled out a beer and downed half of it before she faced Olivia again. Olivia didn't point out that it was a little early in the day for a beer, because, honestly, she wanted one herself. But she had to keep a clear head and figure out what she was going to do about Campbell. What would happen when night fell? Would he leave? Or was she now facing having to walk away from the diner and her home? She'd told him she believed he was a good person, but his nature might trump those good intentions if he got hungry enough.

"Olivia."

She looked up and realized she had more immediate problems—helping Campbell and convincing Mindy to not kill him while he was vulnerable.

Mindy nodded toward the back door. "Did you kill them?"

Olivia shook her head. "No." She hesitated. "It was Campbell."

Mindy took another swig of her beer.

"He saved my life. Again."

Mindy started to take yet another drink but stopped with the bottle halfway to her lips. She scanned the scattered dishes, the busted sack of flour. Olivia knew the moment she figured out what had happened.

"You invited him inside?"

Olivia swallowed. "I had to. I couldn't break free of those guys. I couldn't let them drag me away to... I wouldn't survive a blood den. And Campbell was...burning." Tears stung her eyes at the thought that she could have been forced to watch him go up in flames.

Mindy's eyebrows shot up. "He was here after daylight?"

"He wouldn't leave, not while those men had me."

Mindy sank onto another chair, looking as if she'd been given a good jolt to her core belief system. "Nothing makes sense anymore. Humans working for vampires. Vampires saving humans." She looked one surprise short of a nervous breakdown, and Olivia was afraid she was about to send her over the edge.

"Min, I need your help, and I need you to stay calm." She paused. "He's still here."

Mindy's eyes went impossibly wide. "What! Where?"

"The freezer."

Mindy's gaze shot to the freezer door. "Oh, my God."

"It's okay. He's cuffed."

"As if a pair of handcuffs will hold him."

"He said they've been blessed with holy water. As long as he wears them, his fangs can't descend and he can't feed."

"But he's still strong. He could kill us both in the blink of an eye, break our necks."

"He won't."

"How do you know that?"

Olivia let the question sit there in the air for several seconds. "Because he just risked himself to save me." She was either crazy or naïve—or something beyond her understanding was happening here. It made no sense how her attitude toward vampires had changed so quickly, but it had. And she needed to make Mindy understand.

Mindy stood. "Let's get out of here while we can. You can move into my place."

"I can't leave. This is my home, my business."

"And he can waltz in anytime he wants now and kill you."

"You can leave if you want to. I'll understand. But Campbell has saved my life more than once. It's time I return the favor. The least I can do is let him hide here while he heals and the day passes."

She could see the argument in Mindy's eyes, but she kept quiet. Though her entire body was so tense she might pop soon.

"I've got to call the police," Olivia said. "I'm begging you not to say anything about Campbell."

For a horrible moment, she thought Mindy wouldn't agree. But then she gave what was obviously a reluctant nod.

After Olivia called the police about the bodies and told them a story about hearing a fight in the alley the night before, she and Mindy righted the kitchen.

As the police examined her attackers and questioned her about what she'd heard, she noticed one of the officers looking at her with an odd expression on his face. He approached her as the officer in charge of the scene finished his questioning.

"Olivia DaCosta?"

"Yes."

"You were one of the women who helped stop that kidnapping."

"I was." She did her best to look confused, as if she didn't know there might be any connection between her ticking off the Nefari and the two dead guys outside.

The officer nodded behind him. "You think the two events are connected?"

"Why would they be? To my knowledge, they didn't even try to get in here." *Please don't check the front door. Please don't notice the lock is broken.*

"Someone thought you were in danger even before your

moment in the spotlight. He called the police requesting a protection detail for you."

Shock jolted her, but she couldn't bring Campbell into this. Not when he was inside her freezer and vulnerable.

"You seem surprised."

"I am."

She hoped the officer chalked it up to disbelief that had nothing to do with a vampire. But Campbell had been serious enough about protecting her that he'd reached out to the human police. She fought the urge to run to the freezer and pull him into her arms.

"I can't imagine who it was, or why," she said.

He didn't look as if he believed her, but he didn't press the issue. "Well, whoever it was, looks as if he was right to be concerned. These two have a rap sheet as long as Broadway. We might need to rebuild the human population, but I can't say I'm sorry to see these two out of the gene pool."

The cop, an Officer Cortez, judging by his nametag, looked down at the dead kidnappers, a pinched look on his face.

"Is something wrong?" Olivia asked.

Officer Cortez sighed. "The person who called about protection claimed some humans were working with the vampires. Sounded crazy to us at the time. But recent events have proven he was right about that, too."

Olivia did her best to play dumb. "You think these two were working for vampires?"

"The fact that they were out here at night tells me yes."

"Were they killed by a vampire? I thought they were fighting with each other."

"Maybe. Maybe not. There are no bite marks, but their necks were broken. Hard for them to break each other's necks, don't you think?"

The visible shiver that shook her wasn't manufactured. Campbell had killed them so easily, so quickly. That he'd done it to protect her didn't calm the nausea rising in her stomach. She didn't dare make eye contact with Mindy.

"So whoever they were working for turned on them?" Olivia asked.

"We may never know. But I'd be very cautious if I were you." He pointed toward the bodies now zipped up in body bags. "This is bad news, whatever really happened." With a nod, he walked away and started talking to another of the officers drawing the attention of her neighbors. Just what she needed, curious stares turned in her direction right when she needed people to look the other way.

She did her best not to fidget, irrationally afraid she'd somehow reveal that she had a vampire hiding in her walk-in freezer next to her frozen foods. Would he freeze in there? Did cold affect vampires at all?

"He knows something," Mindy said.

"Shh."

When the police left and the coroner hauled away what was left of her attackers, Mindy strode to the sink and poured a large glass of water. She downed it before turning back toward Olivia. Her face was drained of color. She glanced toward the freezer. "I don't know if I can stay here, not with him so close."

"He can't hurt you."

"Like he didn't hurt those guys?"

"He's in bad shape, Min. Give him the time to heal today and he'll leave."

Mindy didn't speak for what seemed like endless minutes. "I'll stay, but we're both leaving well before sunset."

Olivia nodded, though she didn't think she could leave unless Campbell looked well on the way to mending. She'd deal with that later. Now she had to somehow get Mindy and herself through the day wearing a facade of normalcy.

Mindy started preparing breakfast while Olivia headed to the freezer to check on Campbell.

Mindy stopped her. "Don't."

"It's daylight. He can't step foot out of there."

After a moment, Mindy released Olivia's arm. She even followed as Olivia approached the freezer and gripped the handle.

When Olivia opened the door, she saw that Campbell had managed to drag himself to a sitting position against some cartons of sausage. And he didn't look as if he'd healed at all.

"Hi, Mindy," he said, his voice weak and raspy.

Mindy gasped, though Olivia had no idea if it was because Campbell had spoken to her or because he looked as if he'd walked through hell. Without speaking, Mindy retreated. Olivia would be lucky if Mindy managed to stay in the building.

When Olivia returned her attention to Campbell, beyond the pain she saw a sense of relief in his eyes. As if he was glad not to be alone anymore.

She approached him and he tried to move away. He stilled only when she touched his hand, his badly burned hand.

"Why aren't you healing? Do the cuffs prevent that, too?"

"No. I guess I just got smoked more than I thought."

She met his eyes. "You need to feed to get better, don't you?"

He hesitated before nodding.

"What happens if you don't? It'll just take a long time to heal, right?"

"Afraid not. I'll stay like this. It's too much damage."

She bit her bottom lip. After what he'd done for her, she couldn't let him suffer, too weak to heal or even to leave the relative safety of her freezer.

"If I take off the cuffs—"

"No!"

She flinched but didn't move away from him.

"No," he said more calmly. "I won't take the risk of hurting you."

"But I can't let you suffer like this. I won't."

A look of disbelief invaded his blue eyes. Then he turned his damaged hand over and held hers. "Call St. Patrick's. Tell Chloe what happened. She can help you get what I need."

Olivia tamped down a twinge of jealousy that he was turning to another woman for help. It didn't matter as long as it aided in his healing. And it was Chloe. Through their time together, she knew that Campbell and Chloe were nothing more than friends. Olivia and Chloe had bonded over the fact that they were perhaps the only two humans in Manhattan who could say they were true friends with vampires.

Campbell squeezed Olivia's hand despite how it must make his tender skin pull. "Why are you doing this?"

She met his gaze then jumped off the proverbial cliff. "I think you know." And before she could talk herself out of it, she leaned forward and kissed him gently on the lips. It was over before he had a chance to react, and the look of surprise on his face when she pulled away made her happy.

Despite the seriousness of the situation, she couldn't help smiling as she stood. But she let the evidence of how Campbell made her feel fall away before she left the freezer and closed the door behind her. At least that kiss might give him something to think about other than his condition. Judging by the rapid beating of her heart, she certainly wasn't going to forget it anytime soon.

Mindy looked up from where she was flipping sausage patties on the grill. "Is he dying in there?"

"No, but he's not getting better. He needs to feed."

Mindy fumbled and dropped a spatula. "You...you didn't?"

"No, but I have to help him." Olivia headed to the phone and dialed St. Patrick's. When Chloe answered, Olivia said,

"Hey, Chloe. It's Olivia. I need your help. I need to go to the blood bank."

"If you can wait another couple of hours, I'll go and give my monthly quota, too."

"No, I need to go now. Campbell is here and he's badly burned. He needs to feed."

Chloe gasped. Judging by the sounds coming through the phone line, Olivia guessed Chloe was standing and heading for the door. "I'll be there in five minutes."

"Okay, thanks."

When Olivia hung up, Mindy was staring at her in disbelief.

"You're leaving me here with that thing?"

"If not for him, I'd be suffering a fate worse than death now. Would you have me be so cruel as to let him die for it?"

"He's already dead."

"You know what I mean."

Mindy squeezed Olivia's hands. "I'm glad you're safe, but nothing's ever going to make me like them or trust them. They're savages."

Olivia wanted to cry as she faced the knowledge that she was going to lose her best friend or the guy she was falling for. She couldn't have both. But first she had to help Campbell. Then she'd let him go.

Chloe screeched to a halt right outside the diner.

Olivia gestured to her that she'd be right out. "I've got to go. Help with this and I'll never put you in this type of situation ever again."

Tears pooled in Mindy's eyes but she finally nodded.

"Okay. Be back soon." Olivia hurried through the dining room out to Chloe's car.

"Buckle up," Chloe said as she zipped away from the curb.

Olivia got the impression that even if New York City traffic equaled what it had once been, Chloe would have found a way around it or possibly over the top of it. She very nearly took the right-hand turn at the corner on two wheels.

"Um, we won't do Campbell any good if we kill ourselves getting to the blood bank."

"You said he was bad off."

"He is, but he doesn't seem to be getting worse." At least she hoped not. Would she be able to tell? Suddenly, she wasn't so sure and fear swelled in her. When she met Chloe's eyes, the rush of concern in her own must have been evident because Chloe floored the SUV, honking at anyone who dared get in her way.

Chloe parked behind the blood bank, the same one the team had taken Campbell to after he'd attacked her. "Come on," she said as she hopped out of the SUV.

Olivia followed as Chloe swiped a card through a reader at the back door and stepped inside. Chloe walked into the first office at the back, one totally devoid of windows or any way sunlight could reach it.

"Hey, big brother," she said, and proceeded to hug a tall handsome guy with reddish-blond hair.

"Hey, sis. What are you doing here?"

"Ethan, this is Olivia."

Olivia shook his cool hand and noticed the silver bracelet around his wrist. A quick glance revealed an identical one on his other arm. So that was how he could stand to work in a blood bank. His sister was supplying holy water to more than V Force.

"Seems Campbell got himself a bit scorched trying to protect her this morning, so she needs some AB-neg so he'll heal," Chloe said.

Ethan made a pained expression. "We're running really low. And I have half a dozen vamps coming in who got turned away last night. Two nights in a row of no blood and we could have a serious problem on our hands."

"Take mine." Olivia startled herself with her words.

Ethan looked at her. "How long since you last gave?"

"Long enough."

Ethan hesitated only a moment before leading her to a chair and pulling out the necessary equipment. As he looked for the vein in the crook of her elbow, he met her gaze for a moment. "I've never seen anyone other than my sister give blood to a specific vampire."

"Campbell saved my life this morning. Time for me to return the favor."

"I think it's a bit more than a favor," Chloe said from where she'd seated herself on the countertop that lined the far wall. "I've never even heard of a vampire exposing himself like that for a human, for anyone."

Olivia had known what Campbell had done for her was huge, but it hit her anew. She winced as Ethan inserted the needle into her vein and started the blood flowing through the tubing. The momentary pain was nothing compared to how it must feel to have your flesh burned as if you'd walked through a fire. Regardless of the fact that Campbell was a vampire, it had to be beyond painful.

"I admire your open-mindedness, but you need to be very careful," Ethan said. "You're now in more danger than you can even imagine."

"Ethan!" Chloe said.

He glanced back at his sister. "It's true, and you know it." He returned his attention to Olivia. "You know it, too. The man Campbell is at his core might not want to hurt you, might even care for you a great deal, but he's going to always be battling the vampire side of himself. We all do. Even if he's not hungry, your blood will call to him. That's never going away. Ever."

Olivia swallowed hard at the thought of seeing Campbell in full bloodlust again. She didn't want to think of him that way, but Ethan's words kept echoing off the walls of her mind. Was her kindness and acceptance enough to change him, to keep the vampire at bay, or was she the world's biggest fool? She shifted her gaze to the blood draining from her arm, blood that would feed the vampire who might end up killing her.

Chapter 15

Campbell's mouth watered before Olivia even opened the door to the freezer. His fangs ached to descend but couldn't. He needed to feed soon so he could get out of these cuffs. He was nearing the max time confined before the blessed silver started poisoning him.

When she opened the door, his nostrils flared at the scent of the blood. It was fresh, still faintly warm. And it was... hers. His gaze flew to hers.

"I had to," she said, evidently reading his expression correctly. "They were running too low."

He nodded and reached for the first bag. "Go outside. I don't want you to see this."

"No, I'll stay." She sat on a box of bacon, but she did avert her eyes.

He understood. After all his years of drinking blood, he could still remember his initial revulsion after being turned. It'd taken him a couple of years to get over it.

Unable to wait any longer, he drained all the bags she'd brought him, thankful that no fangs were required for the consumption of bagged blood. He felt his body start to heal as soon as he swallowed the first time.

"Is it helping?" she asked after he was finished drinking.

"Yes. Thank you."

She looked at him then, and her mouth fell open. "I can see a difference already."

"Hopefully I don't look like charcoal anymore."

She slipped off her box and moved closer. "Definitely not."

There was that weird phantom heartbeat again, memories of how his human body would react to a beautiful woman. Truth be told, his vampire body reacted much the same way.

"I'll leave as soon as it's dark," he said.

Her eyebrows scrunched. "There's no rush. You need to heal more."

He lifted his hands. "When the sun sets, I'll need you to take these off. We can only wear them for a max of twelve hours before they begin to slowly kill us."

Her eyes widened and she reached for the cuffs. He pulled them away. "Not yet. I want to make sure that I can leave as soon as you release me."

She shook her head. "I don't understand. Chloe's brother had on blessed bracelets, and he was fine."

"He takes them off as soon as he leaves the blood bank. By the time he goes back to work, he's healed of their effects and can put them on again."

"Why don't all vampires wear them?"

"Some of us need to be able to fang at a moment's notice. The Soulless wouldn't dream of it. The rest? They just don't like how they make them feel, as though you've been sapped of all your energy. And as long as they feed regularly, it's not a problem for the Souled. But they really can make you feel like crap."

She wrapped her hand around his, now more healed than burned flesh. "I'm sorry you were hurt so badly because of me."

He turned his hand over to clasp hers. "This was not your fault."

"But if you'd never met me—"

"I would have missed out on knowing a remarkable woman."

She smiled, and he was unable to believe they were touching each other, that she was close enough that he could feel her breath wafting across his cheeks, warmth against the constant cold. She moved closer and lifted her hand to his cheek. "You're almost completely healed."

"Thanks to you."

"And Chloe and Ethan."

"My trio of heroes," he said. Then he sobered, remembering how close he'd come to losing her to the vampire underworld. "I'm sorry I was so harsh with you before. I thought I was doing the right thing, staying away."

"I know."

He saw a flash of the remembered hurt he'd caused her. It made him feel guilty and amazed at the same time, amazed that she could have even been hurt by his words and absence. What could she possibly see in him? The fact that she evidently did see something worthwhile made him want to give her everything. Of course, he couldn't. Not anything near what she deserved.

Damn, he wanted her. But even though he was fully fed, he didn't trust himself. He broke eye contact. "You should get back to your customers. You don't want to draw unwanted attention."

"Afraid it's too late for that." But she did stand and head for the freezer door. "I'll be back when it clears out."

He sat in the freezer listening to the various conversations in the restaurant. He heard many of the customers ask about the cops and the dead guys in the alley, how Olivia and Mindy did their best to shift those conversations without drawing suspicion. When he detected the last person leaving the dining area and the sun approaching the western horizon, he sat up straighter.

As soon as Olivia opened the freezer door, he said, "It's time I leave."

"Oh, okay." She stopped for a moment as if she'd been surprised by his abrupt statement.

He needed to get away from her for a while, to clear his senses of her smell, the sound of her voice, the rhythm of her breathing. But when she moved close, he clasped her hand and brought it to his lips, kissed her fingers.

"Don't think I don't want to stay," he said. "You have no idea how much."

She met his gaze. "Then stay."

His mouth stretched in a sad smile. "I can't."

"You're not a danger to me, not now."

"I'm always a danger to you. You have to accept that."

"You won't let anything happen."

Her faith in him was almost his undoing, partly because he knew she didn't come to it easily. Even now, some part of her probably struggled with doubt about him, about her safety around him. And still she voiced a confidence in him he didn't deserve, that no vamp did. Maybe he'd allow himself just a little taste. He leaned forward and kissed her, fell into the sweet flavor of her lips, their warmth. It felt like coming home after a long trip away. What was meant to be a simple parting deepened the moment she opened to him. His tongue slid into her mouth and tangled with hers. She moaned and his entire body reacted with need. Not the need of a vampire but that of a man for a woman.

Campbell started to run his fingers along her face, only to

realize he was still cuffed. What the hell was he doing? As if he hadn't put Olivia in enough danger already.

He pulled back. "I need to go."

She hesitated but finally shifted away. Without meeting his eyes, she unhooked his cuffs then stood. He wanted to reach out to her as she headed for the door, but he refrained. He needed to leave before either one of them went too far.

Damn it, he'd already gone too far. He'd kissed her, tasted her, had gotten himself invited into the sanctuary of her home. He followed her into the kitchen, wishing things could be different.

He spotted Mindy at the far side of the kitchen and smelled her fear. She had a firm grip on one of those wooden mallets that were used to tenderize meat. Sometime during the day, she'd shaved the handle down to a sharp point, a very effective stake. Hoping to somehow put her at ease, he nodded. "Thank you."

She pointed the makeshift stake at him. "I know you saved Olivia, but I still don't trust you."

"I don't blame you."

"You need to leave and never come back."

"Mindy," Olivia said from behind him, part scolding and part embarrassment.

He held up his hand. "No, it's okay." Campbell made the mistake of meeting Olivia's bright eyes. In them he saw a yearning that matched his own, her unspoken plea for him to stay. But he couldn't. Refusing to allow himself to speak any words that would even touch how he was feeling, he gripped the knob on the back door.

"Goodbye, Livvi" was all he managed before he fled into the coming night. Fled before his willpower abandoned him totally and he gave in to temptation and did more than simply kiss her.

* * *

One moment Campbell stood in front of Olivia and the next he was gone, literally in the blink of an eye. He'd pulled the door closed behind him, and she knew as she approached the door it was no use looking into the alley behind the building for him. He wouldn't be there. That damned protective trait she so admired about him was now standing in the way of them seeing where they could go following that kiss. That and the knowledge she had to give him up for good. She bit her lip to keep it from trembling.

Remembering the kisses they'd shared, she lifted her fingers to her lips and thought she could still feel his coolness there. It should have freaked her out to kiss someone who was technically dead, but it hadn't. He had felt very far from dead as he'd allowed himself a moment of indulgence. If nothing else, she could hold on to the fact that she was certain he wanted her for something other than her blood.

"Olivia?"

It took a moment for Mindy's voice to penetrate the haze of memory, but when it did, Olivia locked the door before turning toward her friend.

"You didn't have to stay," Olivia said.

"I wasn't going to leave you alone with him."

"If he'd wanted to hurt me, he would have done it the moment I took his cuffs off. He could have killed me and you before we even had time to say a word. But he didn't."

Olivia glanced toward the back door as if Campbell would magically appear there again. After her staring did nothing to bring him back, she shifted her attention back to Mindy. "Looks as if you're stuck staying here again tonight. I'm sorry."

She knew Mindy wouldn't get a wink of sleep knowing she was in a building that was no longer vampire-proof. Granted, Campbell was the only one who could enter, but that was one too many.

"Come on." Olivia led the way up the stairs, flicking the lights off in the diner as she went and trying not to think about how much she wished Campbell was the one following her.

Once they were in the apartment, Olivia closed and locked the door at the top of the stairs. She glanced at the balcony but found it empty.

"If I hadn't been here, you would have invited him up, wouldn't you?" Mindy asked.

Olivia couldn't lie to her best friend, but she didn't want to hurt her either. So she said nothing. But she didn't have to.

The momentary flash of disgust on Mindy's face was enough to tell Olivia that Mindy knew more had happened between Olivia and Campbell than Olivia had admitted. Only days ago she would have felt the same way at the thought of a vamp's lips on hers.

"We had this dog, a black lab named Renfro, when I was a kid," Mindy said. "Best dog you'd ever want, until he wasn't. He'd never shown any hint of viciousness, but one day he lost it and attacked Mom, bit her badly. Nobody knew why he turned like that, other than the fact he was an animal. We had to put him down. I cried and cried, but Mom wouldn't risk him hurting Jess or me."

"Campbell isn't a dog."

"No, but he is an animal who can turn with no warning."

"You don't have to worry about it anymore, okay?" She knew she sounded curt, but it had been a hell of a day.

Mindy didn't look convinced, and Olivia didn't have the energy to try to convince her. She wasn't sure she'd find enough to convince herself.

When Campbell returned to the cave to change into clothes that didn't smell like burned flesh, Sophia met him at the entrance. The strained look on her face put him on high alert.

"What's wrong?"

"There are Imperium representatives here to see you."

"Really? I figured it'd take them longer to get back to me."

"They're not here because of your inquiry about contacting the NYPD."

It took him a moment, but the truth sank in. They were here because he'd killed two humans. His heart sank at the knowledge he might very well never see Olivia again. Probably wouldn't live to see another day. Damn, damn and double damn. He hated the idea of having to give up his life because of two lowlife pieces of scum like the men who'd attacked Olivia.

But he hadn't drained them. Maybe that little technicality would be enough to save him.

"What happened?" Sophia asked. "We called Olivia's diner today, but she wasn't there and we didn't dare ask for you. We were afraid you were dead."

"I very nearly was, as you can probably tell from smelling me. But you might as well hear the story with everyone else. I only want to tell it once."

After hesitating for a few seconds, Sophia turned and headed down into the main room. There Campbell spotted a trio of familiar faces, the Lex Legis of New York. If V Force was the law enforcement arm of the Imperium, the Lex Legis was judge and jury. He'd had dealings with Annabelle Light, Henry Fowler and Chin Lee Wan before, but he'd never been the one on trial.

"Legisters," he said respectfully. "Sorry to appear before you in such a state."

"It seems you had a run-in with the sun as well as the two dead humans," Fowler said without preamble.

Campbell forced his expression to stay neutral. He'd never liked Fowler, and that was why of the three, Fowler was the only one Campbell didn't think of by first name. The guy just seemed to glory in his job a little too much. "Unfortunately," he said simply in response to the guy's comment.

"You know why we're here?" Annabelle asked.

"I'm assuming because of the dead humans."

Annabelle looked genuinely saddened. That sent a surge of concern through him. Would they really execute him? If they did, they'd be stretching the law beyond what it said.

"You know the punishment for killing humans," Fowler said.

"Yes, I do. It says that vampires are to be executed when they kill a human by draining him. I didn't even fang them. I broke their necks."

Fowler started to speak again, but Chin stopped him by simply holding up his hand. Chin was the head Legister and so always had the right to speak before the others.

"Why did you kill them?" Chin asked.

"They were kidnapping humans for the blood-slave trade, we believe at the instruction of the Nefari. I caught them in the middle of trying to kidnap a woman with AB-negative blood." He did his best to keep any inflection or facial expression that might give away his relationship to Olivia out of his response. There was no law against vampire-human relationships, but he didn't want to give them any reason to ask the Imperium to implement one.

"You have identified these men?" Chin asked.

Travis took a step forward. "The human authorities have."

Chin redirected his attention to Travis. "You can track them back to the source, to whoever is responsible for their actions?"

"Yes, sir," Travis said, betting the farm and quite possibly Campbell's life on their ability to solve this case.

"Good. We are done here." Chin headed for the door.

"But, Legister Chin, he killed two humans," Fowler said.

"He has broken no law. The men were not drained, and he

was performing his sworn duty at great personal risk." Chin looked at Campbell. "Thank you."

Campbell gave him a respectful nod. "Thank you, Legister."

Fowler gave him an ugly look as the Legisters filed out of the room. Campbell didn't know what the guy's problem was, and he didn't really give a damn.

Neither Campbell nor any of the other members of the team moved or said a word until they heard the exterior door close behind the Legisters.

"That dude sucked on too many lemons when he was alive," Billy said.

"Where the hell were you today?" Len asked. "Colin said you raced away with dawn on the horizon."

"You wouldn't believe me if I told you."

"Try me."

"Olivia DaCosta's walk-in freezer."

There was a suspended moment; then Colin had the balls to laugh.

Campbell punched him in the shoulder. "You try burning to a crisp and see if you don't think a freezer is paradise afterward."

Sophia made a sound of distress.

"I'm okay now. Chloe and Olivia got me some blood so I'd heal."

"Damn, man," Len said. "You really do like this gal to go through that. I don't mind pain, but growing skin. Hell."

Campbell filled them in on the rest of what had happened then looked at Travis. "How close is NYPD to knowing who those guys were working for?"

"Not very."

Campbell cursed.

"I, however, am a wizard with connections and have a pretty good lead."

"And you didn't tell the Legisters?" Kaja asked.

"They didn't ask if I had tracked them, only if I could. I answered them truthfully."

Len laughed. "That Wall Street sneakiness does come in handy once in a while."

That it did. "Who is it?" Campbell asked.

"I got a couple of hits on them having been in contact with Nicky Salmeri."

Len whistled at the same time Sophia shivered, both with reason. Nicky was really bad news, feared even among the ranks of the Soulless. The Nefari kingpin had the reputation of punishing by baseball bat just so he could watch the vamp in agony as his bones grew back together. Well, he could try tonight, but he would be in for a surprise. If Campbell found out the guy was behind the kidnappings, behind the attempt to take Olivia, he'd be hard-pressed not to use Nicky's bat on him.

"Wow, this just gets better every day," Kaja said as she pulled back her hair into the tight braid she wore when they were about to do some serious ass-kicking.

"What's the plan?" Colin asked as he leaned back against the edge of his desk.

"First I'm taking a shower and changing out of these reeking clothes so I don't have every dog in Manhattan following me. Then I feel the need to go say hi to the Nefari."

Chapter 16

An impressive line of very large vampires slid into a shoulder-to-shoulder barricade, cutting off Campbell's view of Nicky Salmeri. He'd bet money not a one of them possessed a sense of humor. No matter, he wasn't exactly in a joking mood.

"Nicky, you're going to want to have your goons step to the side or have them charged with obstructing justice," Campbell said.

A deep laugh came from the table in the back corner of the restaurant. "Obstructing justice? Sounds like such a human term." He'd heard many a vampire use the same tone of disgust when uttering the word *human* before, but the way Nicky said it really grated on his last nerve.

"You know we have laws, too." Salmeri had certainly broken enough of them, even if he did manage to slither out of paying for his crimes.

Nicky snapped his fingers, which must have been a signal, because the line of guards parted.

"Now, what law have I supposedly broken this time?" Nicky said.

Campbell took his time walking forward, closing the distance between himself and the Nefari boss. Len and Kaja backed him up while the rest of the team had positioned themselves around the restaurant to keep an eye on things and make sure they didn't go sideways fast.

"Hiring humans to do your dirty work during the day."

He sneered. "While a repulsive thought, I fail to see how that would be against our laws."

"It is when those humans are kidnapping other humans for the blood-slave trade."

Salmeri barked out a solitary laugh as he sat back in the corner of the booth, stretching his arms along its back. He wore a slick gray suit that no doubt cost more than Campbell made in a month. Evidently crime paid very well.

"I have no need for blood slaves. I don't lack for food or sources of pleasure." He gave Kaja a long look. "Though I've always got room for another lovely at my side."

Len growled low in his throat, and Campbell had to agree with the sentiment. But Kaja wasn't the type of girl to need guys to take up for her.

Kaja said nothing, but Campbell had no doubt that she was giving Salmeri an "eat crap and die" look.

"Quit trying to divert the conversation," Campbell said.

"Is that what we're having, a conversation?" Nicky asked. "Because it sounds more like you coming in here and accusing me of crimes with no evidence. The Imperium must be dragging the bottom of the recruitment barrel if you are the best it can muster."

Like every other Soulless vampire, Salmeri was no fan of the Imperium. Campbell had his own issues with them, that they were perhaps a bit too much like human politicians, but he kept those thoughts to himself.

Campbell pulled a photo out of his pocket and tossed it onto the table, causing it to slide across the surface until it came to rest in front of Nicky. "So you're saying you don't know those guys?"

Nicky barely gave a glance to the crime-scene photo of the two guys in Olivia's alley, a photo that Travis had procured from the NYPD's server.

"I don't associate with human alley trash. Seems someone did the world a favor by removing them from the population."

"I agree."

Nicky met his gaze and nodded. "Your work?"

"Yes, and when I find the vampire who hired them, he's going to wish he could die as quickly."

"It must be tiring caring so much for your prey."

The muscles in Campbell's jaws tightened. He refused to respond because anything he said would likely be seen as a victory to Salmeri. Man, he hoped the guy was the one behind the kidnappings so he could take him out of play, knocking a big hole in the Nefari.

"Be sure to spread the word that we're looking for the vamp behind the kidnappings. I want him to know we're coming for him."

"You can rest assured your visit and accusations here have already begun to spread. You can't beat the vampire grapevine. I suspect you'll hear something very soon."

Campbell detected a hint of threat in Salmeri's words, but he didn't acknowledge it. The vamp was used to scaring others to get his way. Well, Campbell didn't scare easily.

He nodded to Len and Kaja that it was time to go.

"You're forgetting your photo," Salmeri said.

Campbell looked back at Salmeri, wearing his surface cool with a practiced air. "You keep it. Maybe it'll help jog your memory."

With that, Campbell and the rest of the team filed out of

the restaurant, intently aware of all the eyes on them and the level of malevolence thick inside.

Once they were out on the street, Kaja glanced back at the entrance. "Can I just rip that guy's throat out and be done with it?"

"Get in line," Len said.

"I wouldn't mourn his loss, but we need to watch him instead," Campbell said. "He knows something. I saw it in his eyes."

"Eyes I'd like to poke out," Kaja said quietly.

Though he'd love to let Kaja do whatever she wanted to Salmeri, would even lend a helping hand, he was the leader of this team. The one who had to ensure the rules were followed by all vampires, including his friends.

Including himself.

Olivia thought she might as well get used to not sleeping very well ever again. After several insomnia-filled hours, she finally drifted into REM shortly before dawn. It seemed as though she'd only just shut her eyes when her alarm clock started blaring as though it was trumpeting the end of the world.

"Turn it off before I come in there and shoot it," Mindy yelled from the living room.

Olivia slapped the button to quiet the clock, then lay there staring at the ceiling and trying to remember the last time she'd had a day off from work. She let herself fantasize about what she'd do if business picked up enough to where she could hire another cook and waitress. She'd wander through the Met, eat somewhere besides her own kitchen, hang out in the park with Herbie, Roscoe and their friends, and enjoy the feel of the wind and sunshine on her face.

She let out a long sigh at the elusiveness of all those things. When she finally dragged herself out of bed, she felt as if she were slogging through hip-deep mud. Her brain was sending the appropriate signals to her arms and legs, but they didn't seem to want to obey.

A shower helped marginally, but she was still not up to par when she wandered into the kitchen and grabbed a huge mug of the strong coffee Mindy had made.

"You look about how I feel," Mindy said when Olivia joined her in the living room.

"Then you must feel as if you've been through the wringer a few times and have the energy of a slug."

"That about sums it up."

Olivia took a drink and stared at a random spot on the coffee table. She'd had just one too many shocks lately. Hiding a burned vampire in her freezer and giving him what felt like half her blood was the proverbial straw that broke the camel's back.

"I feel as if I need an energy drink to even make it down the stairs," Mindy said.

"What I wouldn't give for a day at a spa. Massages, facials, manis and pedis, maybe a new hairstyle."

"Now you're just being mean, putting that idea in my head."

"Misery loves company," Olivia said.

This felt right, joking around with her best friend. She tried not to think about what she would have to give up to keep this type of relationship with Mindy.

They slipped into silence as they drank the rest of the pot of coffee.

"Guess we better get to it," Olivia finally forced herself to say. "Don't want to scare poor Rusty by being late to open again."

She beat Rusty to the front door by about thirty seconds. "Morning, Rusty," she said when he slipped inside. "What'll it be?"

"Feels like an oatmeal-and-whole-grain-toast morning."

"Coming right up," she said as Mindy came out with his coffee.

"You girls need a day off. You work too hard."

"We were just thinking the same thing this morning," Mindy said.

"Alas, days off don't pay the bills," Olivia said.

Though she was still tired, some of her fatigue receded as she dived into her morning routine.

"Oh, Lord," Rusty said as he opened his paper.

"What?" Mindy asked from where she was putting the cash in the register.

"Those kidnappers got someone else, a teenage boy on his way to school this time. Poor kid."

A kid in the hands of vampires. Had he been taken because they'd failed in abducting her? Nausea welled up in Olivia and she had to force it down through pure will-power. She couldn't imagine the horror his parents were going through.

And the reality that the threat hadn't gone away simply because Campbell had killed those two guys made her even sicker. How many kidnappers were there? How many people were they after?

As the next several minutes progressed as they usually did, Olivia couldn't get her mind off the boy and what he must be going through. She tried to focus on something else by looking up at the sound of the front door opening again. But instead of a customer, it was a woman carrying a huge vase of roses, pale pink ones with dark pink at the tips of the petals.

"I have a delivery for Olivia DaCosta."

Olivia stared at them for several seconds in disbelief. He'd sent her flowers? When a few curious stares and even a couple

of appreciative sounds came from the customers, she hurried
to the front counter to take the roses.

"I'm Olivia," she said.

"Lucky girl," the delivery lady said. "These are the prettiest roses we have in the shop."

"Thank you." Olivia tried not to be obvious when she grabbed the card and slipped it into her back pocket.

"Looks as if someone's been holding out on us," Rusty said as he gave her a wink. "Do tell."

"Nothing to tell."

"That's not what those roses say."

"Stop embarrassing her, nosy," Jane said from her spot next to the window.

When Rusty shifted his attention to Jane, Olivia took the opportunity to grab the flowers and retreat to the kitchen. She set them in the corner so she could look at them as she worked. It was remarkably difficult to keep the wide, silly grin tugging at her mouth from fully forming. No need in feeding the curiosity fire.

She flipped the bacon and sausage before slipping the card out of her pocket, then out of its little envelope. "Olivia, thank you for everything. Sorry I couldn't stay last night. C."

Mindy brought some dirty dishes into the kitchen and placed them in the sink. "You shouldn't have accepted them."

Olivia bit her tongue. She was tired of the constant Campbell bashing. She took a deep breath, reminding herself that she had no idea what it felt like to lose family members to vampires. Mindy didn't hate without good reason.

"I don't mean to be such a bitch," Mindy said.

"I understand. And…I'll break off contact. It's just…" She stared at the roses until tears pooled in her eyes.

"You have no idea how much I wish this guy was still human," Mindy said. "I'd be planning your wedding already."

The thought of a wedding caused a pang in Olivia's chest.

"I'm sorry. I didn't think," Mindy said.

"It's okay." She'd never thought she'd even want to think about getting married again after losing Jeremy. Now... She shrugged at the situation in which she found herself, falling for a guy who not only posed a very real threat but was also one she'd never be allowed to marry. No church, no human authority would ever recognize it. She glanced at the flowers. "I'm just going to enjoy the flowers because they're pretty."

Mindy surprised her by giving her a big hug before returning to the front of the restaurant.

What she'd told Mindy echoed in her head. She wanted so much more than pretty flowers. She wanted to enjoy being with Campbell, not worrying about what couldn't be or what might happen. She didn't want to have to choose between her best friend and the man who'd captured her heart.

By the time they closed the diner and Olivia convinced Mindy to go home and sleep in her own bed, she wasn't sure if she had enough energy to force herself up the stairs. But a look outside at the deepening darkness sent a shot of fear through her. Sure, her would-be kidnappers were dead, but what if their boss sent more? Clearly there were more human fetchers out there. Was it personal now because she'd eluded capture twice?

With a fear-fueled burst of energy, she grabbed the vase of roses and headed upstairs. After locking the door behind her and shoving a dining chair under the doorknob for good measure, she set the vase in the middle of her table. She lowered her nose to the roses and took a deep breath of their heavenly scent. They reminded her that despite all the pain and suffering and loss in the world, there were still things of remarkable beauty.

She sensed Campbell's presence before she saw him standing on the balcony. It surprised her that his sudden appearance only feet away hadn't startled her this time. Maybe a part of her had expected him to return tonight. How was she going to tell him to leave? That he couldn't come back.

Olivia met his gaze and walked to the door. When she opened it, he took a step away.

"I see you got the flowers," he said.

"Yes, they're beautiful. Thank you."

"They seem so small a gift for all you've done."

"They're perfect."

His mouth edged up at one end. "I'm glad you like them."

"Is that the only reason you came by, to see if the florist did her job?"

"No."

She stared at him, waiting for him to elaborate.

"I wanted to make sure you were okay. You had a big scare yesterday."

"More than one. I was afraid you were going to die in my freezer." She had to bite her bottom lip when the reality of how bad he'd been burned hit her again.

"That would have been difficult to dispose of, huh?" he said.

"Don't joke about it. It's not funny."

"I'm sorry." He took a step forward but stopped himself.

A mixture of longing and caution showed itself in his eyes. She saw the decision there. It should make what she had to say easier, but it didn't.

"What's wrong?" he asked.

She lowered her gaze to the floor. "I am… I'm faced with an impossible decision."

"I just came to say goodbye," he said.

When she looked up at him, she realized what he was doing—trying to make the decision for her so she didn't have to. This time it didn't make her angry. It made her sad, desperate. When he tried to step away, she reached out and took his hand. "Don't go."

He turned slowly and looked at her with an expression that told her he wanted this every bit as much as she did. But there was pain there, too.

"Olivia. You don't want to lose Mindy. Good friends are more valuable now than ever. And she's right about me. It's too dangerous for us to be together, for so many reasons I can't count them all."

She took a step closer to him. "I love Mindy dearly, but I don't want to be alone anymore."

"You're killing me. How much willpower do you think I have?"

"I want this. You want this. We can fight it all we want, list all the reasons it couldn't possibly work, but it's not going away."

His last ounce of resistance evidently fled, because he closed the distance between them.

Olivia felt as if she were the one going up in flames when Campbell wrapped his strong arms around her and kissed her. A desire more potent than anything she'd ever felt consumed her, made her body hum in places that insisted on finding satisfaction. Somewhere amid all the kissing and caressing, she managed to utter a single word.

"Yes."

He wasted no time in scooping her up into his arms and making short work of the space between the balcony and her bedroom. It seemed only a solitary breath escaped her from the time he stepped across her home's threshold to when he placed her gently on her bed. His eyes glowed with a brilliant blue hue that, for the first time, she thought of as beautiful and not frightening.

"I must have lost my mind along with a few layers of skin," he said.

She sat up and captured his mouth, needing to taste him again. His hands slid under her T-shirt and unclasped her bra. And then his hands found their way unerringly to her breasts. Though he possessed incredible strength, he applied only enough pressure to make her gasp in yearning. Needing to feel him, she tugged off his long-sleeved tee and let her hands move wherever they wanted across his sculpted chest, his strong arms, his muscled back.

He was perfect.

"You're so beautiful," he said, his words reverent.

"So are you."

He gave her a crooked smile. "Don't ever say that in front of the guys, or I will never hear the end of it."

Feeling more daring and needy than she ever had, she ran her hand down his chest to the top of his cargo pants. "I don't plan on talking to anyone for many hours."

With a growl that was supercharged with sexual promise, he pressed her back against the bed and kissed her nearly into oblivion. They paused for moments in between kisses to remove and toss clothing. And when he stretched his long body along hers, skin to skin, she nearly cried with need.

"I want you," she whispered against his wet lips.

"You're sure? Because once we do this, I can tell you I'm never going to want to let you go."

She knew he meant it as a warning, but she accepted it as a promise. She placed her mouth next to his ear. "Good," she whispered.

His mouth latched on to her breast, and for a moment the old fear surged into her despite her belief in him. What if his fangs descended? What if he couldn't help himself?

Campbell looked up at her. "I won't hurt you. I swear it." There was such conviction in his words that she believed him totally.

And in the next second she lost the ability to think beyond registering pure sensation. Campbell kissed her all over, making her body tingle in the most delicious way. He drove her to a frenzy just with his mouth and hands.

"I can't wait anymore," she said.

When he entered her in one fluid motion, she cried out, not caring if the neighbors heard her.

He slid out, then back in again, exquisite pleasure and torture all at once. She grabbed his hips and pressed down as she surged her own upward. He growled and pulled her hard against his body, then started pumping. Her breath rasped out in ragged gasps, faster and faster, mimicking his strokes within her. She matched his rhythm, getting closer and closer to her pinnacle.

"Faster," she said, and he complied.

They were beasts of frenetic motion, and with another powerful thrust she came apart. He continued to ride her— and that was what it was, a crazy, beautiful, hammering ride—until he reached his own release and cried out her name.

They collapsed in a tangle of arms and legs, their lungs heaving. Olivia snuggled close to him and marveled at the rise and fall of his chest.

"You're breathing," she said.

"Yeah. It's not essential, but our bodies still remember and react. Running, climbing stairs, making love to a gorgeous woman." He pulled her close and kissed the top of her head.

He held her so carefully that her heart opened up like a blooming flower. As improbable as it might seem, even to her, she loved him. She lifted herself so she could look in his eyes. "Can vampires love?"

He smiled. "I think I just answered that question."

She twirled her finger along his chest. "Not make love. Love."

His expression changed, growing more serious. "Evidently so."

He kissed her with such feeling that her body started to hum again. This time they made love so torturously slow that she thought she might start begging for release before he got around to giving it to her.

In the lazy aftermath of their lovemaking, Campbell wrapped an arm around her and pulled her close to his side. "I'm sorry I have no warmth to offer you."

"It's okay. I think I'm warm enough for both of us at the moment."

He chuckled and she liked the sound of him happy. She knew he had a strong sense of purpose, but she had no idea if this immortal life he was living held happiness. It seemed unreal that she, an everyday diner owner, could possibly be the person who could bring him that. Almost more unbelievable than the fact that the man bringing her happiness was a vampire.

She trailed her fingers over his chest, examining the muscles there.

"Be careful. You might get more than you bargain for," he teased.

She lifted her head to look at him. "How do you know what I'm bargaining for?"

He lifted an eyebrow.

"Is that another of your vampire powers, to be able to make love all night long?"

A wicked grin stretched his lips. "Oh, no. That's all me, one hundred percent Campbell Raines the man."

She smiled back. "Mighty sure of yourself, aren't you?"

"With good reason."

She laughed as he rolled her onto her back and entered her again. Now she was definitely going to hire some help in the diner because she didn't know if she was ever going to leave this bed again.

Chapter 17

When Olivia fell asleep, Campbell lay next to her for a long time watching the slow rise and fall of her breath, the peaceful look on her face. When the vampire side of him tried to think about her blood, he forced himself out of her bed. He should leave, go to work, but he couldn't make himself walk out the door. He stood and watched her sleep for several moments, marveling that she could rest so peacefully with a vampire next to her. That she had wanted to make love to him, to have him hold her.

She'd made him feel alive again.

God, he wanted that memory to go away. Hadn't he had to relive that horrible night enough?

But he could so easily take Olivia's life before he even thought about it. He'd almost done it before. The image of Bridget Jameson lying bleeding in his arms taunted him, whispering that it was only a matter of time before it was Olivia hanging from his grasp like a rag doll robbed of its stuffing.

He slipped his pants on and wandered into the living room. A check of the exterior out both her front window and the sliding glass door revealed quiet, vampire-free streets. When he turned away from the balcony door and headed back toward her small living area, he spotted a framed photo on a shelf full of books. He picked it up and looked at a beaming Olivia with her arms around a sandy-haired guy. They stood on a pier that jutted into the ocean, the sun bright overhead.

He'd never be able to give her that.

"That's Jeremy," she said as she crossed the room from her bedroom doorway.

"I'd assumed. You look happy."

"We were. We'd gone to Florida on vacation, just a couple of months before the virus hit."

He lifted the picture and looked at her. "I can't give you this."

"No, but you have other things to give."

"What? I deal with death and crime and the dark underbelly of vampire society. There are no sunsets or sunrises or building sandcastles on the beach. I can't even take you outside at night for fear I'd have to fight off other vampires. And I can't go outside with you in the daylight. What could I possibly give you?" With each word, he felt as if he were ripping himself more raw inside.

"You." She took the photo from him and placed it back in its spot on the shelf. "I'm going to always love Jeremy. He was my first true love. But even though it felt like it at the time, I didn't die with him. I still have a life to live, however long it might be. And I want you in it."

He shook his head. "I still don't understand why."

"Because you're a good man, Campbell Raines. You are honorable, kind, self-sacrificing, caring."

She wouldn't think so highly of him if she knew everything. He should tell her, push her away for good, but he couldn't. She moved closer.

"Not to mention sexy as hell," she said.

That last part made him smile despite dark thoughts of the past and tug her close. "Sexy, eh?"

"Mouthwateringly so."

He examined every inch of her face and slowly shook his head. Would he ever get enough of this woman? "I could say the same about you."

"Oh, yeah?"

"In fact, I think you've slept enough." He lowered his mouth and captured hers in a hungry kiss. When she answered in kind, he'd swear his body heated from one end to the other.

She unzipped his pants. "You have on entirely too many clothes."

He stood mesmerized as she unbuttoned them and let them drop off his hips. He slid his hands under the long T-shirt she'd put on and lifted it over her head, leaving them both naked. They didn't make it to the bed this time. He lifted her and sat her bottom on the back of the couch. When she wrapped her legs around him and slid her tongue over his left nipple, he made a sound of painful pleasure and buried himself in her to the hilt.

"I can't go slow."

This time she licked his ear. "I don't want to go slow. In fact, I want to see just how fast you can go."

And so he showed her, holding her close and pumping so hard and fast that she gasped and let her head fall back, giving him glorious access to her breast. He sucked and pumped until he thought they might both fly apart, and then he did it some more. He felt her interior muscles tighten around him, and that sent him over the edge. She cried out with her release, and the sound of her pleasure caused his to swell as he slid in and out even faster until he too finally found release.

His legs unsteady, he rolled her backward onto the couch and draped his leg over her. There was no doubt about it anymore. Wise or not, he loved this woman, loved her with all his heart.

Olivia woke up in her bed, though she had no memory of how she got there. Before she opened her eyes, she let herself drift on the memories that came back with a heated clarity. A bird chirped somewhere nearby, heralding the dawn. She smiled in her half sleep at the beautiful sound.

And then she sat up so fast her head swam.

She ran her hand down the other side of the bed, now empty. The rest of her bedroom proved just as lacking in his presence. The fact that she was naked told her that she hadn't just dreamed last night.

"Campbell?"

No answer.

She kicked off the covers and checked the bathroom, then the rest of her small apartment. After wrapping herself in a robe, she checked out the windows but he wasn't anywhere visible outside either. When she turned away from the window, that was when she noticed the note propped against the vase of roses.

"You're beautiful when you're sleeping. I wish I could see you with the sunlight on your face."

She covered the giddy smile that formed on her lips. No matter what they'd shared the night before, she'd never expected such lovely words from a guy like him, a man's man. She giggled at the idea that these were words he'd also never want the other guys on his team to hear.

That was okay. She wanted them all to herself.

It was hard to think about working, but she needed to get

ready before Mindy arrived. She wondered how long she'd be
able to keep how she'd spent her night from her best friend.

It ended up not being an issue.

When she got downstairs and started mixing the ingre-
dients for cherry pastries, the phone rang. Her heart started
beating faster in anticipation of hearing Campbell's voice.
"Hello," she said as she put the phone to her ear.

"Liv, I need to take the day off, maybe two," Mindy said
without preamble.

"Are you okay?"

"Yeah, just exhausted."

Olivia knew it was more. Mindy was reliving the horrible
deaths of her mother and sister, and it was Olivia's fault. She
closed her eyes, searching for the right thing to say. Maybe
it was best not to bring it up, to let Mindy deal with it in her
own way.

"You deserve some time off. Get some rest. Do something fun."

"Hey, maybe I'll get that massage," Mindy said a bit half-
heartedly.

"Tease."

Mindy laughed a little, but it was a shadow of her normal
laughter. "You going to be okay running things on your own?"

"Yeah. Not expecting a big run on the diner."

"Okay. I'll see you in a couple of days."

When Mindy hung up, Olivia felt the void where her friend
should be. It grew bigger with each moment that passed in
condemning silence.

Campbell stood in front of the Imperium the next night.
He'd wanted so much to go back to Olivia's, to hold her again,
but he'd been summoned to the Imperium's North American
headquarters a mere two streets away from the United Na-

tions. At least this time the reason for the meeting was of his own making.

When he climbed the stone steps to the front door, he remembered when this building had used the cover of the private residence of a reclusive billionaire. He remembered driving by when he'd been with the NYPD and wondering about the identity of its owner. He and his partner had gone back and forth guessing how the recluse had made his billions.

He'd had no idea that the owners had amassed their fortune by living for centuries.

When he stepped inside, the unease that he always felt here made a reappearance. He didn't feel threatened, more like out of place, as he had felt at really fancy restaurants when he'd been alive. He'd been more of a takeout-pizza kind of guy.

"Officer Raines, your timing is perfect," said the red-headed vampire at the front desk. "Representative Drogan just finished a phone call and can see you now." The woman stood and led him down a hallway beside the stairs that led to the upper levels of the six-story building. He didn't know what was on all the floors or in all the rooms, only that the courtroom was on the top floor.

As he entered the office the woman indicated, Charles Drogan stood and rounded his desk with a formal-looking stride. Though he'd lived through centuries, he sometimes still showed the mannerisms of King Henry VIII's court, which was where he'd been turned.

"Ah, Raines. Good to see you."

Campbell nodded in acknowledgment. "Representative Drogan."

"What can I do for you today?"

"I've been trying without success to make contact with the NYPD on a matter. I'd like your help in making them listen. Perhaps if a request came from the Imperium—"

"What is this matter?"

Campbell hid his annoyance at being interrupted. People doing that had always irked him, as if they were indicating what they had to say was more important than what he'd been in the middle of saying.

"Protection for a woman."

"A human woman?"

"Yes. She's a target of whoever is behind these abductions."

"All humans could be their targets."

"Yes, but she's escaped two attempted abductions already."

"Sounds to me like she can take care of herself," Drogan said.

Campbell couldn't help his hands fisting at his sides. And by the quick glance he saw, it hadn't gone unnoticed by Drogan. "My team intervened. She wouldn't stand a chance against vampires on her own, not even the humans they have working for them."

"Your team happened to be nearby on both occasions?"

If Olivia's life weren't so important to him, he'd tell this guy what a jerk he was, Imperium be damned.

"The first time, we detected human distress while we were on patrol. The second, we were alerted by a tip from an informant."

Drogan returned to the far side of his desk and sat in his large leather chair. "Protection for a single human hardly seems a concern for the Imperium."

"I thought all humans were important. Isn't that why we changed the laws about tapping veins, why we established the blood banks?"

The tick in Drogan's jaw told Campbell he'd probably just crossed a line and shouldn't expect any help from the Imperium. He forced himself to calm down and remember that Olivia's safety was the important thing here.

"All I'm saying is that if the Imperium and the NYPD were

to work together, perhaps it would be beneficial for everyone. There are others in her neighborhood at risk, too."

"Noted," Drogan said, sounding as if he'd already begun the process of filing Campbell's idea in the "no action" part of his brain's file system. "Though it's my opinion that the less we interact, the better."

Before Campbell could say anything else, Drogan picked up his phone. "If you'll excuse me, I have an important call to make."

Campbell could rant and rave all he wanted, but once an Imperium representative made up his mind, there was no changing it. Anger made his bunched muscles throb as he nodded and turned to go. By the time he hit the hallway, he wanted to punch something, and hard. He was taking such long angry strides that he nearly ran over someone as she came out of the door of the next office.

"I'm sorry," he said a moment before he recognized her. "Baroness. I didn't realize you were in town."

She sighed. "It seems I am always in a town not my own."

"You do have a demanding job." Catherine Flanders, the Baroness of Edgemont, called London home, but her position as a liaison between the Imperium's home and all the offices around the world kept her traveling more often than not. She was what you might call Internal Affairs for the Imperium's leaders in Bucharest.

"Yes, and it only seems to get more so with each passing year."

"What brings you to New York?"

She slid her arm through the crook of his and walked slowly toward the front door. "I'm not at liberty to say. What brings you to the Imperium? I know you didn't just drop by to pass the time."

She knew him pretty well considering they'd only spoken a handful of times, but he'd liked her the moment they'd met when she'd been in town to bear witness at the trial of an Imperium employee who'd drained a teenage girl almost to the point of death. What made it worse was that the vamp had called the girl, posing as a hospital employee, to say her mother had been in an accident to get her to come outside. Because the girl lived, the man hadn't been put to death. But if Campbell had to guess, he'd bet wherever he was now he was wishing he had been. A life sentence had quite a different meaning for a vampire.

The baroness had told the man to his face that he not only was a disgrace to the Imperium and vampires everywhere but also gave pond scum a bad name.

Baroness Flanders was what one might call filthy stinking rich, and so she said whatever she wanted and no one challenged her.

He debated telling her about his run-in with Drogan.

"Come, now," she said as they descended the front steps outside and headed slowly up the sidewalk. "I know you were in with Drogan, and I know that the man is a pompous ass."

He laughed then told her the extent of his conversation.

"You like this girl." It wasn't a question.

He didn't contradict her. "She is a good person. Sometimes it seems those are hard to find these days."

"What makes her a good person?"

"She's kind, selfless, feeds the homeless." He looked down at the baroness. "She's only the second human I've ever met who believes all vampires aren't like the Soulless. Granted, our kind hasn't really advertised otherwise."

The baroness smiled and patted his arm. "She sounds good for you. It sometimes isn't a popular viewpoint among my colleagues, but I think it's very important to remain as close to our human selves as possible. Understanding of differences often takes a great deal of time to come to pass, but I have hopes of one day seeing humans and vampires coexisting in a friendlier, easier way."

"That's a tall order, especially when humanity still has problems with acceptance among themselves."

"Yes, but we will live a very long time. There's no telling what we'll see."

He didn't know why he'd not thought of it before, but it hit Campbell that even if he and Olivia found a way to make their relationship work, it would only be for a tiny fraction of his immortal life.

"You're thinking of your lady's life span?"

He stopped and looked the baroness in the eye. "How did you know?"

"I'm a keen observer, Mr. Raines. How do you think I got this job? Why I'm so good at it?"

"Why do you work, anyway? I know you don't have to."

She pushed some of her dark hair behind her ear. "Because I bore easily." She waved her hand in a swirling motion. "I guess I'm a little like you. Somebody has to keep all these crazy vamps in line."

He looked off into the night. "Sometimes it feels like a losing battle."

"I know."

He returned his attention to her. For the first time since he'd known her, she sounded tired. It was so unlike her that it caused concern to swell in him. What did she know that he didn't? Did it have anything to do with the fact that she was in New York?

Her abnormal moment passed and she met his eyes. "My advice is don't think about how long her life is. It robs you of the joy you can have with her while she is here."

"You sound as if you speak from experience."

"I do. I loved a man very much, but I spent all the years we had together tied in knots over the fact that I'd lose him too soon, that we wouldn't be like other couples who got to spend their entire lives together. When he was gone, I realized how much time I'd wasted, time when I could have been truly happy."

He shoved his hands in his pockets and looked up at the night sky. "If I were sane, I'd stay away from her. I fear hurting her, or worse."

"You know what my favorite saying is?" the baroness asked. "Where there's a will, there's a way." With that, she patted his arm again and turned on her heel. "Well, I better get back. Maybe I'll think of a way to make Drogan's night miserable on the walk back."

He smiled then kissed her cheek. "Maybe I should have fallen for someone like you."

"My dear, you wouldn't be able to keep up with me."

As he watched her walk away, her words reverberated in his head. *Where there's a will, there's a way.*

Was there? He wasn't so sure, not with memories of Bridget tormenting him. But if so, he was damn well going to find it.

Something was wrong. Olivia stared out at the handful of people sitting in the diner, a fraction of the normal morning crowd. And it was too quiet. She'd noticed that as soon as Rusty had shown up. First, he'd been several minutes later than usual. Then he hadn't been able to meet her eyes, and he'd barely said anything.

"What is going on?" she said to herself.

Could the abductions be keeping people away? Or maybe the fact she'd had two dead bodies found in her alley? She shook her head. It was more than that, and she intended to find out what. She headed for the dining room.

She stopped only a few steps in when Rusty simply left his money on the table and left. Dread settled in her stomach. With Rusty's exit, that left only a family of four in the back corner and Jane next to the window. When she met Jane's gaze, the other woman gave her a sad smile. Olivia took it as permission to approach. At least Jane wasn't making a bee-line for the door without a word.

Jane pointed to the chair across from her. "Have a seat."

"Are you sure? Seems everyone else thinks I'm contagious with something."

Jane nodded to the empty chair, and Olivia slipped into it. "Word has gotten around the neighborhood that you're see-ing a vampire."

Olivia jumped as if she'd been stung. "What?"

Jane leaned a little closer. "One of your neighbors saw you together, saw him jump from the street to your balcony."

What should she say? Deny it? Try to explain.

"You are not the first and likely won't be the last," Jane said.

"I… You don't seem upset."

Jane shrugged. "It doesn't affect me. I personally think people ought to mind their own business and not tell every-one else how to live."

Olivia glanced across her nearly empty diner. "You seem to be in the minority."

"Unfortunately." Jane slid her glasses to the top of her head. "You ever wonder what I'm writing in here every day?"

"Yes. Mindy and I have actually debated many times. Our latest guesses are erotic novel—that's Mindy's guess—or spy thriller because you used to be a spy."

Jane laughed. "Maybe it's an erotic spy thriller."

"Hey, new genre."

Jane placed her hand on either side of her laptop. "No. I'm writing about human-vampire relations throughout history."

Olivia scrunched her forehead. "Is there enough material for that? There really hasn't been much interaction."

"See, I don't think that's true. There are too many stories

of vampires throughout history. I'm taking a look at all of them again, along with historical accounts of the same periods when the stories originated. I don't think all of those tales are fiction."

"I was told that those stories sprang up because of rogue vampires who killed too much and didn't make sure no one saw them."

"Maybe part of it. But I don't think all the interactions were deadly. They've just been very well hidden or disguised. Do you think your vampire would consent to being interviewed?"

Olivia couldn't imagine it in a million years. She gave Jane an apologetic smile. "I don't think so. Besides, he's a very young vampire. He wouldn't have witnessed any of these potential historical encounters."

Disappointment fell over Jane's face. "Oh, well. It was worth a try."

"You don't fear them?"

"I wouldn't say that. I'm not so adventurous that I step out of my building after sunset. But they do fascinate me. I want to know the reality versus the myth. Before the Bokor virus, I traveled to remote locations all over the world writing about little-known peoples and places, but this is like nothing I've ever worked on before. I feel as if I could peel back layers forever and still not get the entire story."

"They were very good at hiding their existence." Despite her relationship with Campbell, Olivia still found the vampire world frightening and the fact that they'd lurked in the dark for centuries creepy.

"The most secret of societies." Jane took another sip of her coffee.

"Can I get you a fresh cup?"

Jane closed her laptop. "Sorry, no time. I have a meeting this morning."

"Will you be coming back?" Olivia hated the hint of desperation in her voice. But her dining room sat as sparsely filled as it had in the days after she'd reopened following the pandemic. Just when she'd felt as though things were getting better, bam, the rug got pulled out again. At least Mindy wasn't here to see what Olivia's actions had done to their livelihood.

"Yes, dear. I'll be back again tomorrow." She looked at the empty tables around her. "Hopefully the others will come to their senses soon, too."

Olivia sat at the table for several minutes after Jane left, watching people walk by on their way to work. Could she really blame customers for staying away? Not so long ago, would she have been any different?

She had to find a way to fix this, to fix everything.

Chapter 18

Campbell would swear it'd been ages since he'd seen Olivia rather than the mere day since he'd left her apartment. He needed to feed later tonight, had confirmed with Ethan that there were a couple of units of AB-negative available. He wasn't going to push himself to the breaking point ever again if he could help it. But first he needed to see Olivia, hold her in his arms.

The baroness's words had reverberated in his head ever since she'd uttered them. He didn't know if he could totally turn off the thoughts of her mortality or the danger he posed to her, but he couldn't imagine never seeing her again either.

When he arrived at her apartment, she was lying on her couch watching TV. All he could see of her were her sock-covered feet hanging over one of the couch arms. Hoping he wasn't disturbing her if she was asleep, he knocked on the balcony window.

It took her a moment, but she rose, turned off the TV and

crossed to the door. "Hey," she said when she opened it and ushered him inside.

Once he was standing in her dining room, she pulled the blinds closed over the sliding glass door.

"You okay?" he asked.

She offered a small smile. "Just a long day."

He pulled her into his arms. "Are you too tired for company?"

"No." She wrapped her arms around him and placed her cheek against his chest. "I want you to stay."

Sensing her fatigue, he led her to the couch and urged her to curl up against him. He kissed the top of her head.

"How's the abduction investigation going?" she asked.

Campbell's muscles tightened. "We've got a suspect. Just have to find the evidence to prove it."

"Do you...do you think those people are still alive?"

"I hope so."

When she fell silent again, he knew something was wrong. He rubbed his hand along her arm. "You're hiding something from me. What is it?"

"Just had a bit of a dip in the amount of customers today."

"How much of a dip?"

She let out a long sigh. "A big one. It hasn't been that bad since I first reopened after the pandemic."

He knew the reason without her having to say it. "It's because of me, isn't it? Someone found out about us?"

She hesitated but then nodded. "I guess one of my neighbors saw you."

He cursed, then closed his eyes and let his head fall against the back of the couch. "I'm sorry."

"Don't you dare blame yourself," Olivia said as she sat up.

He opened his eyes and looked at her. "Who do you think is at fault?"

"Me, the neighbor who couldn't keep his or her mouth shut,

any vamp who has ever drained a human. Frankly, whoever is behind these kidnappings. It's not just one thing, though it seems that way."

"Maybe not, but I was the tipping point."

"And I wouldn't have done anything differently."

He shook his head slowly. "How can you say that? It's hard enough to get by now without having someone like me torpedo your business. Not to mention how your best friend feels."

"I'll manage. I always do. I might not be a vampire, but I can be a tough cookie when I set my mind to it."

He smoothed her hair away from her face and let his fingers travel along the edge of her cheek. "I know. I saw that fight in you the first time we met." When he'd almost killed her.

Campbell pulled Olivia close and kissed her. He knew he should leave, figure out some way to make things right, but his need for her overpowered any other thoughts.

"Make love to me," she said in his ear.

"My pleasure." He lifted her effortlessly in his arms and carried her to the bedroom.

The dip of the bed woke Olivia. She fought off the disorientation of sleep in time to see Campbell stand and pull his pants over long legs and lean hips.

"You're leaving?"

He didn't turn toward her. "I have an appointment at the blood bank."

"You're hungry?" Despite how she felt about him, the idea of his vampire hunger still stoked fear in the deepest part of her.

"Yes. I don't like it when I start to think of your blood too much."

She didn't like that thought either. Instead she focused on

the play of his back muscles as he slipped his T-shirt on. She resisted the urge to ask him when she'd see him again, partly because she didn't like clingy women and didn't want to be one. But she had to admit to herself that it was mostly because she didn't want to give him the opportunity to say, "Never."

When she tossed off the comforter, he turned toward her. "No, don't get up. Go back to sleep."

Unease stirred inside her, but she didn't voice it. He leaned over and kissed her forehead, and she became acutely aware of the distance between them.

"I shouldn't have told you," she said.

"Told me what?"

"About the loss of customers."

He stood and slipped on the jacket he didn't need. "I'm not leaving because of that. I've just got a lot to do." He smiled. "Guy's got to work for a living."

Sadness settled in her chest. Though everything he said was true, she knew there was more to it. At least some part of Campbell was running away from her, whether he realized it or not.

As Campbell drank bagged blood at the blood bank a few minutes later, he berated himself for getting so involved in Olivia's life. Not only was he a constant danger to her, as his yearning for her blood tonight proved, but now he'd also endangered her livelihood. And Mindy's. But evidently he was a selfish bastard, because he still didn't think he could stay away forever. Not even close to forever. But he had to figure out how to make things right.

But how was he supposed to undo this damage? He couldn't make someone unsee him, couldn't contact all her customers and tell them he posed no threat and would stay away.

After his feeding and then a fruitless questioning pass

through Little Italy, he headed home. When he walked through the door, Travis looked up from his desk.

"Good news," Travis said. "Olivia's car has been located in Connecticut."

Campbell headed toward his own desk with a nod and a sound of acknowledgment.

"And the award for least excitement goes to…" Travis said. "What's eating you?"

"Olivia's customers have deserted her diner. Guess whose fault that is."

Travis adopted a chastised expression. "Sorry."

Campbell ran his hand back through his hair. "And I have no idea how to fix it."

"That's easy," Kaja said as she walked over from the kitchen with a new mug, this one with a big curly *K* on it. "Buy a big honking ad in the *Times* for her. Replace the old customers with new ones."

Kaja took a drink and sat down at her computer. Instead of work, however, she started playing "Farmville." For the life of him, he couldn't imagine what her fascination with that game was.

He thought about what she said. Maybe an ad would help. Couldn't hurt.

"I just emailed you the details about where to pick up Olivia's car," Travis said.

"I need you to do it."

"Me?"

"Yeah." Campbell didn't use a tone that invited argument, and Travis didn't give him any.

"Fine, whatever."

Len, Colin and Sophia came in from patrolling with only a couple of minutes to spare. Billy rolled in on his skateboard a few seconds later.

"Look who's cutting it close now," Campbell said as he met Colin's eyes.

"One of those nights," Colin said.

"Yeah, if we were werewolves, I'd swear it was a full moon with the way things were going down," Len added. "Fights, more than the usual amount of angry stares coming our way. Some weird vibe in the air."

"At least one of us had a good night," Colin said as he glanced at Billy. "I think Puppy here found himself a skater-geek girlfriend."

Billy skated by Colin and bopped him on the head. "At least I'm getting some action, old man."

"Don't listen to him, Billy," Sophia said. "I think she's cute."

"Thank you." Billy paused to kiss her on the cheek before pushing off on his skateboard again.

Thumping from the street level drew their attention, then the sound of something coming down the drop chute. Campbell was sitting closest to the chute, so he headed for it. "Did anyone put in another order with Chloe?" he asked.

He heard the chorus of noes at the same moment he saw what had been dropped down the chute. He spun and pointed toward the back corner. "Get out!"

They almost made it.

Olivia considered not even opening the diner. She didn't know if she could face another disheartening day of empty tables and the lack of friendly faces.

She remembered how she'd told Campbell she was a tough cookie, however, so she forced herself downstairs. Whatever the day dished up, she'd deal with it.

She was glad to see Jane a few minutes later, her first and perhaps only customer of the day.

"Something must be on fire," Jane said as she walked in.

"I heard a bunch of sirens, and there's a big black plume of smoke coming from somewhere up near the park."

Olivia turned on the TV mounted on the wall. A reporter was on the scene with fire trucks behind her.

"Officials say it appears a bomb has gone off at a vampire-owned building on the east side of Central Park. It is unclear if any vampires were in the building at the time of the bombing, which happened just after daybreak."

A bad feeling started growing in Olivia's middle. After taking Jane's order, she retreated to the kitchen. She grabbed her cell phone and dialed Campbell's number. Her pulse raced faster with each unanswered ring. After his phone rang a dozen times, she hung up and dialed Chloe with shaky fingers.

When she got voice mail, she realized how early it was. She hung up and dialed Chloe's cell phone.

"Hello." The normal pep in Chloe's voice was absent.

"Chloe, it's Olivia. Where is the V Force headquarters? Where does Campbell live?"

Chloe didn't answer, and tears popped into Olivia's eyes.

"Tell me it's not what's on the news."

"I'm sorry, Olivia."

Olivia made an anguished sound. No, not again. She refused to believe it, not unless she saw it for herself. "I'll be there in a few minutes."

"No, don't." Chloe paused for a moment, and Olivia gripped the back of a chair to keep standing. "There's nothing left."

"Just pull it out," Campbell told Len as they sat in the old subway tunnel, dust from the explosion thick in the air. But when Len did exactly that, pulling a large shard of metal from Campbell's back, he couldn't hold in the yelp of pain.

Sophia was ready with a wad of white cloth that he thought was the long-sleeved shirt Len had been wearing over a gray henley. As soon as the metal was free, she pressed it against the wound, stemming the flow of blood until Campbell's body could begin to heal.

Colin walked toward them with his tee shoved against a wound on the side of his head. Blood streaked his bare chest. "What the hell happened back there?"

"It was a bomb." Which they'd thankfully survived, along with the daylight, by picking themselves out from under the rubble and escaping through the emergency exit that led to the network of abandoned subway tunnels. He counted heads and came up one short. "Where's Billy?"

They all stared at each other for a horrible moment, then started digging frantically at the rubble that filled the passage that connected their headquarters with the subway tunnels. "Billy!" several voices called out at once.

"Puppy? Come on, kid," Colin said as he tossed huge chunks of concrete out of the way.

Campbell winced with the pain in his back but dug nonetheless. Dug despite the sick feeling in the pit of his stomach. He found Billy and wished he could hide the boy's body from the rest of the team. But it was too late.

Sophia cried out, "No!" and took Billy's lifeless hand in hers.

The irony was Billy didn't seem any more damaged than the rest of them. It was the large shard of his skateboard through the middle of his heart that had sealed his fate. Curses and crying met Campbell's ears, but all he could do was stare as a cold numbness filled him.

After the initial shock, Colin and Len stepped forward and together with Campbell they finished digging Billy out. Kaja reached over and closed Billy's eyes and caressed his pale cheek.

"I'm going to kill whoever did this," Campbell said. "And he's going to die slow."

"Why the hell did a bomb end up down our delivery chute?" Colin asked.

"Someone wanted to deliver a message," Len said.

"That we're getting close and they don't like us sniffing around," Campbell added.

"That creep Salmeri?" Kaja asked.

"That's where I'd lay my money," Campbell said, focusing on his job, on avenging Billy's death.

"Told you to let me rip his throat out," she said.

"After I'm through with him, if there's anything left, you can be my guest," Campbell said.

Travis stared back at the pile of rubble. "We've lost everything."

Campbell looked around at his dirty, bleeding, bedraggled team. Time to be the leader. "We're going to get whoever did this. And we'll rebuild somewhere else."

"Perhaps I can help you with that."

They all turned toward the new voice, ready to fight. A man in khakis and an expensive leather jacket stepped into the faint glow shed by the emergency light on the subway-tunnel wall.

"Who are you?" Colin asked as he pointed a piece of rebar at the unknown vamp. "And don't take a step farther."

Campbell moved to the front of his team. He placed his hand on Colin's arm, applying downward pressure so he'd lower his weapon. When Colin did so, the guy took a couple more steps toward them.

"I'm Raymond Pierce."

"Raymond Pierce?" Colin said.

"Yes, that one," Pierce said.

Pierce had owned more companies than Campbell could name a decade ago. As rich as Richard Branson, Bill Gates and the entire Walton family put together. So he was dead, as the news had claimed, but not gone.

"How did you know we were here?" Colin asked.

"Baroness Flanders is a good friend. When she heard about the bombing, she asked that I come offer my assistance. You are in need of a new home, are you not? As it happens, I have just the place. If you all feel up to a bit of a walk, I can show you what we can offer."

"We—" Sophia started but choked on a sob.

Len gripped her shoulder in support and nodded toward Billy's body. "We lost a member of our team."

"A friend," Kaja said, her voice sounding shaky, too.

"I'm very sorry," Pierce said. "We can take care of him once we get to our destination. I'll get you whatever you need."

The others looked to Campbell. After a moment of consideration, he nodded. Pierce turned and led them into the darkened tunnel.

Despite Chloe's assertion that she shouldn't come, Olivia hadn't listened. Now she wished she'd stayed away. It felt as though a gaping hole was opening up inside her to match the one in the ground she couldn't stop staring at.

Smoke rose in the air from something still burning below street level. The air reeked with the scents of unnamed objects smoldering. She prayed that Campbell and his team were not amid the burning rubble.

Chloe still had her arm around Olivia's shoulders. Olivia suspected that if Chloe released her, she'd crumple to the ground. Movement among the crowd of officials beyond the yellow crime-scene tape caught her attention. When a man who looked as if he might be a detective stepped away, she spotted Herbie.

"Miss DaCosta?"

Olivia looked to her left and noticed another familiar face. "Officer Cortez."

"What are you doing here?" There it was again, the look that said he knew more was going on.

Trying to think on her feet while her heart was breaking took all her concentration. "I heard about the explosion and wanted to check on a friend." She pointed to Herbie. "But he looks to be okay."

Cortez glanced at Herbie before returning his attention to her. He didn't say anything, and though she knew it was a tactic to get her to reveal more, she spoke anyway. "I deliver meals to the homeless. I've known Herbie and some of the others who spend their days here for several years."

Finally, he nodded. "I'll send him over when he's finished."

"Thank you."

Officer Cortez walked away.

"That man feels like a human lie detector," Chloe said.

"Notice I didn't lie."

After a few more minutes, Officer Cortez led Herbie to the tape and held it up so he could pass back to the outside of the barrier it made. He pointed toward Olivia.

She broke free of her friend and headed for the older man. "Herbie?"

"Olivia? What are you doing here?" He glanced at the position of the sun. "It's early for your meal delivery."

"Why were the police talking to you?"

"Because I saw someone toss a package into the bank deposit chute. Only that bank's been closed since halfway through the virus outbreak."

"What did he look like?"

"I don't know. He was wearing one of those hoodie things. And he ran away as soon as he dropped the package. Had to be a human, though, because it was already daylight."

"What were you doing out here so early? You're not staying out here at night, are you?"

"Lord, no, honey. I got a one-day gig cleaning up after a

show at Radio City Music Hall. They paid me a little and let me spend the night there."

Olivia stared at Herbie, wishing that he knew more. That he could positively identify the bomber. Could assure her that Campbell had somehow escaped.

"Are you okay?" Herbie asked her. "You look as if all the blood has drained from your face."

"She hasn't been feeling well," Chloe said as she put her arm around Olivia's shoulders. "I think I'll get her home."

Olivia didn't fight her. She had no energy left to do so. As Chloe turned her back toward where she'd parked her SUV, neither of them said anything. What could they possibly say to alleviate the yawning ache growing in Olivia's heart? Tears trickled out of her eyes and ran down her cheeks.

This was her fault, for caring again. Though she'd not known Campbell that long, the pain his loss left behind felt too much like what had swamped her after Jeremy had died.

How could Campbell be gone? He was immortal. Why would fate allow such a good man to die not once but twice?

Chloe got her into the car without her realizing it. She leaned her forehead against the window and watched the streets of New York streak by as Chloe drove. Some part of her knew that they were going back to the diner, but she didn't want to. She wanted to keep driving, far away from New York and all the bad memories of loss.

But that wasn't realistic, was it? Nowhere was safe from death. Not even immortality.

Chapter 19

Campbell and the rest of the team followed Pierce as they left the subway tunnels and passed through a thick metal door into what looked like a private corridor. When they reached a set of stairs and Pierce started climbing, Campbell stopped and stared after him.

Pierce looked back. "Don't worry that we're going above ground. I'm a vampire, too, remember?"

After a bit more hesitation, Campbell and the rest of the team followed. They exited the stairway into an expansive library. Floor-to-ceiling bookcases lined a long wall, and several polished wood tables with comfortable-looking chairs filled the middle of the room. Opposite the bookcases was a line of tall windows now covered with thick metal shutters.

"This is amazing," Sophia said as she walked forward and trailed her fingers over the top of one of the tables, its surface smooth.

"It is the least we can do for those among us who try to keep peace. Who fight against the tide of the Soulless."

A tide, that was exactly what it felt like sometimes.

Len, carrying Billy's body in his arms, was the last one up the stairs.

Pierce pointed at a door on the opposite side of the room. "The bedrooms are down the hallway to the right. If you want, you can place your friend in the first one until you can make arrangements."

Len's eyes looked bright with unshed tears as he carried Billy from the room. Quiet settled in the wake of his leaving. Finally, Pierce shifted to face them.

"The baroness asked that I convey that whatever you all need, the Imperium will provide. And if they don't, she and I will," he said.

Campbell extended his hand. "We can't thank you enough, Mr. Pierce."

Pierce took Campbell's hand between both of his. "Call me Ray. And truly, no thanks are necessary. I'm honored to have you here." He gestured at their surroundings. "One of the benefits of being wealthy is that I can help. Feel free to look around and use the house as you see fit. I don't live here, so consider this entire place yours."

Campbell suspected that calling this a house was like calling the *Titanic* a dinghy.

After Pierce left them alone, Campbell met the eyes of his team. Before they did anything, they had to say goodbye to Billy.

Olivia sat in the middle of her empty diner and watched the sun move closer to the horizon. She was dimly aware that Chloe was on the phone with her brother. Chloe had wanted to call Mindy, but Olivia wouldn't let her. She didn't think she could handle facing Mindy when she knew her friend wouldn't mourn the loss of any vampire, not even Campbell.

Surrounded as she was by empty tables and chairs, Olivia

couldn't believe how fast her life had changed from being on the upswing to hitting rock bottom.

She became aware of the fact that Chloe was no longer on the phone.

"Would you like something to eat?" Chloe asked.

"I'm not hungry."

"I know, sweetie, but you have to eat."

"Why?"

Chloe slid into the chair next to Olivia. "Because Campbell cared about you, and he'd want you to take care of yourself."

Realizing Chloe wouldn't give up until Olivia ate something, she said, "Maybe a grilled cheese."

The sandwich ended up tasting like old cardboard, not through any fault of Chloe's cooking but rather through Olivia's utter disinterest in eating it. Her friend must have realized it, because she quietly slipped the half-eaten sandwich off the table and took it to the trash in the kitchen.

"I think we could both use some rest," Chloe said from the doorway into the kitchen.

Olivia realized that night had fallen without her noticing, and that meant Chloe wasn't going anywhere until morning. Reluctantly, she nodded and somehow found the strength to stand. She was halfway to the staircase when someone pecked on the front door. Fear shot through her until she turned and saw a familiar face. She grabbed the back of a chair and still felt as if she might collapse. Whether it was her imagination, a ghost or reality, Campbell stood on the other side of the locked door.

And she couldn't make her feet close the distance between them.

Chloe crossed to the door and unlocked it. She looked as stunned as Olivia felt.

"Hi, Chloe," he said. Then he looked at Olivia. "We found your car." He motioned toward the street, and she saw Colin leaning against the door of her car. He raised a hand and waved.

That movement broke through the veil of unreality that had kept her immobile, and she raced to Campbell. She leaped at him so fast that he stumbled backward but caught her in his arms.

"Hey, hey. It's okay," he said.

She framed his face and met his gaze. "You're alive."

The confusion in his eyes gave way to understanding as he glanced at Chloe.

"How did you survive that?" Olivia asked. "I saw the hole. I just knew you were gone." Tears streaked down her cheeks again, a mixture of remembered sorrow and tremendous happiness that she'd mourned for no reason.

His eyes dimmed in pain, and she realized Colin was quiet, too. Even though she barely knew him, she knew that wasn't normal.

"Campbell?" Chloe said as she stepped forward.

He met Chloe's gaze, then lowered his own. "We lost Billy."

"Oh, no."

Olivia saw the pain, knew he was taking responsibility. She squeezed his hand. "It's not your fault. The police said it was a bomb."

"He's just as gone," he said, his voice thick. This, more than anything else, showed her he had feelings the same as any human.

"I'm sorry."

"How did you get out of there?" Chloe asked.

"We fled into the subway tunnels. The Imperium sent someone to help us set up a new headquarters elsewhere."

"You've got a new place already?" Chloe asked, sounding surprised.

"It's in the Imperium's best interest that we stay on the job, and that means having equipment and a place to lay low during the daytime." He shifted his gaze to Olivia. "I'm sorry I didn't call. I didn't think."

"It's okay. You're safe now."

Campbell caressed her cheek and gave her a sad smile. "I need to go. I hadn't planned to come back tonight."

"Oh." She tried to hide her disappointment. He had too much on his mind already.

"Being with me has serious repercussions, including the fact that I have my own enemies. But turns out I'm not as selfless as I'd like to be. After today, I couldn't stop wanting to see you."

"I'll see you upstairs," Chloe said, and turned away.

"Good night, Chloe," Campbell said. "Thank you for staying with Olivia."

She waved over her shoulder without looking back and headed for the stairs. Colin made himself scarce, too.

Campbell returned his attention fully to Olivia. "I'm sorry you worried about me. The day was chaos, and I never thought you would make the connection between the bombing and V Force."

"Do you really have to go?" After a day of thinking he was lost forever, she never wanted to let him out of her sight again.

He nodded. "We have to follow a lead on the bombing. We think it might be the same person who is behind the kidnappings." He ran his fingers along the curve of her jaw.

"I'm afraid if you go, I'll convince myself the past few minutes didn't happen," she said.

He pulled her close and lowered his mouth toward hers. He kissed her softly, then more thoroughly, full of hunger. She responded with all the joy she felt at having him still be alive.

Campbell growled, not the scary version but rather the kind that made her want to drag him to bed. Suddenly, he broke away and took a step backward. "I need to stop now or I'm going to end up taking you up against this building," he said next to her ear.

The thought shouldn't have excited Olivia but it did. But enough common sense still resided in her that she knew she didn't need to make the current situation with the diner irrevocable by having public sex with a vampire. Plus, Chloe was upstairs waiting for her. And Olivia knew part of what Campbell was feeling likely had to do with the loss of his friend, the need to feel alive after a brush with death.

"Promise me you'll be careful," she told him as she cupped his jaw.

"As careful as I can be."

That would have to be enough.

Olivia went through the motions of running the diner for the next couple of days, but her only regular customer to appear was Jane. And as lovely as Jane was, she and the occasional person who had no idea who Olivia was sure weren't enough customers to keep the diner running. Frustrated and not knowing what to do next, Olivia decided to take a day off. She slept in, had a leisurely cup of coffee then decided it was time to go see Mindy.

She tried calling, but Mindy was either out or ignoring her calls. Whichever it was, she aimed to talk to her friend today even if she had to plunk herself down outside Mindy's apartment door and talk to her through it.

After arming herself with her gun and a knife, she headed out into the brisk wind. She kept in mind Mindy's first rule of self-defense, always being aware of her surroundings. But thankfully all she saw were other New Yorkers going about their days.

When she reached Mindy's apartment building, movers had the elevator filled with someone's belongings, so she took the central staircase. A shiver went up her back as she looked back down the stairs and saw one of the guys watching her. She felt safer with the weapons and the knowledge of how to incapacitate attackers, but he still gave her the creeps. Not every bad guy in Manhattan was working for vampires. There were still plenty of garden-variety rapists, muggers and thieves, too.

She felt better by the time she reached the fourth floor, where Mindy's apartment was one of four units. At least she felt better until she saw Mindy's keys hanging in the door and a bag of spilled groceries on the floor outside Mindy's apartment. Dread settled in her stomach like a cold stone.

"Mindy," she called out as she pushed inside. Her fear ratcheted up several notches as she searched the apartment. Instinct told her Mindy was not inside, and Olivia's thoughts flew back to those movers.

She called 911 for backup as she raced down the stairs. When she hit the lobby, she saw one of the guys loading a bulky object covered in a thick blanket. She shoved her phone in her pocket and pulled the gun from her waistband.

"Put her down," she said with as firm a voice as she could muster when she pushed through the exterior door. She scanned the area but didn't see the second guy.

The guy at the back of the van dropped the bundle and held up his hands. Olivia did her best to stay calm when she saw two feet in familiar athletic shoes tumble out of the end of the bundle. "Move away from her," Olivia said, punctuating her words with the gun.

"You even know how to use that thing?" the guy asked as he took a couple of steps backward.

"You want to find out?" She would shoot him, and she wouldn't hesitate. Not with Mindy's life at stake.

The sound of movement behind her caught her attention just before the other man grabbed her. She forced her elbow back into his gut. He grunted but it didn't stop him for long.

She tried kicking the side of his knee, but he was too fast and she kicked open air, putting her off balance.

"You are more trouble than you're worth," the guy said as she spun and slipped out of his grip again. He snatched at the gun but she stepped backward out of his reach.

Unfortunately, her heel slipped off the edge of the sidewalk. The guy took advantage of her momentary lapse of concentration and grabbed her. She kicked, squirmed, tried to bite him. He managed to get his arm around her neck to limit her struggles. She noticed the other guy was shoving Mindy into the van, so she lifted the gun still in her hand and aimed for the biggest target, his chest. When she pulled the trigger, the other guy flew backward and lay still. Mindy dropped halfway out of the van. She didn't try to free herself, so they must have drugged her or knocked her out.

Fear zipped through Olivia a moment before the guy holding her cursed and covered her mouth with a cloth. Despite his tight hold on her, she struggled to get free as the world around her started to fade and then went black.

For a couple of days after the bombing, Campbell's team got their new headquarters up and running. Though they all wanted to take Salmeri apart chunk by chunk, they knew they had to go in with a solid plan that would ensure they were getting the right guy and he didn't go free this time. So at night they ferried computers, cabling, office furniture and a new collection of weapons into the mansion. During the day, they set everything up and used the new supply of holy water Chloe had delivered to Ray to bless their shiny new handcuffs.

"What's the plan?" Kaja asked as she sat on the edge of Campbell's desk.

He looked up from where he'd been coordinating with Team 2's leader, Matt Calloway, on a combined visit to one Nicky Salmeri. In the midst of setting up the new base of operations, Campbell had been beating the bushes extra hard, too. Turned out that Nicky was part owner of that new club where Campbell and Colin had convinced Charlie Benson to be a little more forthcoming with his intel. Universal Donor—Campbell still hated that name.

A Souled vampire witnessed the abduction of the teenage boy through his building's video security feed. He'd recognized the driver of the van as one of the bouncers from Universal Donor. That'd been the one break they'd needed. But they couldn't go in stakes raised without planning this down to the tiniest detail.

"Team 2 will be holding down the exterior, making sure no one leaves. We will go in and spread out. Word is Nicky likes to hang at the club early in the evening, so we'll set up a perimeter and only go in after we see him."

"When is this going down? Because I want to make short work of this creep and get the humans back where they belong."

"Have some heavy-duty shopping to do?" Len asked as he strolled by to his desk.

Kaja gestured at the ratty jeans and Yankees T-shirt he was wearing. "You ought to think about doing some of your own."

Campbell just smiled. It was good to see his team members showing signs of normalcy. After Billy's funeral and the burning of his body, they'd all walked around in a daze until Colin pointed out that Billy was probably rolling his eyes at them. That had led to stories about Billy and even a bit of unexpected laughter.

"Tonight," he said in answer to Kaja's question.

Kaja laced her fingers together and bent them backward to crack her knuckles. She was ready to kick some Soulless vampire ass.

In contrast, Sophia was sitting on a dark brown leather couch reading one of her science journals. She might not work in a hospital or treat humans anymore, but she liked to keep up with medical science. As he looked closer, he noticed a tight look on her face.

"What's wrong, Sophia?" Campbell asked.

She glanced up at him, but part of her was still far away for a few seconds until she fully reengaged with the world around her. "Maybe nothing."

"That doesn't sound too convincing."

"It's just a story about a couple of scientists who've gone missing."

"Please tell me they're not from here," Colin said.

"No. One, a geneticist, is from Duke University. The other works for the Centers for Disease Control in Atlanta." Sophia looked up with an expression of concern. "She's a phlebotomist."

"A fla-what?" Len asked.

"Phlebotomist. A doctor of the blood."

"Could be a coincidence," Campbell said. "Can't imagine that scientists' blood tastes any better than anyone else's."

"I know. It's just…something feels off," Sophia said.

Campbell didn't much like it either, but the truth was those two scientists could have slipped up and been killed by vampires. They also could have been taken by abductors of their own kind for a purpose that had nothing to do with vampires. Heck, they could have just flown the coop.

Whatever had happened, it wasn't his responsibility. He and his team had enough to worry about in their own backyard. As he finalized the details of the raid on the club, he tried to focus on the fact that he was just doing his job. But the reality was that this was personal. He needed to put an end to these kidnappings so Olivia would be safe, so he could stop worrying about her.

At least stop worrying about this particular threat. The damage he'd caused in her life was another worry altogether.

When he took care of Salmeri's operation, he was going to do what he could to ensure her customers came back or she at least got some new ones.

His cell rang. After glancing at the caller ID, he answered. "Hey, Chloe."

"They've got Olivia and Mindy," she said, frantic and out of breath.

White-hot fear shot through him as he sat up straighter and nearly crushed the phone in his grip. "What?"

"Witnesses in the neighborhood said the kidnappers were in the process of taking Mindy when Olivia showed up at her place. She managed to shoot one of them, but they took her."

Campbell's world spun off its axis. "The guy she shot, is he alive?"

"Yeah. At least he was when they hauled him away in the ambulance."

"Travis, find out where they took a gunshot victim today. Get me his name and everything about him, now," Campbell said, punctuating his words with jabbing gestures.

"What's going on?" Colin asked.

"Kidnappers took Olivia and Mindy." He couldn't believe he was saying those words.

"Campbell, what can I do?" Chloe asked.

"Stay with your brother until we take care of this." He hung up and stared at the door he couldn't yet exit. He'd burned for her once, but that had been only moments and had nearly done him in. As much as it killed him, he had no choice but to wait.

"The NYPD?" Sophia asked.

"They won't be able to go wherever the humans are stashed," Len said.

Campbell roared and cursed the sun.

"We'll get them," Colin said. "We stick to the plan, and we'll save them all."

Somewhere beneath the fear and rage, Campbell knew Colin was right. It didn't make the wait any less agonizing.

"Gunshot victim is a Troy Giani. Has a rap sheet of petty stuff," Travis said. "Looks as if he's picking up his game."

"And got a slug for his trouble," Len said.

"Yeah, right in the chest," Travis said as he pointed to the report on his computer screen.

That Olivia had not gone without one hell of a fight made him proud of her but also afraid she'd be punished more than the other abductees, and before he could get to her. He paced the library. He had to save her. He had to.

When Olivia woke, the first thing she noticed was how parched her throat felt. Next came the throbbing pain in her wrists. She blinked her eyes several times to try to push away the fogginess in her brain. Gradually, memories slipped into place from wherever they'd been floating. Going to Mindy's. The spilled groceries. The movers who weren't movers at all. Shooting the guy who had Mindy. Then something being pressed over her mouth.

That last thought made her jerk more awake. Her movement sent pain shooting down her arms.

"Olivia?"

She turned her head and saw Mindy in the dim light. She was shackled to a stone wall, her arms stretched out above her and her ankles spread. That was when Olivia realized why her wrists hurt. She was shackled the same as Mindy, the same as the rest of the people beyond Mindy.

Oh, God, they were in a blood den. Cold, ripe fear shot through her. She saw it reflected in Mindy's eyes. Tears streaked down her friend's face.

"How long have we been here?" Olivia asked.

"I don't know. I just woke up a few minutes ago." Mindy

looked the other way, toward the other captives. "We're going to die here."

"No, we're not. We will figure out a way. Campbell will find us."

"Campbell? He's the reason we're here in the first place."

Olivia flinched at the ferocity of Mindy's words. She told herself that Mindy was scared, and if anger kept her going, that was okay. Olivia did her best not to give in to panic and fear herself. She pulled as hard as she could at the restraints, but they didn't budge.

The door at the top of the stairs opened, and loud music filtered through. Bile rose in Olivia's throat as three well-dressed vampires descended, a woman and two men.

"You have impeccable timing tonight," said the guy in the front to the others. "We just acquired two new sources today. One is already spoken for, but the other is the blood type you require. She's young and healthy, so you can both tap her together."

The vampire couple looked at each other and smiled. Olivia got the feeling that simultaneous feeding was somehow erotic to them, that it would be a sexual act as well as the gaining of sustenance.

The guy in the front met Olivia's eyes, and she hated him on sight. She would have hated him if he'd been human. He had that slick "I can get away with anything" look about him.

"This one proved a challenge," he said as he gestured to Olivia. "But I have a distinct feeling she'll pay for it later to-night." He gave her a knowing smile that sent cold rushing through her veins. Then he led the couple to Mindy, who struggled in vain against the restraints holding her.

"You're wasting your energy," the guy said. "You might as well stop struggling and enjoy it."

Mindy spat in his face. He slapped her with such a ferocity that Olivia gasped and worried that he'd killed her. But then Mindy moved.

"Leave her alone," Olivia said.

The guy moved slowly toward Olivia. "Can't stand to watch what you caused?"

Olivia forced herself not to flinch from him. His kind thrived on seeing fear in others. "You can keep me. Just let her go."

"No," Mindy said.

"She's right. We're not letting either of you go," he said. "You might as well set that pretty little head to accepting your new existence because it's all you'll ever see for the rest of your miserable little life." Suddenly, he grabbed her breast and ran his other hand down her stomach. His vile touch turned her stomach. "Too bad you're spoken for or I'd enjoy banging you against this wall while your friend watched helplessly." He smiled, showing the tips of his fangs. "Instead you will be the one to watch as your friend lives her worst nightmare."

He stepped away suddenly and motioned for the couple to come forward. In a flash, they were at Mindy's sides. When they both sank their fangs into Mindy's neck, she screamed the most horrible scream Olivia had ever heard. Olivia struggled as fat tears streamed out of her eyes. Her pleas for them to stop fell on deaf ears.

The man who evidently ran this den headed up the stairs, looking very pleased with himself.

"You're going to die for this, you monster!" she yelled at him.

He smiled at her. "That I highly doubt."

She'd never hated anyone so much in her life. She closed her eyes and prayed that Campbell found them soon, before the couple drained Mindy dry. Before the sound of Mindy's screams drove Olivia mad with grief and guilt.

* * *

Sometime during the feeding, Mindy passed out. Olivia's tears flowed a long time after the vampires left. She wanted nothing more than to be able to pull Mindy into her arms, but she was as helpless as anyone else hanging from this cold stone wall.

"I'm sorry about your friend."

Olivia looked beyond Mindy to a young woman and realized it was Jennifer Watson, who'd been abducted behind her apartment building. "Me, too. How are you doing?"

"Still here," she said with a shaky smile that seemed to cost her all her energy. "Not sure how much longer I can take this, though. I wonder if I'll die or go crazy first."

Though her own hope had suffered a lot in the aftermath of Mindy's ordeal, Olivia found she wanted to give this young woman a reason to believe they'd be rescued. "I have faith someone will find us."

"Someone named Campbell?" Jennifer shook her head. "There's no way anyone can find us down here. There are too many vampires."

Olivia looked toward the door and wished she had just one bit of knowledge—what time it was, where they were, if Campbell even knew she'd been taken. Deciding to focus on something she could determine, she looked past Jennifer. She recognized the teenage boy who'd been snatched up on his way to school. There were four others, but she didn't recognize them. The reporter, Leila Russell, wasn't among them.

"Has there been anyone else kept down here?"

Jennifer leaned her head back against the wall and closed her eyes. Were it not for the shackles holding her up, Olivia had no doubt Jennifer would crumple to the floor.

"A couple," Jennifer said. "One…one boy died. Another woman was taken somewhere else."

"Leila Russell?"

"Yeah." Jennifer shook her head slowly. "I'm not sure if I saw this or dreamed it, but I'd swear a man in a black cloak took her. I couldn't see his face, but…there was something terrifying about him. It was more than him just being a vampire."

Olivia swallowed past the dryness in her throat and prayed again that Campbell and the rest of V Force found them soon.

Jennifer lapsed into silence and Olivia thought maybe she'd fallen asleep or passed out. Endless minutes passed with the occasional moan from someone else in the room. The minutes stretched until Olivia wondered if they'd become hours.

"Liv?" Mindy said, sounding weak.

"I'm right here. I'm so sorry, Min. I never meant for any of this to happen. I'm sorry I wasn't able to prevent them from taking you."

"It's not your fault."

"It is." Fresh tears ran down her cheeks.

Mindy was quiet for several moments before she spoke again. "It's not your fault. The world just isn't a good place anymore."

Olivia didn't like the tone of Mindy's voice, as if she was giving up. "Min, listen to me. We will get out of this. I swear to you, I will figure out a way." She thought she saw a weak smile on Mindy's lips, one of those that said she didn't believe a word she was hearing but appreciated the effort.

The door at the top of the stairs opened and the slick vampire descended, thankfully alone this time. He didn't even spare them a glance as he walked the length of the room and opened a door at the end. After a long moment passed, three people in cloaks walked in. Hoods obscured their faces as they seemed to glide into the room, ever closer to Olivia. When she could see them better, she noticed two of them wore red while one was cloaked in deep black. The story Jennifer had told about Leila caused Olivia's heart to accelerate.

If they took her out of here, she feared she'd never be found and be doomed to a life of horror.

"This is the one I told you about," the slick guy said. "She's not been tapped, and she's AB negative just like you requested."

Olivia pressed her back against the wall as if she could dissolve into it. The pain she'd seen on Mindy's face as she'd been fanged made Olivia's neck burn in dread.

The person in the black cloak nodded once, and the ones in red stepped forward and unshackled her. Immediately, she fought them, but it did no good. Their grips were ironclad.

"No," Mindy said, her voice still weak but determined. "Let her go."

They ignored Mindy's pleas as much as Olivia's struggles as they dragged Olivia toward the door at the end of the room.

"Liv!" Mindy called out, a bit more forcefully.

"Stay strong," Olivia said right before she was dragged into a dark corridor and the door shut behind her.

She couldn't help the thought that the door had just shut forever on the life that she'd known.

When night finally fell, everyone was already geared up without any direction from Campbell. They knew their jobs and did them well. They all had their own reasons for wanting to put lowlife vampires like Salmeri away.

An hour before Salmeri was supposed to be at the club, Campbell texted Matt with Team 2 that they were heading out and his team should do the same. Everyone had their assigned positions and would be in them within minutes.

Campbell had to tell himself over and over to stay in control, stick with the plan. It was the best way to ensure Olivia, Mindy and the others stayed safe. The best way to make sure they found them and made certain this time Salmeri paid for his crimes. That he didn't hurt anyone else.

They fell into the premission silence as they walked the now familiar series of hallways to the garage. They climbed into their new truck and Colin drove them out on their first foray since the bombing. Campbell could tell by the focused look on everyone's faces that they were eager not only to save the human abductees but also to dish out some retribution for Billy's death.

Colin parked in the dark alley they'd chosen for the express purpose of staying hidden from any vamp who might tip off Salmeri. Still without speaking, they all slipped out into the night and blended with the shadows as they walked the final three blocks to the edge of the Tribeca vampire-club strip. Campbell held up his hand, indicating everyone should stop while he checked in with Matt.

"You guys ready?" he asked over the radio as he looked up to the rooflines surrounding Universal Donor.

"All set here," Matt said back, and gave Campbell a two-fingered salute from his post across the street. Dressed as he was all in black, he blended against the night sky behind him.

Despite the fact he didn't need it, Campbell took a deep breath, then exhaled slowly. "Okay, here we go. Move in hard and fast, and don't let anyone get in your way."

When Campbell moved forward at full speed, he sensed the rest of his team doing the same. The bouncer saw them at the last second and started to block their path inside. Campbell knocked him aside so hard that the guy crashed into the side of the building next door.

The moment they were inside, internal security descended. If this were a law-abiding club, no one would have messed with a V Force team. The fact they were meeting resistance was all the proof Campbell needed that something illegal was going on here.

Colin and Kaja parted a path for him, and he scanned the

club until he spotted Salmeri sitting in a corner yet again, this time with a leggy brunette draped over him. He dumped her on the floor the moment he saw Campbell and tried to make a smooth getaway.

"No such luck, you bastard," Campbell said as he sped after Salmeri and tackled him in a flying leap. Before Salmeri could buck him off, Campbell clamped a set of silver cuffs on him behind his back.

"You better have a damn good reason for assaulting me," Salmeri spat over his shoulder.

Kaja placed her booted foot on his head and shoved it back to the floor. "We're just taking out the garbage, and you're stinking up the neighborhood."

"Bitch."

"Big mistake," Kaja said then called Salmeri a rather unflattering name. She pressed down until his cheeks flattened.

Campbell let her have her bit of payback then signaled for her to back off. She did so with a final sneer in Salmeri's direction. Campbell jerked him to his feet, and not gently. A quick glance around the club showed him his team had trussed up the security goons, and the club's patrons had been herded onto the opposite side of the glowing dance floor.

He returned his attention to Salmeri and leaned in close. "One chance. That's all you get to come clean about the abductions and the location of the people you took."

Salmeri answered by spitting in his face. Campbell responded with a fist to the other vampire's jaw. Then he simply stood and looked at the crowd.

"Everyone stay where you are. There's another team outside armed with stakes and enough holy water to float the U.S. Navy." Matt came through the front door then. "Watch this no-good piece of garbage."

"With pleasure," Matt said as he settled his hand atop a stake at his waist.

Campbell looked at his own team. "Tear this place apart. Look for anything that might lead us to the captives."

They searched every room on every floor, but it wasn't until they descended the stairs to the basement that they found what they were looking for.

"They're here," Colin called up the stairs.

Campbell couldn't get to the basement fast enough.

A line of humans stood against the wall, their hands chained to it above their heads and their feet manacled and secured to large metal rings in the stone floor.

"Oh, my God," Sophia said.

One of the women looked up and started whimpering. "Please, not again," she said. Though she'd only been gone a few hours, Mindy was pale from multiple feedings.

"We're not here to hurt you," Sophia said as she moved toward her.

Mindy flinched and tried to get away even though she had to know it was no use trying. But the human survival instinct was strong.

He scanned the faces of the rest of the captives but didn't see Olivia. Was he too late? No, he couldn't be. He refused to believe it.

"Mindy, where's Olivia?" he asked. His question was more like a command, and it made her recoil.

Colin gripped Campbell's shoulder. "You're scaring her."

"I need to find Olivia."

Colin centered himself a few feet in front of Mindy. "Hi, Mindy. I'm Colin. I know you're scared, but I also know you want to save Olivia. Do you know where she is?"

"She needs to go to a hospital," Sophia said to Campbell. "They all do."

Mindy stared at Colin in confusion. "I've died, haven't I? Or I'm having a dream."

"No, you're awake and if you'll let me come closer, I'll take the restraints off you," Colin said. "We can free all of you."

Tears streaked down Mindy's cheeks, and Campbell knew exactly what she must be thinking. That she'd thought she'd never see the outside of this basement ever again. But he desperately needed her to focus.

With what little energy Mindy had, she nodded. Campbell motioned to the rest of the team to start releasing the prisoners. Colin moved forward slowly. Even with freedom not far away, Mindy couldn't hide her vivid fear of him. Once the chains were off Mindy, Colin helped her slide to a sitting position on the floor and offered her a bottle of water they'd brought in the hope they'd find the prisoners alive. With shaking hands, Mindy sucked the bottle dry in seconds. It seemed to push away some of her hysteria. When she looked up, she appeared to be thinking more clearly.

Mindy closed her eyes and took a shaky breath. "Olivia. They sold her, to someone really scary."

"Scary how?" Campbell asked.

"These people came in wearing red cloaks with hoods, then a guy with the same kind of cloak, only black. He never said a word, but...there was something about him. Cold, made my skin crawl."

"Some vamp with a weird fetish?" Len suggested.

"Maybe," Campbell said, but he was getting a distinctly bad feeling. "How long ago did they leave?"

Mindy looked confused for a moment, as if she'd lost all track of time. "Not long."

Campbell headed for the stairs.

"No," Mindy said with more force than she'd exhibited since they arrived. She pointed toward the other end of the room, toward a half-hidden door in the shadows. "They went through there."

Campbell nearly ripped the door from its hinges in his haste to reach Olivia. He heard more feet pounding behind him, but he didn't look back to see who it was. He ran as fast as he could through a series of dark corridors. He'd lost count of how many turns they'd made when he rounded another and saw movement up ahead, the fluttering of cloaks. Two big guys in red turned toward him, and he saw Olivia hanging between them. If they'd hurt her, he was going to slice the flesh from their bodies before he staked them.

They shoved Olivia into the darkness ahead of them and turned to fight. Campbell and Len hit them full steam. Fists flew and Campbell took a couple to the jaw and an elbow to the gut. Another blow busted his lip and rattled his fangs. Not in the mood to let this guy live any longer, he pulled his stake-shooting gun from his hip and pressed it against the guy's chest. He pulled the trigger and the fight went out of the guy like a light switch being turned off.

Campbell let him drop and stood in time to see Len make a powerful swipe with a knife that severed the other guy's head from his body.

When Campbell looked ahead, Olivia was gone. "Damn it." He raced past the dead vamps. He refused to believe he'd gotten so close only to lose her. He rounded another corner and skidded to a halt. Olivia lay in the middle of the floor, struggling to lift herself. He ran to her and dropped to her side. She yelped and tried to crawl away.

"Shh, Livvi. It's me."

When she saw him, tears sprang to her eyes and she crawled into his arms. "I knew you'd come for me," she said. "I knew it."

He held her close. "Are you okay?"

She nodded against his chest. "Now I am." She sat back suddenly. "Mindy?"

He framed her face with his palm. "Safe. The rest of the team is getting them across the street to a human-owned building."

"Mindy needs to get to the hospital. She's lost a lot of blood."

He ran his hand over her mussed hair, needing to reassure himself that she was really there in front of him, really safe. "We'll take you both to the hospital." He glanced down the darkened corridor, considered sending Len after the guy who got away. But he was probably long gone, and getting the humans help was more important at the moment. He didn't let go of Olivia as he led her back through the maze of corridors.

When they reached the basement where the captives had been held, all of them were gone but Mindy. Colin had just lifted her in his arms. Olivia raced forward. "Min?"

"She's passed out," Colin said. "But alive. She's strong."

"How are the rest?" Campbell asked.

"Weak but okay. They hadn't been fed on in a couple of days, and it looked as if they'd been given food."

"They wanted to make sure they were able to keep making blood," Campbell said with disgust.

"Everyone else went up under their own power," Colin said.

"We'll guard them until morning when the ambulances start running, but we're taking Mindy and Olivia to the hospital now."

Colin didn't argue and started up the stairs with Mindy.

When they reached the club, Campbell stopped and looked down at Olivia. "Go out with Colin. I'll be there in a minute."

She gripped his arm.

"It's okay. I just have a bit of business to finish."

He watched as Olivia followed Colin out the door. Then he turned his attention to Salmeri. "You have no idea how much I want to kill you right now and save the Imperium the trouble of a trial. I'll settle for shutting you down and anticipating seeing which horrible punishment they hand you."

"You may have won the battle, but you'll lose the war," Salmeri said with a contemptuous sneer.

"It's war, is it?" Campbell asked. "That why you tried to blow us to the hereafter?"

"You're nothing more than a nuisance, but I don't like nuisances."

"Then you're really not going to like where you're going."

Salmeri had the gall to laugh. "I won't be there for long."

"You seem mighty sure of that," Campbell said. "Think your Nefari friends are going to break you out?"

Salmeri snorted. "You think like the small-minded vampires you are, as if the Nefari were your biggest problem."

There it was again, that skittering feeling up his back that told Campbell something bigger was going on.

"Feel free to stop being cryptic at any time," he said.

"You'll know soon enough," Salmeri said, evidently deciding to stay with the cryptic. "That or the next time someone bombs you, your merry little band won't be so lucky." He met Campbell's gaze with hate-filled eyes. "When they do kill you, I plan to watch the tears pool in your little human's eyes, delight in her mourning for her poor dead vampire." Salmeri smiled, causing rage to swell inside Campbell.

Fed up, he jerked Salmeri to his feet and shoved him at Len and Kaja, who had returned from escorting Salmeri's victims to safety. "Get this piece of garbage out of my sight before I kill him."

Kaja wrapped a silver chain around Salmeri's neck and dragged him out like the dog he was.

"You think he was just blowing smoke with all that mysterious crap?" Len asked.

Campbell stared toward the door and thought about Salmeri's words. "I don't think so."

"What do you think he was talking about, then?"

Campbell shook his head. "I don't know, but I'm sure we're not going to like it."

Chapter 20

Having been checked out and given a clean bill of health, Olivia sat beside Mindy's hospital bed as her friend slept. Mindy had been through so much, new horrors she didn't deserve. The press had wanted to interview them again, especially since the viewing audience was already familiar with them from when they'd halted the earlier kidnapping attempt. But Olivia had simply denied them access, focusing instead on Mindy's recovery. Despite what Mindy had said when they'd been held captive, Olivia still felt guilty.

A scrolling Breaking News banner on the muted TV caught her attention, so she adjusted the volume just enough to hear the reporter.

"An unbelievable story is coming out of Mount Sinai Hospital this morning. Eight people, the victims in a rash of recent abductions, were rushed to the hospital this morning just after daybreak. All had suffered significant blood loss and other less threatening injuries after having been kept as blood slaves beneath a new nightclub popular among vampires. Officials say that the victims confirmed that they were abducted by humans working for vampires. But what is truly surprising to everyone who has spoken to the victims is that they are all claiming they were also rescued by vampires. One of the rescued abductees, Jennifer Watson, spoke with some of the vampires who raided the club and freed the people being held captive."

"I didn't believe it at first," Jennifer said from her hospital bed. "I thought I'd either died or was hallucinating. But there was this…team of vampires who busted in and set us free. They unchained us and led us across the street to a human-owned building so we could wait for the sun to rise. Just after dawn several ambulances arrived, so I can only assume they kept their word and called them for us." She shook her head slowly. "These vampires captured the one behind our abductions, said he would be made to pay. I still half can't believe it, but it makes me wonder about all my assumptions."

When the filmed clip ended and the camera refocused on the reporter outside Mount Sinai, she looked every bit as stunned as Jennifer Watson.

"Law enforcement officials have indicated to us that they had their doubts about the story at first, but each abductee relayed the same details in separate interviews. This is one of those events that has just left everyone scratching their heads, but rest assured we will stay on the story and bring you more information as we have it."

As the news anchor shifted to another story, Olivia lowered the volume. When she turned back toward the bed, Mindy's eyes were open.

"I'm sorry. I didn't mean to wake you," Olivia said.

"It's okay." Mindy glanced at the TV. "So it wasn't all a dream?"

"No. I'm sorry."

"It's not your fault, so stop acting as if it is." She didn't seem upset, just put out. In fact, she sounded enough like her old self that hope swelled in Olivia.

"Can I get you anything?"

Mindy shook her head on her pillow then stared at Olivia.

"What?" Olivia asked.

"You love Campbell, don't you?"

She'd hoped to not have to face this conversation so soon.

"It's okay if you do," Mindy said.

Olivia couldn't believe her ears. "It is?"

"Yeah. If it wasn't for him and his team, we might be dead now. How many times has he saved you now, four? Even I can't argue that he's evil after that."

Tears popped into Olivia's eyes as she squeezed Mindy's hand. "Are you sure?"

"Yes. I should have listened to you sooner."

"You had reason not to. More than once I thought I was crazy."

"Don't get me wrong," Mindy said. "I still believe most of them are monsters, just that there are a few exceptions when they're not thirsty."

Olivia couldn't argue with that, because she agreed with every word. She shivered as she remembered Salmeri's hand on her, the cold, hopeless feeling she'd gotten the moment she'd seen the nameless vampire in the black cloak. She hated the idea that he was still out there somewhere. She just hoped V Force's raid forced him to flee and stay far, far away.

Despite her experience, hope bloomed inside Olivia. Hope that this story would start to change people's minds about all vampires being evil. Maybe if the details of vampire society started to come out, Campbell would stop being so resistant to being with her, might stop worrying that he'd bring her nothing but sorrow. Even as he'd rescued her and held her close, she could feel some sort of barrier still between them. She needed to find out what it was so she could break it down.

She told Mindy she was going to the cafeteria, but when she reached the end of the hallway she called Chloe. "Hey, it's Olivia."

"I was just about to head to the hospital to see you and Mindy. How are you?"

"We're fine. Listen, I have a question. Do you know where the new V Force headquarters is?"

Chloe hesitated before answering slowly. "Why do you ask?"

"Because I want you to take me there. I need to see Campbell."

"I can't do that."

"Why not? Campbell won't hurt me, and the rest of the team doesn't have my blood type."

"They're not the only vampires there, and not every vampire has the strength to resist the call of the blood like Campbell does. Hell, even he can't always overcome it. You know that."

"Chloe, please. If I could just talk to him."

"No, Olivia. No matter how much you beg, the answer will remain no."

"But—"

"No. And it's not just for your safety but also for theirs. The fewer people who know, the better. The only reason I know is because I have to deliver the holy water."

Olivia understood, could even appreciate her friend's concern for her, but it was getting really damn old. She was going to find Campbell, one way or another.

Campbell stared at the pencil he was twirling between his fingers. He despised Nicky Salmeri for many things, but perhaps most of all for the thought he'd put in his head. The one that someone was eventually going to take Campbell out, and that if he let his relationship with Olivia continue, she would be the one left behind grieving. She'd already been through that once. And he'd seen how thinking he'd died in the bombing affected her. She didn't deserve to be subjected to it again.

And then there was the fact he had not shared his darkest secret with her. Each time he thought about doing so, he wondered if he could face seeing her horror, watching as she realized she'd been wrong about him all along. Realized that he really was a monster and ran away from him forever.

"When you get that look on your face, it means you're thinking too much," Kaja said from where she sat with her booted feet propped on the edge of her new desk. "And if I were a betting vampire, I'd say it has something to do with Olivia. When are you going to stop being an idiot and go see her again, anyway?"

Campbell tossed the pencil onto his desk. "Well, haven't you made a one-eighty on that topic."

"What? I'm an incurable romantic."

Len literally choked on a drink of blood he was taking, this time from his own cup. Kaja had threatened him with castration if he ever drank from hers again, and even vampires wanted to keep that particular body part intact and functioning properly.

"It doesn't seem fair to her when I could be killed tomorrow."

"Seriously, that's the excuse you're going with?" Kaja asked.

"It's not an excuse. It's true." And he couldn't tell Kaja the bigger reason.

"For you and every cop in the world. Pretty sure a lot of them have girlfriends or, gasp, even wives."

"They don't have the strike of having died once already against them."

"Do you think she cares? Seems to me you're the only one hung up on that anymore."

"You don't know what you're talking about. Until you've found someone you really care about, you can't know."

Kaja dropped her feet to the floor and stood. "You know, Campbell, I respect the hell out of you. But sometimes you can be a real ass."

He didn't try to stop her, because she was right. But didn't that just prove his point that he was no good for Olivia? Vampire, the constant target of the Soulless who would love to take out a V Force member, jerk. Three strikes and you were out.

The door opened and Ray walked in. But he wasn't alone. When Campbell saw who was with him, he stood.

"Baroness."

She made a dismissive wave. "Please, call me Catherine. After so many years of hearing myself addressed as *Baroness*, it's grown quite stuffy." She and Ray came farther into the room.

"Can we get you anything?" Sophia asked.

Catherine smiled. "No, dear, but thank you. I'm here to congratulate you on a successful mission. It is a good thing to have so many humans back where they belong through the help of Souled vampires."

"We were just doing our job," Campbell said.

"Yes, you were. You'll be happy to know the trial date has been set for the detestable Mr. Salmeri. And if I have anything to say about it, he will no longer be a problem."

"I'd be happier if I could just toss him out into the sun to roast," Kaja murmured, but Catherine didn't miss it.

"You never know," Catherine said. "He might end up with a date with daylight."

Campbell winced, not because he didn't think Salmeri deserved such a punishment but rather at the memory of his own brush with the sun.

"I am sorry to not be able to let you all enjoy a much-deserved break," Catherine said. "However, I need to discuss something of the utmost importance with you. I'm afraid that your job will only grow more challenging in the days and months ahead."

Campbell knew vampire crime was on the rise, but something told him theft and assaults weren't exactly what she was talking about.

"What I'm about to tell you is classified to the highest levels of the Imperium. I do not agree with that decision, so I'm not going to abide by it."

Sophia gasped, and a couple of the others shifted uncomfortably. The Imperium's law was absolute.

"It must be something very serious to cause you to make that decision," Campbell said.

"It is indeed. It's why I've been traveling like a crazy woman lately, why I'm in New York now. I've been meeting with the heads of the various Imperium offices around the world. We believe there is a building and significant threat to the Imperium itself."

"The Nefari has gained that much power?" Colin asked.

"I wish it were as simple as the Nefari. Them, we know how to deal with. Common crooks, if ones with a lot of resources." Catherine sighed, though she hadn't required breath in more than a century. "I'm afraid the Nefari are child's play compared to the Pravus."

"The Pravus?" Campbell asked. "Sorry, but I'm no expert in Latin."

"Evil, pure and simple," Ray offered.

"We do not know who is behind it or what the specifics of their plans are, but what little we have gleaned points toward it being a plot by the Soulless to take over the Imperium and substantially change vampire society."

"Oh, my God," Sophia said, and sank heavily into her chair.

Campbell watched the baroness for a moment before speaking. "Why are you telling us this?"

"Quite frankly, because I trust you more than I do some of my colleagues in the Imperium."

"You think someone in the Imperium is involved?" Kaja asked.

"That I don't know, but I've been around long enough to know I should always trust my instincts. And those instincts are telling me that your team members are trustworthy. You all have proven that by how you interact with humans." She looked directly at Campbell. "You, more than the vampires at the highest levels of the Imperium, see them as more than a food source. You see the potential for our two species to coexist, to do more than just share a world without crossing paths."

He felt like squirming but refused to do so or make eye contact with any of his fellow team members. There were many reasons he shouldn't be with Olivia, but he didn't feel he should have to enumerate them. They ought to be obvious to anyone with eyes to see.

"What do you need from us?"

"Right now, simply be observant. If anything seems beyond what you normally see from the Soulless, let Ray or me know. I have a handful of Imperium representatives I trust investigating, as well. I also need for you to just be on standby." She paused. "But before you agree, you need to know that should I call on you, what I ask of you must take precedence over everything else. You may have to deliberately disobey the Imperium."

The full impact of what was going on descended on the room, but Campbell didn't look away from Catherine. Like her, he trusted his instincts. And they were telling him that the vampire world was on the precipice of something huge, and Catherine was standing on the right side of the battle.

"I'm with you, but I cannot speak for the rest of my team.

This is too big." He shifted his attention to the others. "Each of you has to make the decision for yourself."

"Well, I'm in," Len said with no hesitation.

"Me, too," Colin said.

Kaja flipped her hair over her shoulder, and a sort of defiance flashed in her eyes. "I don't like authority figures who take advantage of their positions, so if there's a chance that's happening here, I'm with you one hundred percent."

Travis followed suit, and finally Sophia, who unsurprisingly had the most difficult time with going against authority. She had a good heart and always wanted to do the right thing, but she wasn't by nature a rebel.

Campbell returned his attention to Catherine. "There you have it."

"Good." She smiled. "I knew I was making the right decision. Until you hear from me again, go about your normal duties. I have no idea when I might need you or for what. It could be hours, days, even months."

Campbell couldn't say he liked the sound of that. If a threat existed, he'd much prefer to dedicate all his energy to rooting it out and destroying it for good. But for now, he'd trust Catherine and just keep his eyes and ears open.

Catherine and Ray shifted as if to leave. "Campbell, walk with me," she said.

He fell into step with her and noticed that Ray lagged behind.

"I know how you think, so I would bet my considerable fortune that you consider this new threat yet another reason to not be with the lovely Olivia."

He wasn't even surprised that Catherine had found out Olivia's name. She probably had Olivia's entire family history committed to memory by now.

"You're wrong," Catherine said.

Campbell stopped walking. "How do you know that?"

Catherine halted and shifted halfway toward him. "Remember those instincts I mentioned? They tell me that you are stronger with her in your life than without."

"But what about her? Her life is more dangerous, more full of problems with me in it."

"Is it? Or could it just be you're afraid?" She turned to fully face him. "Tell me, would she be safer with or without someone with your power watching over her? Loving her?"

Campbell paced several steps away. "I could kill her so easily."

"But you won't."

"You talk as if you're all-knowing."

"Hardly. But I have been around for a long time. And I know that cutting people out of our lives because we think we're protecting them is never the answer. It just makes us resent this forever life we lead. How much sense does it make to be lonely for eternity when you have the option not to be?"

Campbell didn't have an answer. The truth was his resolve to stay away from Olivia was weakening more with each word Catherine spoke. He didn't know if he could convince himself that going back to her was even remotely safe, but there were things he could do for her while he tried to decide.

Catherine had started to walk away when he spoke again. "I need a favor."

When she turned back toward him, she wore a victorious smile.

Now that the abduction case had been put to rest, Olivia expected Campbell to come see her. But two days passed with no visit, no call, no word of any kind. Her mood was not improved by the continued emptiness of the diner.

"I don't know why I even opened," she said to Mindy, who sat across from her in the dining room. "I sure don't know why you came in. You should be resting."

"If I *rest* any more, I'm going to go bonkers."

Olivia sighed and looked out at the deepening darkness. "At this rate, I can't afford to keep the diner running much longer."

"I don't like that sound of defeat in your voice."

"I don't either, but sometimes we have to face the truth, no matter how much it hurts."

"Why do I think this has as much to do with Campbell as the diner?"

Olivia shrugged. "Maybe it's just time for a change, a big one."

Mindy glanced beyond Olivia. "Hold that thought." She grabbed the remote control for the TV and turned it up. "Look."

Olivia turned and was stunned to see Campbell on TV, Colin at his side.

"With us outside the studio tonight is Campbell Raines, the head of the team of vampires who rescued the eight human abductees from that vampire nightclub two nights ago. Mr. Raines is a former NYPD officer. With him is Colin O'Shea, a former firefighter with the FDNY."

Olivia stood motionless as she listened to the reporter ask Campbell and Colin question after question, and they answered, sharing with the viewing public all the information Campbell had shared with her. The differences between Souled and Soulless vampires, the Imperium, vampire law.

"But none of this changes the precautions humans should take," Campbell said. "The night is still deadly, and humans should stay indoors after sundown. It's the only way to ensure their safety."

"I can't believe they're doing this," Mindy said.

"Me neither." Everyone they used to know would see them and know that they'd not perished during the pandemic or at the hands of vampires, that they had in fact become vampires.

"I understand you have something else you want to share with our viewing audience tonight," the reporter said.

"Yes." Campbell looked directly into the camera that must have been mounted outside the TV station and handled remotely from inside. "A private party has purchased an apartment building here in Manhattan and will be donating it for housing for the homeless, a safe place for them to live."

"Is this private party a vampire, and if so, how does that make the homeless any safer than they'd be on the streets?"

"Because the title to the property will be transferred to a human before anyone moves in."

"Which human?"

"Her name is Olivia DaCosta, and she already works with the homeless, taking them meals when no one else will. She's put her own life at risk to help those society has continued to forget in the wake of the Bokor virus and the emergence of vampires."

Olivia lifted her hand to cover a gasp. She couldn't believe what she was hearing.

"This is the Olivia DaCosta who prevented a kidnapping recently, then was a victim of one earlier this week?"

"Yes. Olivia is a remarkable person, strong, determined," Campbell said. "Not only does she help the less fortunate, but she's been able to see something in me that I couldn't even see myself."

"And what would that be?"

"My humanity, that I'm not a monster just because I was attacked. That with obvious differences, I'm still the man I was before I was turned. But it's cost her. People who can't see the same things have abandoned her diner, leaving her without the means to support herself or her employee. She's done nothing wrong, and yet she's paying the price."

"It sounds as if you care for Miss DaCosta."

"I do. I love her."

"Oh, Olivia," Mindy said, and grabbed her hand.

Olivia was too stunned by Campbell's public declaration of love to respond. She just kept staring at the TV screen, even after the video feed cut away from Campbell and Colin. The two TV anchors looked stunned.

"I don't know what to make of the past few days, Frank," the woman said to her co-anchor.

"I'm right there with you, Candice. Only time will tell what new revelations will come from the vampire community. But remember what Mr. Raines said, ladies and gentlemen. This makes no difference in just how dangerous the world continues to be at night."

When the news shifted to the weather, Mindy lifted the remote and turned off the TV.

Olivia continued to stare at the black television screen. "Did that just happen?"

"Unless you and I are having the same dream, yes, it did."

Olivia felt Campbell's presence before she saw him. Slowly, she turned in her seat to see him standing outside.

"I suddenly feel the need to be anywhere but here," Mindy said.

Olivia paid her no attention as she crossed to the front door and opened it. "I saw the news," she said. She had no idea how to voice everything she was feeling. All she knew was that she wanted to grab him and never let go.

"Mindy," Campbell said.

"Yeah?" she said.

"Colin will take you home."

Suddenly, Colin stood in the doorway, too, his forearm propped against the outside since he couldn't cross the invisible barrier.

"No, I'll stay here tonight." Even though Mindy had thawed a little toward Campbell and his team, Olivia doubted her deep fear of vamps would ever go away.

Colin gave Mindy a crooked grin that Olivia knew was meant to help alleviate her fear. "You're safe from me. I couldn't drink from you even if I wanted to. I do and I die, for good this time. So you have a choice. You either allow me to take you home or you can stay here and listen to these two make wild monkey love all night. I'd vote for going with me. I'm really kind of fun to be around."

Campbell made a sound of frustration, and Olivia's face flamed with embarrassment. Mindy stood slowly and pulled a wooden stake from where she'd hidden it in her waistband below her shirt.

Colin placed his hand over his heart. "Now you're just hurting my feelings."

"He won't hurt you," Olivia said. "He's the one who carried you out of the club."

Mindy averted her gaze, but not before Olivia saw that Mindy remembered what Colin had done without being reminded. She sensed a struggle going on in her friend—the beliefs she'd held for so long against the fact that she was standing across from the vampires who had saved her life.

"I'm leaving in thirty seconds. Your call—monkey sex sounds or my sterling taxi service." He retreated to the truck to wait.

Mindy rolled her eyes and muttered something about big egos but approached the door nonetheless. She paused and looked up at Campbell. "How you ended up with that for a best friend has got to be one of life's great mysteries."

"He has his good qualities."

"If you say so."

Her hand firmly around the stake, Mindy glanced up and down the street and headed for the armored truck. Colin sped off the moment she got her door closed.

"Alone at last," Campbell said.

"Whatever will we do with ourselves?"

He gave her a wicked grin. "I have a few ideas."

She tugged him inside, and he locked the door behind him. In a blink, he lifted her in his arms and made quick work of the stairs up to her apartment. When he placed her on her feet, she lifted to her toes, took his face in her hands and kissed him. With an animal sound that had nothing to do with him being a vampire, he pulled her close against him and deepened the kiss until her head spun.

When their lips parted, she said, "I've missed you so much. I was afraid you were never coming back."

"I considered staying away. I thought it would be easier for you."

She leaned back so she could meet his eyes. "How could living without you make my life easier? I've already lost one man I love. I don't want to go through that again."

"It could happen. Every day that I go out and do my job, it could happen. That's one of the reasons I wanted to shield you."

She bit her lip at the thought of him dying the final death. "I choose not to think of that. But if it's a choice between living with that knowledge but having you in my life and not having you at all, I know which one I'll choose. Every time."

He framed her face with his big hands. "I love you, Olivia DaCosta."

"I know. I saw it on the news. After all, they do say it's News You Can Trust." She smiled.

"I hope you don't mind that all of New York knows now."

"I'm guessing it's probably spread across the whole country now," she said. "I'm hoping my mother hasn't had a stroke. But no, I don't mind. A lot of people will hate me for it, but I don't care. I'm not listening to them. I'm only going to listen to my heart. And you know what it's telling me to do right now?"

"No."

"Take you to bed and not let you leave until daylight forces you to."

He smiled. "I like that idea." But then his smile faded and sadness took its place. "First I have to tell you something that might change your mind."

"I can't imagine what."

He walked across the room and stood staring out the front window. "I've never told anyone this before."

"You can tell me anything." She wanted to cross to him, but she sensed he needed the distance.

He said nothing for so long that she grew nervous. Finally, he turned toward her. "I'm responsible for someone's death."

"Yes, I know. I was there."

"Not the guys who attacked you. Right after I was turned, I almost drained a girl, a college student named Bridget Jameson. She was walking home after a night class."

Olivia had said he could tell her anything, but she hadn't expected this. She sank onto the arm of the couch and pushed an instinctual fear away.

"The vampire who turned me, my sire, was a criminal I was chasing. He'd attacked a deli owner in his store, but something made him run. I still don't know who he was, because I never saw his face, and the deli didn't have a security camera. He bit me, forced me to drink his blood then didn't stick around to usher me through the transition."

"Why did he turn you instead of killing you?"

"I don't know. Maybe he thought that was a better way to get me off his trail, strike back, who knows. But when I came out the other side hungry for blood, I attacked the first person I came across. When I realized what I was doing, I was horrified. I thought I'd gone suddenly insane. I dropped her and ran. I was on the verge of jumping off a building when another vamp found me and talked me down. Even when I told him what I'd done, he helped me. He'd been a doctor but since he couldn't treat patients anymore, he found ways to help vampires."

"He didn't turn you in?"

"No. I didn't actually kill Bridget. I learned later, though, that I might as well have. I just left her lying there, and the scent of her blood drew another vampire. He finished her off. I wanted to die for good. I still think of her, wondering what her life might be like now."

"She might not have survived the virus," Olivia said.

He stared at a spot on the floor. "But she would have had the chance." He paused, lost in what-ifs. "David, the vampire who took me in, helped me learn to live as close to a human life as I could."

Olivia swallowed, trying to take in all this new information and determine if it changed how she felt about Campbell. Despite how she cared for him, she was surprised her survival instinct hadn't yet sent her fleeing. That had to mean something, right?

"Why didn't you tell me before now?" she asked.

He met her gaze. "It's a heavy secret to bear. And…I was afraid of how you'd look at me when I did."

She tried not to think of that poor girl, instead focusing on the good Campbell had done since. He'd once said he was atoning, and now Olivia realized it was for much more than his attack on her.

"It wasn't your fault," she said. "You didn't ask to be turned, didn't ask to be left with no direction on how to deal with that."

Campbell shook his head. "How do you do that?"

"What?"

"Forgive so easily."

"I'm not discounting that what happened to Bridget was awful, but you were a victim that night, too. It's no different than having a baby then abandoning it, expecting it to learn to walk and talk all by itself."

He stared at her for a long time. "You're amazing."

"I just see you carrying too much on your shoulders. You have team members to help. Friends. Me."

"You still want to be with me?" he asked.

"More than ever." Wanting to push away the past, she gave him a wicked grin. "It's not every vampire I invite into my bed."

He stalked toward her slowly, a graceful animal. "I was afraid to tell you."

"I'm glad you did. Your secret is safe with me. There's nothing to be gained by its revelation. And if I know you, you've beaten yourself up about this since the moment it happened."

He stopped close to her and rubbed his thumb over her bottom lip. "Thank you."

"How about you thank me with something more than words?"

She squealed when he swept her off her feet and carried her into the bedroom. He fell with her to the bed and started trailing kisses up her neck to her ear. He bit her lobe just hard enough to send an erotic surge of need through her body. The words he'd said into that TV camera, that he loved her, fueled her need to touch him, to consume him and have him consume her.

She jerked his shirt out of the waistband of his pants and ran her hands up his back, then raked her fingernails back down all that cool, sinewy muscle. He responded by grabbing the front of her button-up blouse and ripping it open, sending buttons flying in all directions.

His mouth descended to the swell of her breasts above her bra, his lips and tongue working her into a frenzy. In a movement too fast for her to track, he ripped off her bra and sent it sailing across the room.

"Don't like my bra, huh?" she asked between ragged breaths.

He met her gaze with eyes blazing with desire. "I don't like anything between the two of us."

"Then take it off. Take it all off."

With another of those wicked smiles playing across his lips, he rid her of her jeans and panties, leaving her bare under his gaze. Then he stood and oh-so slowly unbuttoned and slid down the zipper of his pants.

"You enjoy torturing me, don't you?" she asked.

"You're more than welcome to help."

Olivia lifted to her knees and slid her hands slowly below the top edge of Campbell's pants, never taking her eyes off his. Then even more slowly, her fingers found their way into his underwear and started pushing them and his pants down over his lean hips, then his thighs. When they dropped to his ankles, he stepped out of them, but she didn't let go. Instead she ran her fingers up his thighs, then his taut stomach. She broke eye contact only to place her mouth on his chest. She rained kisses across his smooth skin then trailed her tongue along the same path.

Campbell growled, and his nonessential breath became ragged. "Now who's torturing whom?"

"You can end the torture," she whispered in his ear. "Make love to me like you've never made love to anyone before."

"Gladly."

He lifted her effortlessly to his waist. "Wrap your legs around me."

As she did so, he entered her in one swift motion. Olivia gasped and let her head drop backward, her hair coming loose in the process. Campbell's mouth captured her right breast and sucked as he withdrew, only to drive into her again.

She laced her fingers behind his neck as he grabbed on to her hips with both hands, holding her firmly against him as he increased his pace.

"Yes," she said. "Faster."

He complied, and she lost the ability to focus on anything but the pulse and frantic motion where their bodies joined. As she felt her climax building inside her, the muscles beginning to contract, she held on to him even tighter and tried to meet each of his thrusts with strong ones of her own. Somehow she felt his climax growing ever closer, too, and it spurred her lust even more.

"Don't hold back," she managed to say between gasps.

His in-and-out motions built until she'd swear they were a blur. Her body grew slick with sweat, but he didn't lose his grip on her.

Her insides spasmed, signaling the beginning of her climax. Campbell pulled her body next to his, her wet breasts pressed against his chest, as he sent her over the edge, then followed. She was vaguely aware that she cried out, but she didn't care if all of Manhattan knew that she'd just had the best orgasm ever. As the final waves drifted away, she collapsed onto Campbell's shoulder.

"That was, hands down, the best sex of my life," she said against his ear.

"We're just getting started," he said back, his voice so deep and gravelly that she was impossibly ready to start all over again.

Campbell laid her back on the bed and gently smoothed the hair away from her face. "I dreamed once of seeing you like this, with your hair fanned out across your pillows."

"I thought you didn't sleep."

He smiled. "I can still daydream." He planted a soft kiss on her lips. "What about you? Any hot fantasies about me?"

"A few. Don't let it give you a big head," she said.

He laughed. "That's half the fun."

She playfully punched his chest, not that she could even hurt him if she hit him with the full force of her strength.

He stopped her assault by gently gliding into her. Olivia's breath caught and she arched against him.

"I like how you respond to me," he said against her lips before he captured them in a long, agonizingly slow kiss.

"I love how you feel inside me," she said next to his ear.

Compared to a few minutes before, this time they made love virtually in slow motion. But it was every bit as wonderful and left Olivia just as out of breath. There wasn't an inch of her body he hadn't loved in some way, bringing every single one of her nerve endings to full, glorious attention.

After they'd both found their release again, Campbell pulled her close to his side and she wrapped her arm around his waist.

"You should get some sleep," he said against the top of her head.

"No, I want to experience every moment of this night with you. I'm afraid if I go to sleep, you'll be gone when I wake up."

"I wouldn't leave without saying goodbye."

She propped herself on her elbow and met his gaze. "I don't want us to ever say goodbye again. Maybe a see you later, but never goodbye. I'm done with goodbyes."

He lifted his hand to her face and caressed her cheek with a gentleness that made her heart fill with love. "Are you sure? There has to be someone out there who'd be better for you."

"Someone who isn't a vampire?"

"Yeah."

"You've got to let that go. The vampire doesn't define you." She placed her hand over his still heart. "This might not beat anymore, but it's what makes you who you are. Not the fangs."

"You're wonderful, you know it?"

She smiled. "I try."

He pulled her face to his and they spent the next several minutes kissing and exploring.

"What you said on the news, is it true?" she asked.

"Yes, every word."

"The apartment building. How did you do it?"

"I have a friend who is very wealthy and very influential with the Imperium higher-ups. The funds partially came from her, partly from another wealthy source. But the Imperium kicked in some money, too. My friend convinced them that this would be a strong goodwill gesture from the vampire community."

"I still can't believe it. Where's the building?"

He pointed toward the window. "Right there."

She glanced out into the night toward the darkened windows next door. "Really?"

"Yes, really. I remembered what you told me that night, and this way it'll be convenient for you and for the residents. They can come to the diner to eat and you won't have to roam all over Manhattan to feed them." He caressed her shoulder and down her arm. "And I admit to having a selfish reason."

"You think this will help keep me out of harm's way."

"Just because we got Salmeri doesn't mean the world is suddenly danger-free. We still haven't identified or located the cloak guy, for one."

She shivered then saw some new concern in his expression. "What is it?"

"Nothing. I'm just always prepared for the next thing to come down the pike."

She didn't quite believe him, but she let it go. He'd tell her when he was ready, or she'd figure out a way to get it out of him. As a few tactics came to mind, she smiled.

"Why do I think I should be worried about that smile?" he asked.

She feigned innocence. "I haven't a clue."

He grabbed her and rolled her onto her back. She giggled before being consumed in lovemaking once again.

Despite her best efforts to stay awake after they'd made love a third time, she felt herself drifting toward sleep. She snuggled close to Campbell and latched on to the thought that she'd never been happier in her life. Her thoughts found their way to Jeremy, but no guilt resided there. As sleep descended, she saw him. He was whole again, like he'd been when they met. And he was smiling.

Chapter 21

Campbell wished he could let Olivia sleep, but he'd promised he wouldn't go and leave her to wake up alone. What he wouldn't give to be able to stay and watch the sunrise with her, see the sunlight on her beautiful face. Instead he kissed her forehead then ran his fingers along the curve of her jaw.

He still couldn't believe he'd told her about Bridget and that Olivia still wanted him. Something miraculous had happened when he'd confessed to her—his heart had grown lighter than it'd been in years.

"Livvi, wake up."

She curled against him. "You're ready to go again?"

He laughed against her hair. "I'd love to, but dawn has other plans."

She jerked fully awake and looked toward the window.

"It's okay." He sat up and pulled her back against him. "I've still got an hour, but I don't want to cut it so close that I'm smoking when I get home."

She turned in his arms. "I wish this could be your home."

"Me, too."

She glanced at the clock on her nightstand. "So, an hour, huh?"

He cocked an eyebrow at her. "Why do you sound as if you have plans for that hour?"

"Because I do." She stood and took his hand. "Come with me."

He went willingly as she led him into the bathroom. His body responded as he watched her enticing curves while she reached into the shower and turned on the water.

"You are a temptress, Miss DaCosta."

Her smile was full of an invitation he couldn't refuse. "What do I tempt you to do, Mr. Raines?"

"Give the sun the finger and make love to you all day."

"But since we don't want you to be extra crispy again, you'll just have to manage whatever you can in the next few minutes. Is that enough time?"

"Let's find out." He backed her into the spray of water and lifted her against the tiled wall. As the minutes ticked down toward daybreak, he made hot, wet, soapy, steamy love to the woman who'd become everything to him. As he climaxed, his whole body shuddered. Even his fangs throbbed. When they threatened to descend, he concentrated all of his energy on keeping them in place.

"I've got to go," he said next to her ear.

She grabbed him as if she feared she'd never see him again. "Campbell."

He made himself smile while keeping the tips of his slowly descending fangs hidden. "See you later."

Fueled by panic, he engaged his fastest speed to dress and return to his private room at the mansion. He leaned back against the door and let the night with Olivia replay in his mind. Those memories forced his fangs the rest of the way

out. Though he'd had sex more times than he could count
with more women than he cared to remember, it was the first
time he'd experienced a fang drop for any reason other than
feeding or fighting.

He'd promised Olivia he'd never say goodbye, had finally
decided he was going to have a life with her. But he couldn't
see her again until he figured out a way to keep her safe from
the biggest threat to her safety—him.

After Campbell left, Olivia just managed to reach her bed
before collapsing. What a night. What a man. She couldn't
believe half of the things they'd done, and all within the span
of a few hours.

She lay in bed well beyond when she normally rose, but
why should she hurry? Business had trickled to the point of
near nonexistence. Plus, she could really use the day to sleep
and recuperate. She was still lying on the bed naked when
she heard Mindy enter the restaurant's back door, once again
refusing to stay at home and rest. Wishing she didn't have
to burst her bubble of happiness by going downstairs to face
what little was left of her business—so little that she might
not even be able to afford to feed herself, let alone the homeless who would be moving in next door—she dragged herself
to her feet and dressed.

"Olivia, you better get down here," Mindy yelled up the
stairs.

"Coming." What the devil was wrong now?

When she reached the bottom of the stairs, she couldn't
believe her eyes. The dining room was already full. Familiar faces sat alongside ones she'd never seen before. And still
others waited for an empty table.

"Looks as though you could use an extra hand or two."

She turned and saw Herbie and Roscoe, all cleaned up and
smiling. "What? How did you get here?"

"Honey, we've walked all over this city. Ain't nothing to meander over for some breakfast at the most famous diner in town," Herbie said.

"I don't understand."

"We saw your friend on the news last night, saw what he's doing for us. Half of me still can't believe it, but if it's not a miracle, I don't know what is."

"I was a cook when I was in the army," Roscoe said. "So I could help you out in the kitchen if you'd like."

"And it won't be any hardship to work alongside your pretty friend," Herbie said with a nod toward where Mindy was handing out menus left and right.

"You're both hired."

Things didn't slow down until midway through the afternoon. Olivia heard an ugly remark a couple of times about her being a vampire lover, but she was shocked by how overwhelmingly positive everyone was.

"I haven't made this much in tips in forever," Mindy said as she came to stand by the cashier counter with Olivia.

"That makes two of us," Herbie said as he joined them. "Maybe I'll hire me a maid in my new place."

Olivia laughed. "I just plan to take a day off. That will feel more like the world used to be than just about anything."

A tall, good-looking man in a dark suit came in the front door and headed straight for them. "Olivia DaCosta?"

"That's me."

"Darren Stuart," he said as he extended an envelope to her. "This is the deed and transfer papers for the apartment building next door. As soon as you sign them, the building is yours."

She accepted the envelope, pulled out the documents and started scanning the text.

"You'll notice there's a provision that the property taxes

have been waived as long as the building is not used for profit and for its intended purpose, to house the homeless."

Olivia couldn't believe how quickly things were happening, and good things this time. As she read the documents in full, Mr. Stuart talked to Herbie and Roscoe about the building and accepted a cup of coffee on the house from Mindy. When Olivia was satisfied that the papers looked legit, she grabbed a pen but hesitated with it over the first signature line.

"Is there something wrong?" Mr. Stuart asked.

"This is just such a big moment part of me doesn't believe it's real."

He nodded. "It's a good thing you're doing."

With that, she signed everywhere he indicated. Then the deed was done, so to speak. She owned a twenty-story apartment building.

Stuart accepted his copy of the forms and gave her a ring of keys about the size and weight of a car tire. Then he slid a business card across the counter to her. A simple elegant off-white card with black ink said simply Darren Stuart above Barnes, Herron and Stuart, Attorneys at Law.

"If you have any legal needs, please let us know. And good luck with being a landlord."

He smiled, and if she weren't already in love with someone else, Olivia might have experienced a heart flutter at the sight.

"Thank you."

He nodded then looked at Mindy. "Thanks for the coffee." He turned and headed for the front door.

When she glanced at Mindy, she grabbed a napkin and gave it to her friend.

"What's this for?"

"Your drool."

Mindy wadded up the napkin and tossed it at Olivia, which set all four of them to laughing again.

They started the end-of-day cleanup, and by the time the last customer left, they were all ready to kick up their feet and relax.

"I'm going to go home and collapse on my couch, eat an entire pizza and watch mindless television until I fall asleep," Mindy said as she grabbed her coat.

They all waved at Mindy as she headed out the door. Then Olivia eyed Herbie and Roscoe. "How do you all feel about having second jobs, on a volunteer basis at least for now?"

"What do you have in mind?" Roscoe asked.

"She needs help with the new building, getting it up and running," Herbie answered for her. He got a twinkle in his eyes. "If Roscoe and I can scope things out and pick our places first, we'll help out with cleaning, maintenance. And tomorrow we can get a lot more people to help."

"Sounds great." When she looked at Roscoe, his eyes looked extra watery. "What's wrong?"

"I just can't believe I'll never have to stay in a shelter again."

She gathered him to her and gave him a big hug. "It's the least I can do for my two adopted grandpas, right?"

His face lit up, and when she looked at Herbie, he was smiling widely, too. Then he leaned over and kissed her on the cheek.

"Come on, Roscoe, we got some apartment shopping to do."

Olivia laughed as she handed over the monster ring of keys then watched the two of them walk across the alley and through the gateway in the fence that led to the apartment building. Finally alone, she dragged her tired body up the stairs to her own apartment and pulled some leftover macaroni and cheese from the fridge. After nuking it, she sat down at the table to eat and watch daylight fade from the sky.

She'd just finished the final bite when Campbell dropped effortlessly onto her balcony.

When she slid the door open, she said, "You know there are less dramatic ways to make an appearance. You can come up the fire escape or even knock on one of the doors downstairs."

He gave her a crooked grin. "Where's the fun in that?"

"Show-off." She pulled him to her and kissed him thoroughly.

"What was that for?" he asked after she broke the kiss.

"I had a very good day."

"Oh?"

"Seems your little TV appearance had a positive effect on my bottom line," she said.

"Your customers came back?"

"Plus a boatload more. I couldn't believe it. I kept thinking I was dreaming and I'd wake up and the diner would still be empty."

"I'm glad business is better."

Olivia noticed how he was looking at her, as if he was holding on to some important piece of information until she was finished sharing hers. "What?"

He took a step back and shoved his hands into the pockets of his jacket, the one she'd worn the first night they met. "I had a big day myself."

"Oh? Catch a lot of bad guys?"

"No, still plenty of them around."

"Wow, thanks for that uplifting slice of news."

"Sorry. Guess you'll just have to get used to my shoptalk because I plan to stick around." He removed his hands from his pockets and turned them palms up. In each lay a thin silver bracelet similar to those worn by Chloe's brother when he was at the blood bank.

Olivia gave Campbell a questioning look.

"I want to be with you, Livvi, but the only way I'm ever

going to feel safe doing that is if I wear these when I'm with you."

"But you said they make vampires feel ill."

"It's manageable, and nothing like the fear that I could hurt you or worse when I'm hungry. And when we made love that last time, my fangs descended even though I didn't need to feed. That's never happened to me before."

Olivia's face flushed at the thought that she'd caused a sexual reaction in him that he'd never experienced with another woman.

"I still don't like the idea of you making yourself sick," she said.

"It's only if I wear them too long, which I won't, because I'll have to split my night hours between you and work I can't do at headquarters. I either wear them when I'm with you or stop coming by, and that would be odd if I didn't see my wife sometime."

Olivia would swear her heart stopped for the span of a couple of beats before it kicked itself in gear again. "Your wife?"

Campbell pulled something else from his pocket and held it up between his thumb and forefinger. She stared at a silver ring that matched his bracelets.

"If you'll have me," he said.

Olivia couldn't believe what she was hearing, couldn't fathom how her day, which had already been wonderful, had just skyrocketed into new levels of greatness.

"Are you sure?" she asked, silently hoping she didn't prompt him to change his mind but needing to know he was completely sure about his decision. "I'm mortal. You'll be here long after I'm gone."

A momentary glimpse of pain showed on his face before disappearing. "A wise woman told me none of us are guaranteed tomorrow, let alone eternity, so we should grab on to happiness and enjoy it for however long it lasts."

Olivia smiled. "She does sound smart, so smart that I'm going to take her advice."

"Even though the human churches, human authorities won't recognize the marriage? And we won't be able to live like normal couples?"

"Yes, and yes." She nodded toward the floor. "This is the part where you get down on one knee."

A moment of shock registered on Campbell's face, as if he'd expected her to finally come to her senses, realize he was a vampire and kick him out of her life. But after it sank in that she was serious, he lowered himself and held up the ring.

"Olivia DaCosta, will you throw common sense to the wind and marry me?"

She didn't hesitate. "Yes, I will."

He slid the ring onto her finger and the bracelets onto his wrists. Only then did he rise and pull her into his arms. "No matter what the world throws at us, I think we just might make it."

"I know we will." How could they not when they'd already been through so much, defied so many odds and lived to tell the tales?

Campbell pulled her even closer. "Do I have to worry about Mindy staking me for this?"

"I think Colin has more to worry about there. Or really any vampire other than you."

"Good to know." Campbell looked outside. "I should get to work."

"Oh, no. You're not going anywhere but to bed."

His wicked grin made an appearance. "I don't sleep, remember?"

"Sleep's not exactly what I had in mind." She ran her hand over a sensitive area to make her point.

Campbell growled in that way that set her body on fire with

wanting, and he carried her to bed. She thought they might have set a new speed record for getting naked.

The phone ringing was such a surprise that she jumped.

"Ignore it," he said as he nuzzled her neck.

"It might be Mindy."

With a sound of frustration, he stopped nuzzling and rolled away.

She took a moment to appreciate the gorgeousness that was his body.

"Either answer the phone or make good on what your eyes are promising," he said.

She picked up the phone, though her lips yearned to go exploring. "Hello."

"Hey, Olivia, it's Colin. Is Campbell with you? I haven't seen him since last night."

"He is."

"He's not barbecued again, is he?"

She laughed a little at the morbid humor. "No."

"Can I talk to him?"

Olivia looked over to where Campbell lay with his arms above his head, his magnificent chest asking for her touch. "Actually, he's busy right now. And he's going to be busy for the rest of the night."

She heard the deep laughter on the other end of the line as she hung up the phone.

Campbell wore the grin of a man very proud of himself. "I'm going to be busy all night, huh?"

"Yes. Is that a problem?"

"Not at all." He pulled her down beside him. "Not at all."

* * * * *

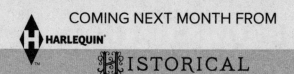

COMING NEXT MONTH FROM

HARLEQUIN®

HISTORICAL

Available October 22, 2013

A SPRINKLING OF CHRISTMAS MAGIC
by Elizabeth Rolls, Bronwyn Scott and Margaret McPhee
(Regency)

This Christmas, indulge in three gorgeous wintry Regency romances from Elizabeth Rolls, Bronwyn Scott and Margaret McPhee. What will happen under the mistletoe this year?

REBEL WITH A HEART
by Carol Arens
(Western)

Trace Ballentine, investigative journalist, has gone undercover to expose corruption at a remote South Dakota hospital. But when his long-lost sweetheart appears out of nowhere, he can't risk blowing his cover!

RUMORS THAT RUINED A LADY
by Marguerite Kaye
(Regency)

Among the gossip-hungry *ton* no name has become more synonymous with sin than that of Lady Caroline Rider. There's only one man who can save her—notorious rake Sebastian Conway.

THE HIGHLANDER'S DANGEROUS TEMPTATION
The MacLerie Clan
by Terri Brisbin
(Medieval)

Highlander laird Athdar MacCallum has had a tragic past and has vowed never to marry again. Until he is utterly disarmed by the innocent beauty in the eyes of Isobel Ruriksdottir...

REQUEST YOUR FREE BOOKS!

2 FREE NOVELS FROM THE PARANORMAL ROMANCE COLLECTION PLUS 2 FREE GIFTS!

YES! Please send me 2 FREE novels from the Paranormal Romance Collection and my 2 FREE gifts (gifts are worth about $10). After receiving them, if I don't wish to receive any more books, I can return the shipping statement marked "cancel." If I don't cancel, I will receive 4 brand-new novels every month and be billed just $22.76 in the U.S. or $23.96 in Canada. That's a savings of at least 17% off the cover price of all 4 books. It's quite a bargain! Shipping and handling is just 50¢ per book in the U.S. and 75¢ per book in Canada.* I understand that accepting the 2 free books and gifts places me under no obligation to buy anything. I can always return a shipment and cancel at any time. Even if I never buy another book, the two free books and gifts are mine to keep forever.

237/337 HDN F4YC

Name _____ (PLEASE PRINT) _____

Address _____ Apt. # _____

City _____ State/Prov. _____ Zip/Postal Code _____

Signature (if under 18, a parent or guardian must sign)

Mail to the **Harlequin® Reader Service:**

IN U.S.A.: P.O. Box 1867, Buffalo, NY 14240-1867
IN CANADA: P.O. Box 609, Fort Erie, Ontario L2A 5X3

Want to try two free books from another line?
Call 1-800-873-8635 or visit www.ReaderService.com.

* Terms and prices subject to change without notice. Prices do not include applicable taxes. Sales tax applicable in N.Y. Canadian residents will be charged applicable taxes. Offer not valid in Quebec. This offer is limited to one order per household. Not valid for current subscribers to Paranormal Romance Collection or Harlequin® Nocturne™ books. All orders subject to credit approval. Credit or debit balances in a customer's account(s) may be offset by any other outstanding balance owed by or to the customer. Please allow 4 to 6 weeks for delivery. Offer available while quantities last.

Your Privacy—The Harlequin® Reader Service is committed to protecting your privacy. Our Privacy Policy is available online at www.ReaderService.com or upon request from the Harlequin Reader Service.

We make a portion of our mailing list available to reputable third parties that offer products we believe may interest you. If you prefer that we not exchange your name with third parties, or if you wish to clarify or modify your communication preferences, please visit us at www.ReaderService.com/consumerschoice or write to us at Harlequin Reader Service Preference Service, P.O. Box 9062, Buffalo, NY 14269. Include your complete name and address.

Tillman took her hand and led her closer to the water.

Her sudden pleasure at his touch disappeared. Being in a pool was fine, but if her feet made contact with the ocean's salt water, her body would automatically transform. When the bare skin of her feet mixed with the alchemy of the sea, webs formed between her toes. All it took was an unexpected splash around the knees and both legs would fuse into a single tail, iridescent scales would burst forth, coating human skin, completing the metamorphosis from legs to fins.

She hung back. "Let's walk here where the sand is dry and warm."

Tillman pulled her to his side and she snuggled up against his hard body, her head against his chest. The fingers of his right hand traced the outline of a wicked scar on her shoulder. A nasty souvenir from an encounter two years ago, when she'd swum too close to a charter fishing boat and a hook had sunk into her flesh.

"Where did this scar come from?"

"Childhood accident from swimming too close to a pier." Only a half lie.

"Ouch."

His hand explored further to a smaller scar by her collarbone. "And this?"

"I don't remember," she lied. She could hardly tell him it was from struggling to get out of a tuna net last summer. Her torso bore several such scars, especially since returning to live in the Gulf. She hung her head, wondering what he would make of a close examination of her body.

He tilted her chin up with a firm hand.

"I'm too curious," he said gruffly. "Another occupational hazard. Great for my job, not so much with people."

"It's okay," she whispered, fascinated with the darkening of his gray eyes. He wanted her every bit as much as she wanted him. Surely there was no harm in a little kiss. She had wanted to get close to him for so long, had fantasized about this moment for over a year.

Then his lips were upon hers, hot, demanding and probing. The sweet, fierce hotness made her toes curl into the warm sand. The pounding of the waves matched the pounding in her blood.

**Find out what happens next in
SIREN'S SECRET by Debbie Herbert
Available November 5, only from
Harlequin® Nocturne™!
Available wherever books are sold.**

HARLEQUIN®

NOCTURNE™

This holiday season, armed with love and passion,
can the Keepers stop the reign of Darkness?

Christmas is coming to Salem, but so is an evil force that
threatens all mankind. In this memorable collection, four powerful
Keepers must save their community as a strange, eternal night
creeps over the town. Forced to choose between their
time-honored responsibilities or the lovers their hearts desire,
these four extraordinary women must risk their own happiness to
save the holiday. But Christmas is a time for miracles, and as each
Keeper's greatest longing is met, the season of light returns.

THE KEEPERS:
CHRISTMAS IN SALEM

by

NEW YORK TIMES BESTSELLING AUTHOR

HEATHER GRAHAM,
DEBORAH LEBLANC, KATHLEEN PICKERING
and BETH CIOTTA

**Don't miss this magical holiday collection,
only from Harlequin® Nocturne™.**

Available November 5

www.Harlequin.com

HN88581